Body of Lies

Iris Johansen is the author of eighteen novels and consistently hits the top end of the bestseller lists in America. She lives in Georgia, USA.

IRIS JOHANSEN

Body of Lies

PAN BOOKS

First published 2002 by Macmillan

and simultaneously in America by Bantam Books,
a division of Random House, Inc, New York

This edition published 2002 by Pan Books
an imprint of Pan Macmillan Ltd
Pan Macmillan, 20 New Wharf Road, London N1 9RR
Basingstoke and Oxford
Associated companies throughout the world
www.panmacmillan.com

ISBN 0 330 48871 6

3 5 7 9 8 6 4

A CIP catalogue record for this book is available from
the British Library.

Printed and bound in Great Britain by
Mackays of Chatham plc, Chatham, Kent

Body of Lies

Chapter One

THE FLATBOAT GLIDED SLOWLY THROUGH THE BAYOU.

Too slowly, Jules Hebert thought tensely. He had deliberately chosen a flatboat rather than a motorboat because it would be less obtrusive at this time of night, but he had not counted on this case of nerves.

Keep calm. The church was just up ahead.

"It will be fine, Jules," Etienne called softly as he wielded the oars. "You worry too much."

And his brother, Etienne, didn't worry enough, Jules thought in despair. Ever since childhood it had been Jules who was the serious one, the one who had to accept the responsibility while Etienne ambled along through life with endearing blitheness. "You arranged for the men to be waiting at the church?"

"Of course."

"And you told them nothing?"

"Only that they would be paid well for the work. And I parked the motorboat to bring them where you told me to."

"Good."

"It will all go very easily." Etienne smiled. "I promise you, Jules. Would I let you down?"

Not intentionally. The affection between them was too strong. They had been through too much together. "No offense. Just asking, little brother." Jules stiffened as he saw the dark looming silhouette of the ancient stone church in the faint moonlight as they rounded the corner. It had been deserted for over ten years and exuded dampness and decay. His gaze flew to the sparsely scattered plantation houses on either side of the bayou.

No one. No sign of anyone stirring.

"I told you," Etienne said. "Luck is with us. How could it be otherwise? Fortune is always on the side of the right."

That had not been Jules's experience, but he wouldn't argue with Etienne. Not tonight.

Jules jumped out of the boat as they reached the landing, and the four men Etienne had hired streamed onto the boat.

"Be careful with it," Jules said. "For God's sake, don't drop it."

"I'll help them." Etienne leaped forward. "Christ, it's heavy." He put his massive shoulder beneath one corner. "On the count of three."

With great care they lifted the huge black coffin onto the landing.

LAKE COTTAGE
ATLANTA, GEORGIA

Coffin.

Eve Duncan woke with a start, her heart pounding.

"What is it?" Joe Quinn asked drowsily. "Something wrong?"

"No." Eve swung her feet to the floor. "I just had a bad dream. I think I'll get a glass of water." She moved to the bathroom. "Go back to sleep."

Good heavens, she was actually shaking. How stupid could she get? She splashed water on her face and took a few sips of water before going back into the bedroom.

The lamp on the nightstand was on and Joe was sitting up in bed. "I told you to go back to sleep."

"I don't want to go to sleep. Come here."

She went into his arms and cuddled close. Safety. Love. Joe. "Want to make love?"

"The thought occurred to me. Maybe later. Right now, I want to know about your nightmare."

"People do have bad dreams, Joe. It's not that uncommon."

"But you haven't had one in a long time. I thought you were over them." His arms tightened around her. "I *want* them to be over."

She knew he did, and she knew he tried desperately to give her the security and contentment that he thought would rid her of them. But Joe should know better than anyone that the nightmare would never entirely go away. "Just shut up and go back to sleep."

"Was it about Bonnie?"

"No." Eve felt a ripple of guilt. Someday she had to tell him why the dreams of Bonnie were no longer painful. But not yet. Even after this last year with him, she still wasn't ready. Someday.

"The new skull? You've been working hard on it. Maybe too hard?"

"I'm almost done. It's Carmelita Sanchez, Joe. I should be able to notify her parents in a couple days." Then there would be closure and, perhaps, peace for them. "And you know my work never brings me anything but satisfaction. No bad dreams there." Just sadness and pity and a driving passion to bring the lost ones home. "Stop probing. Bad dreams don't have to have deep psychological implications. This was just a crazy, disjointed . . . It was probably something I ate. Jane's pizza was a little too rich for—"

"What was it about?"

Joe wasn't going to give up. He would pick at the subject until everything was out in the open. "A coffin. Okay? I was walking toward this coffin, and it scared me."

"Who was in the coffin?" He paused. "Me? Jane?"

"Stop trying to read something into it. It was a closed coffin."

"Then why were you scared?"

"It was a dream. For heaven's sake, I deal with dead people every day of my life. It's perfectly natural I should have an occasional macabre—"

"Why were you scared?"

"Drop it. It's over." She pulled his head down and kissed him. "Stop being a protective ass. The only therapy I want from you right now is strictly physical."

He went still, resisting. Then he relaxed and moved over her. "Well, if you insist. I suppose I'll have to be a gentleman and let you seduce me."

Eve was surprised. She knew how stubborn Joe could be. She smiled and gently tugged at his hair. "Damn right, you will."

"We'll talk about the coffin later. . . ."

SARAH BAYOU

The coffin was in place in the altar of the church.

Jules bent to check the pedestal beneath it to make sure it was sturdy enough to bear the weight of the specially reinforced airtight coffin. He'd had it built to his own specifications and had been assured there would be no problem, but it was his responsibility and he was determined not to fail. Nothing must damage the coffin's precious contents.

"I've paid them off. They're on their way back," Etienne said from the doorway. He came toward Jules, his gaze fixed on the coffin. "It looks so strange there. . . . We did it, didn't we?"

Jules nodded. "Yes, we did it."

Etienne was silent a moment. "I know you were angry with me, but now you understand, don't you?"

"Yes, I understand."

"Good. Well, here it is. We did it together." Etienne put his arm affectionately around Jules's shoulders. "It gives me a good feeling. You, too?"

"No." Jules closed his eyes as the pain surged through him. "Not a good feeling."

"Because you worry too much. But it's over now."

"Not quite." Jules opened eyes that were full of tears. "Have I ever told you how much I love you, what a good brother you've been to me?"

Etienne laughed. "If you had, I would have been the one who was worried. You're not a man who—" His eyes widened in shock as he saw the gun in his brother's hand. "What are you—?"

Jules shot him in the heart.

Disbelief was frozen on Etienne's face as he fell to the floor.

Jules couldn't believe it, either. Dear God, let him take that moment back.

No, for he would only have to do it again.

Jules fell to his knees beside Etienne and gathered him in his arms. Tears ran down his face as he rocked him back and forth. Little brother. Little brother . . .

Control. He had one other task to perform before he could allow himself to grieve. The motorboat taking the men away from the church should be out of the bayou and on the widest part of the river by now.

He fumbled in his pocket for the switch and pressed the red button. He could not hear the explosion, but he knew it had happened. He had set the charge himself and he never allowed himself to make a mistake. There would be no survivors and no evidence.

It was done.

Jules turned back to Etienne and tenderly brushed the hair from his forehead. Sleep, little brother. He prayed Etienne was at peace. He was glad it was too dim in the church to see the shock and pain frozen on Etienne's face.

No, the church was not that dim. It was the coffin, huge, dark, and casting its shadow over both Jules and Etienne.

Casting its shadow over all the world.

———————

"No, Senator Melton," Eve said firmly. "I'm not interested. I have enough work to keep me busy for the rest of the year. I certainly don't need any more."

"It would help us enormously if you could see your way clear to changing your mind. It's a very sensitive situation and we need your help." The senator paused. "And, after all, as a citizen, you do have a patriotic duty to—"

"Don't give me that crap," Eve interrupted. "Every time a bureaucrat wants to be put first on the list, he pulls out patriotic duty. You haven't even told me what this job is going to be about. All I know is that I'd have to leave my home and my family and go running off to Baton Rouge. I can't imagine a job important enough to make me do that."

"As I said, it's a very sensitive, confidential situation and I'm not at liberty to discuss it with you until you're committed to—"

"Get someone else. I'm not the only forensic sculptor in the world."

"You're the best."

"I've gotten a lot of press. That doesn't mean—"

"You're the best. False modesty doesn't become you."

"Okay, I'm damn good." She paused. "But I'm not available. Get Dupree or McGilvan." She hung up the phone.

Joe looked up from his book. "Melton, again?"

"He won't give up. Lord save me from politicians." Eve went

back to the pedestal and began smoothing the clay over the skull. "God, they're pompous."

"Melton has the reputation of being fairly down-to-earth. He's certainly popular. They say the Democrats are grooming him for president."

"I wouldn't trust any politician. They're all bedfellows in Washington. They scratch each other's backs."

"Sounds a little disgusting." Joe studied her. "But you're intrigued. It's sticking out all over you."

"So, I'm curious. Melton's evidently experienced at piquing people's interest." Eve didn't take her gaze from the sculpture. "The only thing he'd tell me was that it was my patriotic duty. Bull."

"No more than that?"

"He said we'll discuss it when I commit." She smoothed the area under the eye crevice. "I wonder who they think it is. . . ."

He watched her for a moment without speaking. "Louisiana in October isn't too unpleasant. We could take a jaunt down to New Orleans. The department owes me some time, and Jane might like it."

"You're not invited." She made a face. "Highly confidential and top secret."

"Then screw him." He thought about it a moment. "Was that a little lacking in tact and understanding? I know better than to try to get in the way of your job. If you're tempted, I guess we could put up with being without you for a few weeks."

"Why should I be tempted?" She wiped her hands on a towel and moved over to stand at the window. The lake was glittering blue on this fine autumn afternoon, and Jane was down on the shore playing with the new puppy Eve's friend, Sarah Patrick, had given her. The girl was tossing a stick for Toby, and the mixed-breed dog was running crazily to retrieve it. They both looked so alive and healthy and wonderfully happy.

Well, what was there not to be happy about here in this place at this time?

"Eve?"

She glanced over her shoulder at Joe, her protector, her best friend, her lover. He was the bedrock of her life, and every moment with him and Jane was precious. She smiled at him. "Hell, no, I'm not tempted. Screw Melton."

"She refused," Melton said when Jules Hebert picked up the phone. "She suggested I get Dupree."

"I don't want Dupree," Hebert said curtly. "We need Eve Duncan. I told you that from the beginning. It has to be her."

"It looks like you'll have to make do with Dupree. He has a decent reputation."

Hebert drew a deep breath. He had seen examples of Eve Duncan's work on academic Websites and compared it to that of other leading forensic sculptors. It was like comparing a da Vinci masterpiece with a cave drawing. He couldn't entrust this skull to a Neanderthal. It was too important to him. It was important to Melton and the rest of them, too, but Jules didn't care about them. Not now. Melton had a safe job in a safe world. He sat in his office and lifted his finger and sent men like Hebert out to take his risks and do his bidding. "You told me I had to find a way to verify. Give me Eve Duncan and I'll do it."

"You made the mistake; it's your job to correct it."

Jules's hand tightened on the phone. "There's always a way to get what you want, if you work at it. What's the problem?"

"My bet is that she's so mired in domesticity that she can't see beyond her little cottage in Georgia. It's only what you'd expect from a woman."

"Never underestimate women. I've known some that I'd rather avoid than come up against. Duncan is obviously very strong-willed. You approached her in the way that I suggested?"

"Yes, she seemed interested, but that didn't make her accept."

"Then we didn't press the right buttons. There has to be some way. Tell me about her."

"You know her reputation, or you wouldn't be so sure she's the right one for the job."

Jules looked down at the newspaper with the picture of Eve Duncan that had first led him to call Melton. It was a photo of a woman in her early thirties with a strong, intelligent face framed by curly red-brown hair. She wore wire-rimmed glasses and looked out at the world with an odd mixture of boldness and sensitivity. "I know about her professional capabilities. I need to know more about her background. I need to know how to manipulate her."

"She's illegitimate and grew up in the slums of Atlanta with a crackhead for a mother. In later years, the mother gave up drugs, and she and Duncan became close. Eve got pregnant herself when she was sixteen and gave birth to a child, Bonnie. She went back to school and was working her way through when her seven-year-old little girl was murdered by some nut who had killed eleven other children. They couldn't find the body, and that spurred Duncan to become a forensic sculptor. She studied at Georgia State and became one of the top forensic sculptors in the country. She works freelance and also with several police departments nationwide."

"And her personal life?"

"She's living with Joe Quinn, a detective with the Atlanta Police Department. They've been friends since her daughter was murdered over twelve years ago, but they've only been living together for the past two years. She's recently adopted a twelve-year-old girl, Jane MacGuire, who grew up on the streets just as Duncan had done. They live in a lake cottage outside of Atlanta. Her daughter, Bonnie, is buried on the grounds."

"You told me the body had never been found."

"Until last year. New information emerged, and they located the skeleton in the Chattahoochee National Forest. DNA tests confirmed that the skeleton was Bonnie Duncan."

And Eve Duncan was now at peace, Hebert thought. He knew the value of closure. He could imagine the dark world Eve Duncan had lived in all those years.

"Anything else?" Melton asked. "I've got all the details; I can cross the T's and dot the I's if you need it."

So cut-and-dried. Jules was sure Melton would relate all those details in the same detached way he'd revealed Eve Duncan's past history. "That won't be necessary."

He couldn't leave this to Melton, he thought wearily. He'd have to work on Eve Duncan's weaknesses himself.

She's so mired in domesticity that she can't see beyond her little lake cottage in Georgia.

She had a man and a child, and her own personal cross was buried on that property near her home. She was probably very happy. And why not? She had earned her peace.

So the only way to get what he needed was to destroy that peace. And he knew he would do it, just as he did everything that needed doing. Drop everything and get to the airport. He had to get her to leave Atlanta immediately.

But there was one thing he had to do before he left.

"I'm going to Atlanta."

"I'm glad to see you're taking action. This had better be solved soon. Remember, you don't have much time to clear up your mess. Boca Raton is set for October twenty-ninth."

"You don't have to remind me. I can take care of both matters."

"We've trusted you for a long time, but the Cabal isn't too pleased with you after that blunder with Etienne."

And Melton was even less pleased. He was probably looking over his shoulder and thinking he'd be next. Lily-livered bastard.

"I had to shoot him. It was self-defense."

"Was it?" Melton paused. "I admit I've been wondering if you're playing a double game."

"You have no reason to accuse me of that."

"Well, then, you'd better make sure your mistake has no repercussions."

"That's why I'm going to Atlanta. I'll find a way."

"See that you do." Melton hung up.

The threat had been veiled, but Jules couldn't mistake Melton's intention to pressure him. He smothered the anger and tried to compose himself. It was the first time in years that any of the Cabal had been in the least critical of him. He had served them faithfully. Wasn't he entitled to their trust?

Well, they had trusted him with Etienne, and he must make amends for that.

Boca Raton.

It would be all right. Jules had made the advance preparations and the plan was proceeding nicely. He could leave the matter alone while he concentrated on the Duncan project.

Eve Duncan. Hebert leaned back and closed his eyes. He would go soon, but another few moments wouldn't hurt. You'd think after all these years that he'd become hardened, but it had never happened. Not with the innocents.

Get a grip. He had killed Etienne; anything else would be easy in comparison.

Joe Quinn, Jane MacGuire, and hadn't Melton mentioned Eve Duncan's mother?

Which one would he have to choose?

———

"Look at him." Jane's expression was glowing with pride as she gazed at her puppy. "I think he's even smarter than his daddy, Monty, don't you?"

"Well . . . he's very good. But rolling over isn't exactly the same as saving lives after an earthquake." Eve smiled as she packed Carmelita's reconstructed skull in a box. "He's got a way to go."

"Well, he's only four months old. I have to train him." Jane snapped her fingers and Toby bounced to his feet. "Maybe I should go out to California and let Sarah help me. I bet she could teach him in no time. She offered to do it when she gave him to me."

Providing Sarah had time to do it, Eve thought ruefully. Besides traveling all over the world with a canine rescue group, Sarah was trying to adjust to marriage and keep her golden retriever, Monty, and his mate, Maggie, content and peaceful. Peaceful wasn't that easy when it came to dealing with an un-tamed wolf like Maggie. "That could be a good idea. We'll ask her when she might have a chance to do it." She addressed the label on the box ready for collection. "But not until your school breaks for the Thanksgiving holidays."

"I could make it up. I'm ahead anyway."

In more ways than in her studies. Jane's background had ensured that in both experience and character she was twelve going on thirty. Eve was glad to see this wild enthusiasm over the puppy. Heaven knows the girl had been cheated out of most of the joys of childhood. "Maybe. We'll talk about it."

"Are you going to the FedEx office? Can Toby and I go with you?"

"Sure. Right after I go and put some fresh flowers on Bonnie's grave. I haven't been up there this week."

"The chrysanthemums by the side of the house? I'll get them. Toby and I will go with you. He needs to stretch his legs."

"What are you talking about? That puppy dashes around every minute of the day."

"Running up hills is different. It's good training and helps the lungs." She ran out of the cottage. "We'll meet you."

Eve smiled and shook her head as she went out onto the porch. They'd be there long before she reached the grave, and she'd be lucky if Toby didn't tear up the flowers Jane put down on it.

Not that it mattered. Flowers were only flowers. And Bonnie would have loved to see the puppy tearing around, full of life and joy. She started on the path around the lake.

To her surprise Toby was being comparatively sedate, lying on his back beside the grave while Jane scratched his tummy. "I told you hills were different," Jane said. "He got tired. He needs to get in shape." She turned around and began picking weeds from the grave. "It doesn't need much cleaning at this time of year. I was up here three days ago and there was hardly any clover or anything."

"You were up here?"

"Sure. I know it's important to you. You love Bonnie." Jane straightened the flowers "There. I was going to brush those maple leaves off, but the red color looks kind of pretty. Like a cozy little blanket."

"Yes, it does." Eve looked down at the fallen leaves. A blanket for her Bonnie. The phrase spoke of home and shelter from harm. Everything she'd wanted for her daughter.

"Is it okay?" Jane asked.

"It's beautiful." Eve swallowed hard. "Have I told you lately how much I love you, Jane?"

"You don't have to tell me." Jane didn't look at her as she jumped to her feet. "You keep thinking you're cheating me or something. It doesn't have to be even. I don't expect it."

"It is even. It's just . . . different."

"Right. I'll see you at the car. Maybe we can rent a video while we're in town, now that you're finished with Carmelita. Joe said he wanted to see that new sci-fi spoof." The girl streaked off with Toby romping at her heels.

Still a few problems there, but they'd come a long way. They had such a strong foundation that Eve couldn't believe they wouldn't work everything out eventually.

Time to go. She looked down at the grave. "Good-bye, Bonnie," she whispered. She turned and started to follow Jane.

A sudden chill went through her.

She whirled and looked back up the hill. "Bonnie?"

Nothing. No sound. No rustle of trees . . .

Yet, had there been . . . something?

Imagination. She must have been working too hard on Carmelita. Bonnie never gave her this sense of menace. . . .

"Eve!" Jane was waving at her from the bottom of the hill. "Toby's treed a squirrel. Or maybe it's a raccoon. Come and see."

Eve turned around and her pace quickened. "I'll be right there."

Chapter Two

THE CHILD COULD BE THE KEY.

Jules Hebert faded away into the bushes as Eve left the grave site. The expression on the woman's face had told it all. She was a mother, and radiated the love, endurance, and tenderness that all mothers possessed. The death of a child could move a woman to do almost anything.

Jane MacGuire?

The idea made him sick. He did not like to kill children. He stopped and leaned against the birch tree at the bottom of the hill. He could do it. He could do anything he had to do. He had proved that.

But maybe it wasn't necessary. He had to clear his head and think. Would he have to do this? Would it even bring the result he wanted? The situation was critical, but wouldn't it be better to explore other avenues? Everyone had secrets. Suppose he probed and pried until he knew every detail of these people's lives. He had always been good at that. He might be able to find something he could use. . . .

It would take time.

Not if he bent all his will and effort to the task. He had come to admire Eve Duncan. With her strength and intelligence, she reminded him of his own mother. Surely, he could wait a few more days.

Boca Raton.

Three days. Taking any more time would be irresponsible. He could allow himself three days to find another option.

Then he would have to kill the child.

———

"I need to talk to you." Jane's voice was hesitant. "Could you spare a moment, Eve?"

"I don't have time to—" Eve looked up from the skull she was charting and saw that Jane was so pale her freckles stood out. "What's wrong? Is it Toby?"

"Toby's fine." Jane moistened her lips. "I didn't know what to do. I thought about telling Joe, but it's really you . . . I tried to fix it, but I couldn't. And then I didn't want you to go up and see—I had to tell you."

"What are you talking about, Jane?"

"Will you come with me?" Jane moved toward the door. "You have to see—"

"See what?"

"Bonnie . . ."

"What do you mean—"

Jane was gone, running down the porch steps and down the path.

"Jane!"

Eve ran after her but didn't catch up until she was almost up the hill. "Why are you—"

Then she saw it.

"I didn't know what to do." Jane's voice was uneven. "I tried to clean it up."

Blood smeared, dripping over the headstone.

Eve shuddered. "What did you— What happened here?"

"I don't know. I came up today to clean off the weeds and it was like this. No, not like this. I made it worse. I'm sorry, Eve."

"Blood."

"No, I don't think so. At first, I thought . . . But it's paint or something." She edged closer to Eve. "I couldn't get it off."

"Paint?"

Jane nodded. "Someone drew a big X through Bonnie's name and everything else on the tombstone." She took Eve's hand. "Who would do this to you?"

Eve couldn't imagine who would commit a horror like this. She felt . . . bruised. "I don't know." It was hard to think. "Maybe some kid who thought it was funny to desecrate a grave." But not her Bonnie's grave. Not her Bonnie. "I can't think of anyone else."

"I'm gonna get him," Jane said fiercely. "Maybe he'll come back. I'll wait here and when he does, I'm gonna get him."

Eve shook her head. "It would only make it worse." She turned away. "Come on, we'll get back to the cottage and see if we can find something to clean it off with."

Jane fell into step with her. "We'll tell Joe as soon as he gets home. He'll get him."

"Not until we clean up the tombstone."

"You're afraid he'll be so mad, he'll do something to him. He should do something. I'll help him."

Jesus, she couldn't handle this right now. Eve knew very well Joe's response would be just as violent and protective as Jane's, and she was too shaky to play peacemaker. Besides, she didn't want to be a peacemaker. Shock was quickly being replaced by anger. She wanted to wring that sicko kid's neck. Not a good example for Jane. And Joe was an ex-SEAL and would think little of doing just that. "Just go to the shed and see what you can find. There may be some turpentine left from last spring when we painted the porch."

———————

"Having trouble?"

George Capel glanced impatiently at the man in a blue Saturn who had cruised to a stop beside him on the side of the road. What a stupid question, when he was standing here with his head under the hood of the Mercedes. "Not unless you're a mechanic. It's dead as a doornail."

"Sorry. I'm a computer salesman." The man in the Saturn grimaced. "And believe me I've had my share of breakdowns. I remember once in Macon, it was the middle of the night and I—" He stopped. "But you're not interested in that. What about a jump?"

"We can try." Capel glanced at the man's neat blue suit. "Better be careful. I've already got grease on my shirt."

The man smiled. "I'm always careful."

Ten minutes later Capel was cursing a blue streak when the car still failed to start. "Piece of crap. For God's sake, it's a Mercedes. Do you know how much this car cost me?"

"A bundle. New?"

"Last year."

"Sorry I couldn't help. Maybe you'd better call for a tow truck."

"When my car's dead, my car phone's dead, too. Do you have a cell phone?"

The other man smiled. "You seem to be having trouble with mechanical objects. I remember a Stephen King book about machines gone amok. I listened to it on Books on Tape when I was driving through Iowa."

Capel tried to keep his temper. "Do you have a phone?" he repeated.

"Sure, but it's back at the motel on the charger. I was only going to go out and find a restaurant to have dinner." He wiped his forehead with his handkerchief. "But hop in and I'll give you a lift to the nearest service station. I'm new in this area. Do you know where one is?"

"There's a Texaco two miles ahead." Capel hesitated, gazing at the Mercedes.

"I don't think it's going anywhere."

"That's for sure. Piece of lousy junk." Capel strode over to the passenger side of the Saturn and got in. "Let's go. I didn't need this. I left the office early because I've got tickets to the basketball game tonight. And then this has to happen. Damn, I hate car trouble. The sooner we get this over with, the better."

"That's what I think. I hate unpleasantness." Jules Hebert got into the driver's seat. "Let's get it over with."

———————

Joe turned away from the grave. "We'll replace the headstone."

"I've got almost all the paint off."

"But every time you look at it, you'll remember. We'll get a new headstone. I'll see to it when I go into work tomorrow." He looked at her. "You haven't seen anyone around the place in the past few days?"

Eve shook her head.

"Don't worry, it won't happen again."

"It's a big property. It's hard to keep trespassers off it."

"It won't happen again," Joe repeated. "Go on back to the house while I take a look around."

She looked at him warily.

"Hey, I'm a cop. Let me do my job."

But this wasn't a cop standing before her. He was in protective mode, and Joe could be lethal when he was this angry. "I don't want you to do your job too well. It was vandalism."

"It hurt you," Joe said flatly. "I won't allow that. Never again."

"And I won't allow you to kill some kid who thought this was just one big giggle."

He was silent a moment. "If it's a kid, he may get by with learning a lesson he won't forget. Satisfied?"

"No." But it was all she was going to get from him. Eve was beginning to hope they'd never find out who did this awful thing. "You can't call a forensic team out here to solve a case of vandalism."

"I'm pretty good on my own." Joe turned away. "Go on back to the cottage. Jane needs you. She's pretty shook up."

"Not any more. She wants to do the same thing as you. She said she was 'gonna get him.' "

"Good. Smart girl. But she doesn't have to bother."

Eve watched in exasperation as Joe disappeared into the bushes. He was on the hunt, and there wasn't anything she could do about it.

She turned and went down the hill.

———

Joe found the footprints almost immediately.

Not running shoes or mountain boots like most kids wore in this area. Regular shoes. Size eight or nine, and the imprint was shallow so the wearer wasn't very big.

And he hadn't tried to brush the footprints away. It was stupid enough to be a kid. Joe followed the prints down the hill.

Car tracks.

It was getting dark. Joe turned on his flashlight as he knelt down and looked at the tracks. He didn't know enough about tire imprints to identify them. He'd go back to the cottage and get some plaster to make a mold, and then run it through the database at headquarters.

He didn't like any of this. His hand clenched on the flashlight as he thought about the grave and Eve's expression when she'd told him about the defacement.

He was going to get that son of a bitch.

———

Hebert's phone rang as he was getting back in the car.

"I hadn't heard from you," Melton said. "Do I have to remind you that time is of the essence?"

"No."

"The situation may be escalating. Have you thought any more about getting Dupree?"

"Forget Dupree." Jules wearily leaned back in the seat. "That may not be necessary."

"Why not?"

"Things are looking up. I want you to wait one day and then call Eve Duncan again and make her the same offer."

"She was quite adamant."

"Try her."

"Whatever you say. It's good that things are proceeding so well." Melton hung up.

There was nothing good about this but the end result, Jules thought. It had been a hideous night. The man had been harder to break than he had thought, and torture was always worse than a clean kill. As he punched the end button, he noticed there was blood on the phone. He looked down at his hands. Blood on them, too.

He wiped his hands with a tissue, and then the phone. He glanced at the sheet of paper on the seat beside him. Good. No blood on the paper. He didn't want to leave any traces.

He looked out the window at the drainage ditch several yards away from the road. The water should wash away any evidence he had left behind.

He wished he could cleanse his mind and soul as easily.

"I ran into the FedEx man outside." Jane dropped her schoolbooks on the coffee table and tossed the FedEx letter on Eve's desk.

"Who's it from?"

"Search me. No return address. Where's Toby?"

"Outside by the lake. He chased some ducks this morning."

"Well, he has retriever blood."

"And he turned tail when one got mad and bit his nose." Eve grinned. "Some retriever."

"Poor Toby." Jane started for the door. "That must have hurt his pride. I'll have to go soothe his feelings."

"He's forgotten already. I saw him chasing a butterfly an hour later. Maybe he thought that wouldn't be quite so dangerous."

Jane giggled. "A little more respect, please." She ran out the door and down the steps. "Toby!"

Eve was still smiling when she picked up the FedEx letter and tore it open. Thank heaven for Toby. He had completely taken Jane's mind off that horror of two days ago. She only wished Joe would be similarly distracted by—

My God.

———

"Come home, Joe," Jane said as soon as Joe picked up the phone. "Right away. You've got to come now."

"Easy. What's wrong?"

"Eve. She's just sitting there. She told me nothing was wrong, but she's just sitting there."

"Maybe nothing is wrong."

"Don't you tell me that." Her voice was shaking. "You come home, Joe."

"I'm on my way."

———

"Eve?"

It was Joe. She curled up tighter at the end of the couch. Go away. Go away.

"What the hell's wrong?"

She put it into words. "Go away."

He sat down beside her. "Stop closing me out. I'm not going anywhere. Now what's wrong?"

"I don't want . . . to talk about it right now."

"Well, I do. That's what a relationship is about. Sharing."

"Sharing what? Sharing lies?"

He went still. "What are you talking about?"

"I told you, I don't want to talk at all." She just wanted to close herself away and try to heal the raw wound. "Go and see about Jane. I think I scared her."

"You're scaring me. Did something happen to Bonnie's grave again?"

"I don't know," she said dully. "It doesn't matter."

"Jane said you got a FedEx. May I see it?"

She got to her feet. "Not now."

He was silent a moment. "Let me help you. You're not being fair to me, Eve."

She whirled on him, her eyes blazing. "*I'm* not being fair? My God, how do you have the nerve to say that after what you've done to me?"

He went still. "And what have I done to you?"

"Lies. You lied to me, Joe. The cruelest lie, the cruelest thing you could have done to me." She drew a deep breath, her gaze fixed desperately on his face. "You're not asking what that was. Because you know, don't you, Joe? I wasn't really sure until I saw your face. I couldn't believe it. I couldn't believe you'd do this to me."

He glanced around the room. "Is that the FedEx?" He crossed to the desk and picked up the single sheet of paper and scanned it. She could see the line of his spine stiffen as if he was bracing himself before he turned to face her. "Was there a return address?"

She stared at him, stunned. "Christ, is that all you have to say?"

"No, but I have to know who wanted to hurt you this much." He grimaced. "And who wanted to hurt me."

"I don't care who it was. All I care about is that you lied to me." She closed her eyes as waves of fresh pain broke over her. "And that the little girl I buried on that hill is not my Bonnie. Jesus, I can't believe it."

"But you clearly do believe it. And I'm sure you verified this particular scrap of poison."

"It's not a scrap." She opened eyes glittering with tears. "It's the official report from the Georgia forensic lab stating that the DNA of the little girl found in Chattahoochee National Park did not match Bonnie Duncan's. It was signed by Dr. George Capel."

"And you called George Capel?"

"I tried, but he was out of the office. So I talked to the head of the department. He couldn't find the official paperwork on the results, but he finally tracked down some of the transcripts from the work in progress. Shall I tell you what they were?"

"Don't bother."

"I was in Atlanta and you took the call that day. When I came home, you told me that Bonnie had been found."

"Yes, I did."

"You deliberately lied to me."

"Yes."

The agony was exploding inside her. "How could you do that?" she whispered.

"How could I not do it?" Joe's voice was harsh with pain. "I'd watched you suffer for twelve years. I'd seen you search for Bonnie in every one of those faces you re-created. It was a wound that never healed, that would never heal until you found Bonnie. Sarah Patrick searched all through that National Forest, and we'd almost given up hope when they found the skeleton. The chances of another skeleton being found there were practically nil at that point. So I prayed every night that skeleton would be Bonnie's." He threw the report on the desk with barely controlled violence. "And then it didn't happen, Goddammit. It was going to go on and on. But it didn't have to. All I had to do was tell one lie, and you'd be at peace."

"A terrible lie. You . . . cheated me."

"You want me to say I'm sorry? I'm not sorry. Yes, I am. I'm sorry you found out and it's hurting you. But I'd do it again if I thought I had a chance of keeping it from you." His words came fast, hard, and full of passion. "I *love* you. You've been the center of my life for over twelve years. I'd do anything to take you away from the hell you've been going through all that time. I'd lie. I'd kill. Anything to keep the pain away."

"Well, you didn't do it."

"No, I didn't do it."

Eve raised a shaking hand to her lips as she thought of something else. "Jesus, I received an official notification two weeks later, verifying the telephone call. You did that, too?"

"I bribed someone in the lab to do it for me. I knew you'd expect it."

"You were very . . . thorough."

"It was important to me. Maybe the most important action I'd taken in my life." Joe was silent a moment, his face pale, strained. "So now what?"

"I don't know. I trusted you, and you betrayed me in the most terrible way possible. I can't even think." Eve moved heavily toward the bedroom. "I'm going to bed. All I want to do is sleep."

"You won't sleep. You just want to get away from me."

"I can't look at you right now."

"You *love* me, Eve."

She did love him. She doubted if that could ever go away, and that was part of the pain she was feeling. "But could I ever trust you again? You don't lie to people you love."

"The hell you don't."

She shook her head and closed the bedroom door. She leaned back against it. Jesus, she felt empty. It was as if everything had been drained out of her, leaving nothing but an aching hole. Was Joe feeling this emptiness? No, he'd be full of sorrow for her, and anger and desperation at the situation. She knew him so well, his mind, his character, his body . . .

But not well enough. She'd never have guessed he'd do this.

She moved over to the bed and lay down, staring into the darkness.

———

"I made you some coffee." Jane handed Joe the mug and sat on the porch step beside him.

"Thanks." He set the coffee down on the step.

"Do you think we have a chance of getting Eve to eat something?"

He shook his head.

She didn't look at him. "I eavesdropped, you know. I had to know why she was hurting."

"Me."

"Yeah. You shouldn't have done it, Joe."

He didn't answer.

"Unless you were sure you wouldn't get caught."

He looked at her.

"I was sitting out by the lake with Toby, thinking that maybe I would have done the same thing if I hadn't been scared of her finding out. She's been really happy since we brought Bonnie home. I mean . . . that other little girl. So is it better for her to be happy or to be sad?" She shook her head. "I don't know. . . ."

He should have known that Jane wouldn't see everything in black or white. She had been in and out of foster homes since she was a baby and had seen too much in her short life. "Let me clarify. It was a wrong thing to do for a right reason."

"You told her you'd do it again."

"I probably would." His lips twisted. "And that wasn't a lie."

"Well, be smarter about it next time."

"There may not be a next time. I may not get the chance to be close enough to her to—" He rubbed his aching temple. "And I thought I was being smart, or at least careful. I bribed the supervisor who ran the test very well to lose that result sheet."

"But he sent it to Eve. Did you make him mad?"

Joe shook his head. "And he didn't even try to hit me up for more money."

"What would you have done if he had?"

"Scared the hell out of him. Capel was money-hungry, but not stupid." He sat up straighter. "I shouldn't be talking like this to you. The welfare people would whisk you away from us in a heartbeat if they could hear me."

"I wouldn't go." She leaned against his shoulder. "Screw them all."

"And that comment would be another mark against me." He put his arm around her. "I want to make sure of something, Jane. Don't ever take my side against Eve. I'm wrong and she's right. Do you understand?"

"Sure."

"Then hadn't you better go in and talk to Eve?"

She shook her head. "She won't want me. Not when it's about Bonnie. She's never been sure how I . . . She'd worry about not hurting my feelings, and she's hurting enough herself right now."

He closed his eyes. "God, you've got that right." He had felt her pain as if it were his own. It *was* his own.

She took his hand. "So maybe I'll just stay out here with you for awhile. Okay?"

His hand tightened around Jane's. "Okay."

———

Eve was still awake when Joe came into the bedroom a few hours later.

He knelt beside the bed. "Don't stiffen up. I won't stay long. I won't even touch you." He was silent a moment. "I just want you to remember a couple things while you're thinking what a bastard I am."

"You're not a bastard."

"I want you to remember what we have together. I want you to remember what we are to each other." He paused. "And sometime it's going to occur to you that I lied because I wanted Bonnie out of our lives. It's not true. If I'd thought you could heal and live a halfway normal life, I'd have kept searching for her till the day we died. But it's still an open wound for you." Eve could see his hand clench in the half darkness. "And it *hurts* me. I wish I'd known her. I wish she'd been our daughter. Then maybe you'd forgive me for doing this. Because I would have done the same thing if Bonnie had been mine. Do you believe me?"

"I believe . . . you believe it."

Joe bent and rested his forehead on the bed only an inch from her hand, but not touching her. "I guess that's all I can ask right now. The ball's in your court, Eve." He got to his feet and moved toward the door. "I'll see you in the morning. Try to sleep."

Not likely. Every word he'd spoken had been like little knives, tearing her apart. *He* was tearing her apart. She was so full of anger and a bitter sense of betrayal, and yet she had wanted desperately to reach out and comfort him. It seemed impossible that those conflicting emotions could exist side by side.

How could she stand this?

Jesus, she wished she could cry.

————

Jane knocked, then opened the door. "Hi, do you want me to fix some breakfast?" Her gaze went to the suitcase on the bed. "Uh-oh."

"It's after eight. You've missed the school bus."

"Joe said it was okay if I stayed home today. He told me to take care of you." She came into the room. "Where are you going?"

"I'm glad you didn't go." Eve put a smock and pair of jeans into the suitcase. "I thought we'd go and spend a week or two with my mother. Why don't you go pack a bag?"

"Can I take Toby?"

"Of course. Mom loves that silly mutt." She threw tennis shoes and socks into the bag. "We'll do all kinds of neat things. Maybe go to the zoo to see the new pandas. What do you think about that?"

Jane didn't answer; Eve glanced at her inquiringly.

Jane moistened her lips. "I know what Joe did. I listened last night. He feels real bad about it, Eve."

"I know." Eve went to the bathroom and brought back her toothbrush and an armful of toiletries. "I know he does, Jane."

"Are you going to come back?"

"I don't know right now. I can't seem to think. I have to put some space and time between us. It was a . . . terrible thing he did, Jane." She closed the suitcase. "I know you love Joe, but I can't look at him every day without—" She swallowed hard. "Why don't you go get packed?"

Jane slowly shook her head. "I'm going to stay here."

"What?"

She crossed the room and put her arms around Eve. "You said you needed to think. I'd only get in the way. If I were you, I'd want to just hide my head under a blanket and not see anyone or anything." She stepped back. "And besides, Joe needs me. He needs me a lot."

"And you think I don't?"

"Not now. Maybe later." Jane smiled. "It doesn't mean I don't want to be with you or don't love you. You know that?"

"I know that."

"Good." Jane turned away. "I'll fix you some breakfast before you leave. Bacon and eggs?"

"Fine." Eve's gaze followed Jane as she left the room. Jesus, the girl's instincts were on target. Eve had felt guilty for wanting to run away and isolate herself from Joe and everything that reminded her of him. She had responsibilities, and Jane was one of them. But it seemed Jane had made her mind up, and Eve wasn't included in that decision.

She was on her way to the closet to get another armful of clothes when the phone rang.

"Ms. Duncan, I'm sorry to trouble you," Melton said when she picked up the phone. "But I felt bound to try one more time, since the task is so extremely urgent. I wonder if you'd reconsider your decision . . ."

———

"You won't change your mind?" Joe asked. "I don't like the idea of you traipsing off somewhere without my knowing more—" He stopped as he saw Eve's expression. "Okay, it's none of my business." He frowned. "The hell it's not. You'll always be my business."

Eve ignored the last remark. "Take care of Jane. I've told her I'll call her every three days and touch base." She picked up her suitcase. "I've called Mom and asked her to take Jane whenever you're working."

"Very efficient."

"I'm trying to be." She met his eyes. "It's not easy right now, and concentrating on this job will help."

"You won't phone me?"

"Probably not. That would defeat the purpose." She moved toward the door. "Good-bye, Joe."

He watched her get into the car and drive down the road.

He felt hollow and lonely . . . and scared.

"Shit." He turned, got out his phone, and dialed. "She's gone," he said when Logan picked up. "What did you find out about Melton?"

"Nothing really bad. Politically savvy. Elected to the Senate two years ago from Louisiana and done a fairly good job. He has friends in high places and may be up for the presidential nomination in a few years."

"Why would he be connected with a hush-hush job like this reconstruction?"

"Search me." Logan paused. "If you're that concerned, you could follow her."

"I told you what happened. Unless I have a damn good reason, she's not going to want me on the same continent. Maybe not even then."

"Well, I can't give you a good reason yet. I'll keep checking. Maybe you should just give her some time to herself. That would be the smart move."

"I'm not feeling very smart right now. And I don't want advice. Do you think I would have called you if I hadn't known you knew every politician in Washington?"

"No, you've never forgiven me for that year I lived with Eve. You should know that's water under the bridge. We're just friends now." Logan paused. "Which appears to be more than I can say for your relationship at the moment."

"If you're friends, then find a way to protect her. God knows I can't do it right now."

"She may not need protection."

"I don't like what was done to that grave. And Capel hasn't shown up for work for the last four days."

"I don't see a connection with Eve's trip."

"I don't, either. I just don't like it. And I don't like not being able to make sure there's no connection." Joe paused. "Get Galen to go to Baton Rouge, will you?"

"The U.S. government doesn't exactly approve of Galen."

"Tough."

"And Galen is freelance. He takes jobs where he pleases."

"You're friends. Use it."

"An order?"

"Please," Joe said through gritted teeth. "Send Galen."

"That's better. I'll ask him and call you back."

Joe went back to the window, but Eve was already out of sight. Soon she'd be on that plane for Baton Rouge, traveling far away from him at jet speed.

She couldn't be any farther away from him than she'd been a few minutes ago in this very room. She couldn't wait to get away from him. The wall she'd put between them had been almost tangible, and her expression . . .

Forget the hurt. He couldn't expect anything else. He should even have anticipated Eve would take this reconstruction job. Whenever she was in pain or lonely, she always submerged herself in her work.

And that's what he should do. He'd take that tire print down to the precinct and then go see what he could find out about Capel.

Maybe if he kept himself busy enough, he might be able to block out the memory of Eve's face before she'd walked out the door.

Maybe.

Chapter Three

A BIG, PORTLY MAN IN A dark blue suit hurried up to Eve as soon as she got off the plane. "Welcome to Baton Rouge, Ms. Duncan. I'm Paul Tanzer with the mayor's office. Senator Melton thought you'd be more comfortable with a fellow southerner. He asked me to meet you and make sure you were comfortable. Did you have a good flight?"

"Fine." It was a lie. It had been a lousy flight. The air had been smooth, but she'd felt hollow and alone and completely depressed every mile of the way. "I thought Senator Melton was going to be here."

"He'll be here tomorrow. He has to attend a fund-raiser dinner tonight in New York." Tanzer was guiding her toward his

Cadillac in a parking space. "But I'm going to get you settled. Don't you worry, little lady."

Eve gritted her teeth at that patronizing last sentence. "I'm not worried. I just want to get to work. That's what I consider settled."

"Very admirable." Tanzer helped her into the car. "But I know you'll want to see a little of Baton Rouge while you're here. Actually, you're very lucky the senator picked me to take care of you. I know everything that's going on in this city. Is this your first visit?"

"Yes. I'm not much of a traveler."

"Then by all means we must see that you get a taste of Baton Rouge."

Tanzer wasn't listening to her. "What hotel did you book me into?"

"Senator Melton decided it would be better if you didn't stay at a hotel. We've rented a wonderful plantation house about an hour outside the city. It's close to the church where you'll be working. It will be much more pleasant for you to just stroll over the bridge, and I'm sure you'll like your quarters. The house is very old and elegant. Of course, many things are old here in Baton Rouge. It has a real atmosphere of—"

"Wait." She tried to slow him down. "I'm going to be working at a church?"

"Well, it used to be one. It's been shut down for the last ten years. It was built in the 1800s and is pretty decrepit. Our city government can't decide whether to tear it down or pour money into restoring it, and welcomed Senator Melton's offer to rent it for awhile. Is there a problem?"

"I don't care. If I'm on site, then maybe I could start this afternoon."

"That's not possible. We'll have to wait for Senator Melton." Tanzer beamed. "But I'll tell him how eager you are to start. He'll be very impressed with your initiative."

"I don't have any desire to impress Senator Melton." Eve tried to hold onto her patience. After all, the man was just doing his job. "And if you'll give me his number, I'll tell him myself."

"Certainly." Tanzer wrote a number on one of his cards and handed it to her. "But it may be difficult to get in touch with him. He's a very busy man. Now, let me point out a few of our local sights to you . . ."

Tanzer never ran out of either sights or conversation for the next hour. Eve was deeply grateful when he finally nodded at a white-columned house up ahead. "Here we are. I told you it was pleasant. Rather like Tara from *Gone with the Wind*. Very picturesque, and the bayou winding in front of it is quite lovely. It will be like being in Venice, and our weather isn't bad at all this time of year."

That's what Joe had said. Eve quickly blocked the thought. Stop thinking about Joe. Easy to say. Joe was such an integral part of her life that everything reminded her of him.

Tanzer helped her out of the car. "Most of the house is closed, but you have quite a charming apartment. Four bedrooms and a lovely marble bath. There's even a very well-stocked library. I've seen that there are several romance novels there for you." He knocked on the door. "Marie Letaux is the cook and housekeeper. She's Cajun, and has a real flair for the local cuisine. She comes highly recommended. We were very lucky to get her." The door was opened by a small, dark-haired woman in her late thirties. "Good afternoon, Marie. This is Ms. Eve Duncan. I've just been telling her what a marvelous housekeeper you are and how well you're going to take care of her."

Marie Letaux gave him a cool glance. "I'm Madame Letaux. And she takes care of herself. I take care of the house and cooking."

For the first time in two days Eve felt a smile tug at her lips as she saw Tanzer blink. "Absolutely right, Madame Letaux," she said. "I wouldn't have it any other way."

The housekeeper looked at her appraisingly and then slowly nodded her head. "You may call me Marie."

"Thank you."

Tanzer forced a smile and turned to Eve. "I'll just carry your suitcase up to your room. Isn't this place as great as I told you?"

She glanced around the foyer. A gleaming oak floor led to a staircase that might have come straight from the house in the novel to which Tanzer had compared it. Fine wood everywhere and delicately painted murals on the walls. "It's very nice."

The bedroom was even nicer, with its fourteen-foot ceiling and huge four-poster bed. Eve threw her handbag on the satin-covered bed and went out on the wrought-iron balcony facing the bayou.

The view was lovely. The winding waters of the bayou snaked past the house, and cypress and willow trees formed a green veil over the banks. An arched footbridge crossed the murky waters leading to what appeared to be a mossy island. Near the bend of the bayou was a dark looming structure that she—

"Didn't I say it was picturesque?" Tanzer said, behind her. "Now, how about going out to dinner at a nice seafood restaurant I know, and then I'll take you for a tour of the city."

Lord, he was persistent. "I don't want to go anywhere. I'm tired and I just want to take a shower and rest. Thank you for the offer."

He nodded. "You see? You couldn't have worked anyway. It's just as well that Senator Melton was delayed in New York."

"I'm seldom too tired to work." Eve turned back to the bayou. "Is that the church?"

"Yes." Tanzer nodded at the ornate entrance of the huge crumbling structure a few hundred yards away. "See, it's only a short distance."

"It looks completely deserted."

"Perhaps it is. I wouldn't know."

"Is that where the skull is now?"

He shrugged. "I wasn't told. It's where you'll be working."

"Is there someone I should contact?"

"Senator Melton will know."

It was like trying to draw blood from a turnip, and Eve had had enough. She held out her hand. "I won't keep you any longer. Thank you for everything."

"Oh." Tanzer shook her hand. "You're sure you'll be all right?"

"I'll be fine. Thank you."

"Well, you only have to call my office if you change your mind. I'm at your disposal."

"I'll remember." She waited until he'd left the bedroom before crossing to the phone on the desk to dial the number on the card.

"I brought your towels." Marie stood in the doorway.

"Thank you. I'll be with you to help in a moment."

"Why? This is my job." She crossed the room and disappeared into the bathroom.

Melton was not at the hotel, and Eve had to leave a voice mail. Great. Just great. She didn't need to spin her wheels this evening. She needed to work until she was so exhausted she could sleep tonight.

"Do you need help unpacking?" Marie had come back into the room.

"No, thanks. I didn't bring much." Eve smiled. "And I don't want to impose on you. That isn't your job."

"Unless I choose." Marie smiled back at her. "There's nothing shameful about being a servant. It's hard, honorable work. I just don't like being patronized by a *trou du cul*." She turned to leave. "Dinner will be ready in thirty minutes."

What was a *trou du cul*? She had an idea, but she'd have to see if she could find it in a French-English dictionary in that library Tanzer had mentioned.

She went back onto the balcony and looked at the main entrance of the church. There might be someone there. Maybe she'd take a walk over there after dinner. . . .

But that dinner was going to be ready in thirty minutes and she should take a quick shower. She'd have to hurry. If she was late, she wouldn't be surprised if Marie threw the meal into the bayou.

And what was a *trou du cul*. . . .

———

"This is delicious." Eve ate the last bite of food on her plate. "What is it?"

"*Spezzatino di Manzo coi Fagioli,*" Marie said.

"And that is?"

Marie grinned. "Beef stew."

"Is it a Cajun recipe?"

"No, Italian. I don't only specialize in Cajun food." She made a face. "I know Tanzer probably pigeonholed me in a neat little corner of his mind, but I'm not as predictable as he'd like."

"It's not like any beef stew I've ever eaten. What's in it?"

"Everything. But I can't tell you. It's my mother's recipe and it's a big secret. If I told you, then I'd have to kill you."

The woman's humor no longer surprised Eve. She had found Marie's conversation interesting and her knowledge well rounded. Marie was unusual, to say the least. "Heaven forbid. Your mother taught you to cook?"

"Partly. I went to the cuisine school in New Orleans after I left the university. I was going to be this magnificent, temperamental chef who would dazzle all the world with my delicious concoctions."

"Well, you dazzled me. You changed your mind?"

Marie shrugged. "Life changed it. I got pregnant and I had to make adjustments. You can't take chances when you have to care for a baby."

"You have a child?"

"A boy. Well, a man. Pierre's at Tulane University in New Orleans himself now. He's very smart and kind. He's going to be a wonderful physician, but it takes a lot of money." She looked at Eve. "You have children?"

"I have an adopted daughter, Jane. She's only twelve, but she's pretty wonderful, too."

"Then you understand how I feel about Pierre," Marie said soberly. "I would do anything for him. He's my whole world."

"Yes, I do understand."

"Good." The housekeeper drew a deep breath. "More wine?"

Eve shook her head. "I need to keep a clear head. I thought I'd walk over to the church and see if I can find something to do."

"What work do you do?"

"I'm a forensic sculptor." That was seldom explanation enough. "I reconstruct faces from skulls."

"I saw something on the television about that." Marie made a face. "Very creepy."

"It all depends how you look at it. You get used to it." Eve got to her feet. "Thank you for a great meal, Marie."

"Who are you going to . . ." She searched for the word. "Reconstruct?"

"I try not to know. I might be influenced. Will I see you when I get back?"

Marie shook her head. "I'll wash up and go home."

"Where do you live?"

"I have my own house in the city. The key to the front door is on the table in the foyer. I'll lock the back door. I'll be back at seven in the morning to fix your breakfast."

"I'll see you then." But Eve hoped she'd be up and working by that time. "Good-bye, Marie."

Marie smiled and turned away.

Nice woman, Eve thought as she left the house. Thank God, she would have someone around that she liked and understood in this strange place. She was already feeling more at home here.

A few minutes later she was walking across the bridge spanning the bayou. This ancient church was a strange choice for a work site, she thought. Or maybe not. It was certainly private enough, and Melton had stressed confidentiality.

The brass knocker on the huge double doors made a resounding noise.

No answer.

She knocked again.

Silence, dammit.

Well, it had been a long shot anyway. She knocked one more time, waited for a few minutes, and then turned away and started back toward the bridge. It was clear she'd have to be patient and wait until tomorrow.

But Eve didn't want to be patient. She wanted to get to work. Why couldn't Melton have been here as he'd prom—

What was that?

She stopped, her gaze flying back to the main entrance of the church.

Had someone come to the door and called her?

The door was still shut.

Yet she would swear someone had called her. The impression had been so vivid . . .

Well, it hadn't happened. It was probably a case of so badly wanting that door to open.

It was still early, but she'd go to bed and try to sleep. When she woke, she'd grab some breakfast and try the church again.

She stopped before going back into the house to glance back at the church.

The door was still shut.

Déjà vu.

She had a sudden memory of last week, when she'd had that sense of . . . something . . . up on Bonnie's hill.

Not Bonnie. It wasn't Bonnie. That had all been a lie.

But maybe that feeling she'd had on the hill had not been a lie. Maybe the bastard who'd later desecrated the grave had been there.

But this feeling was . . . different. She would swear she'd heard someone call.

Nonsense. It was because her nerves were stretched taut and she was an emotional wreck. The only thing she'd heard calling her was the work she'd been hoping to do tonight. Everything would be better after a good night's sleep.

———————

Eve woke three hours later and barely managed to get her head over to the side of the bed before she threw up.

"Oh, God."

Sick. So sick.

She staggered down the hall toward the bathroom, but threw up twice before she reached it.

Her stomach wouldn't stop wrenching. Pain. Nausea.

She dropped to the floor beside the toilet.

She threw up again and again and again.

The stew . . .

Her ribs hurt. She couldn't breathe.

Food poisoning . . .

She was going to die.

Bonnie.

She threw up again.

Nobody was here. Empty house. No one to help her.

Get to the phone.

She was too weak to walk. She crawled back down the hall to the bedroom. It was a million miles away and she had to stop to heave several times.

Her ribs . . .

The phone . . . 911. No dial tone.

She tried the operator. "Help . . . me. Please, help . . ."

The phone dropped from her hand. She was going to pass out.

Not here. She'd die here.

The balcony. Someone might see her. Maybe she could call . . .

She wasn't going to make it.

That was okay. She'd be with Bonnie. Why did she keep trying? It would be so easy to give up.

Joe.

She kept crawling. She was out on the balcony, her cheek pressed against the wrought-iron bars. The metal felt cold, clammy . . .

She couldn't see anyone near the bayou and the houses were too far away for anyone to hear her if she called. The church loomed huge and dark and silent.

"Help . . ." Her futile cry was barely audible even to her. Jesus, she couldn't stop retching. "Help . . . me."

She was sliding down, her face was on the tiles. She could no longer see the bayou, only the tall, dark doors of the church. It filled her vision. Would that be the last thing she saw . . .

Darkness.

———

"No. You mustn't sleep. Not yet."

She opened her eyes.

She was being carried down the stairs.

A man . . . dark hair . . . She couldn't see his face in the darkness of the hall, but his tone was desperate.

Desperate? Why? she wondered vaguely. She was the one who was dying.

"We'll be there soon. Hold on."

Be where?

She gagged again, but there was nothing to throw up.

Oh, God, her ribs hurt.

———

"Are you there? I'm coming, Bonnie."

"Don't you dare. It's not your time." Bonnie was bending over her. *"You fight, Mama."*

"Too tired. Too sad."

"That doesn't matter. Things will get better."

"I want to be with you."

"You are with me. Always. Why won't you believe me?"

"I'm too tired . . . I have to . . . give up."

"No, you don't. I won't let you. Do you hear me, Mama? I won't let you. . . ."

———

The house was dark, but he didn't turn on the light. He moved quickly through the foyer and then down the hall.

Quick. He had to be quick. He didn't know how much time he had.

The kitchen smelled of lemon and the clean scent of soap, and the white refrigerator gleamed in the moonlight streaming through the window.

Hurry.

He opened the refrigerator and took out the only covered

bowl on the shelf. He popped the lid and checked the contents before closing the refrigerator door. Then he wiped the handle and moved toward the door.

It was done.

As he reached the street, his gaze was drawn to the doors of the church, as it always was when he was near it. He felt his stomach muscles clench as the tension and horror gripped him.

No, it was only partly done.

Hurry. . . .

———————

White.

White everywhere. White walls, white sheets on her bed.

"Do you want some ice chips? They said you'd probably want some as soon as you woke up."

A deep voice with just a hint of a British accent.

Her gaze shifted to the dark-haired man sitting in the chair beside the bed. It took a moment for her mind to clear enough to recognize him. "Galen?"

Sean Galen nodded. "The water?"

She nodded. Her throat felt so sore and parched that one word had rasped it.

He put the glass to her lips. "You're hooked up to an IV to help the dehydration, but this should feel good."

The cold liquid slowly flowing down her throat did feel good. Even though the actual act of swallowing was painfully difficult.

"What are you . . . doing here?"

"That hurt, didn't it?" Galen leaned back in the chair. "I'll try to fill in the gaps. I have to ask a couple of questions. You nod or shake your head. Talk as little as possible. You're at the Assisi Hospital in Baton Rouge. Do you remember how you got here?"

She shook her head.

"You contracted the granddaddy of all food poisonings. You nearly died. You were brought in after midnight, and it's nearly four now. They had to work on you for a long time."

"Food poisoning?"

He nodded. "That's what they said. Did you eat in a restaurant last night?"

She shook her head. "At the house. Marie . . ."

"Who is Marie?"

"Marie Letaux. Housekeeper. She made me stew."

"Did anyone else eat any of it?"

She shook her head.

"That's good. What room did you eat in? Do you know if the rest of the stew is in the refrigerator at the apartment? We need to get rid of it."

"I ate in the kitchen." She tried to remember. She had a vague memory of Marie putting foil over the bowl, but she didn't recall her putting it in the refrigerator. "Probably."

"I'll check it out." He poured more water into her glass and held it to her lips. "Though it wouldn't surprise me if she left it on the counter, if she's this careless in her cooking."

"Don't blame . . . Nice. Probably not her fault. Someone must have sold her some bad food in the market."

"Maybe."

"What are you doing here?" she asked again.

"Logan gave me a call and asked me to go and see what was shaking with you." He grinned. "What was shaking was your tummy. More like an earthquake. Right?"

She nodded. "Logan? How did he know where—" She knew the answer. "Joe."

Galen nodded. "Logan said Quinn asked him to make sure you were all right. He was uneasy about the setup here and said the two of you were on the outs. Since Logan and Quinn are still not on the best of terms, Logan thought it must be serious enough to give me a buzz."

What had Joe been thinking about? Eve had met Galen only once before, but Logan had told her about his extremely dubious background. He had been everything from a mercenary to a troubleshooter for various corporations. She shook her head. "Don't . . . need you."

"Well, Logan paid me in advance. I may as well stick around for a few days." He smiled. "You'll find me very useful. I'm fabulous company, I'm a great cook, and I promise I won't give you food poisoning. What else could you ask?"

"I don't need company. I'll be working."

"Not until you get over this case of food poisoning. The doctor won't release you until tomorrow, and said you'll be weak as a kitten for a few days."

She could believe it. She had just woken up but she could hardly hold her eyes open.

Galen's gaze narrowed on her face. "If you won't accept my services, maybe I should call Quinn and tell him about your bout with food poisoning."

And Joe would be on the next flight here. She couldn't face that right now. "Blackmail."

He nodded cheerfully. "Do it well, don't I?"

Oh, what the hell. It didn't make any difference. "You can stay, if you promise not to tell Joe about this."

"Done." He stood up and headed for the door. "Now, I'll let

you rest. Paul Tanzer is out in the waiting room. He was pretty insistent about seeing you, but I held him off. Do you want me to send him in?"

She shook her head. "Tiresome. Marie called him . . ." What was the word? "*Trou du cul*. What does that mean?"

He chuckled. "Asshole. I'm beginning to realize your Marie isn't as thick-witted as I thought."

"She's very smart. She'll wonder where I am when she comes to the house in the morning. Will you tell her?"

He nodded as he opened the door. "I'll take care of it. Do you know where she lives?"

"No."

"Then I'll ask Tanzer."

"Galen."

He looked back at her.

"It wasn't you who found me and brought me to the hospital, was it?"

He shook his head. "I came to the hospital was his contact Logan found out from the hospital? bed when he got the here. as I remember?"

thing I remember was being out on the balcony thinking I was going to die. Then there was a man . . . dark hair."

"That figures. The emergency room people said you were admitted by a small, dark man who handed them your purse with a card that had Paul Tanzer's name and phone number. He told them to check for food poisoning. He left before they could get any other information. Recognize the description?"

Eve shook her head. "I only remember him carrying me and telling me not to go to sleep."

"How did he get in? Was the house unlocked?"

"I locked the front door myself, and Marie said she was going to lock the back door. She might have forgotten."

"Maybe." Galen shrugged. "And maybe he was a Good Samaritan who heard you calling for help and broke in. I'll check the doors. We may hear from him again. Good Samaritans who don't expect compensation are rare these days." He lifted his hand. "See you. I'll pick you up tomorrow and take you back to the apartment."

He was gone.

Good Samaritan. If what Galen said was true, he had probably saved her life.

But how had he gotten into the apartment? Well, maybe Marie had forgotten. She'd ask her tomorrow. She was too sleepy now . . .

Chapter Four

THE SMALL HOUSE ...k lived was on a twist- ...ton Rouge. Like the rest of the ...geraniums bloomed on the doorstep.

...d: ...an't answer Galen's first knock. Nor the second or ...

He waited for a few minutes and then tried the door. Locked.

He examined the lock. Piece of cake. It took him only a few minutes to spring it.

He entered a living room that contained comfortable furniture, but nothing ostentatious. He noticed there were more geraniums on the coffee table. Several family pictures in matching maple frames stared at him from the bookcase across the room. The overall impression was that this was a nice house occupied by nice people.

But Galen's experience was that things were rarely as they appeared to be. He walked over to the desk and went through it. Letters with a New Orleans return address. A checkbook and savings account passbook, a receipt for the rental of a safety-deposit box dated two days ago. More pictures, unframed, showing a young man in a green T-shirt.

He closed the drawer and moved across the room toward the far door that must lead to the kitchen. He could see the white refrigerator with small colorful magnets against the far wall. Marie Letaux obviously had a taste for whimsy and showed it in little things with which she surrounded—

He stopped inside the door, his gaze drawn to the woman crumpled on the floor beside the stove.

A small, dark-haired woman with hair swept back in a chignon,

Probably Marie

open, as if she was staring up at him.

Undoubtedly dead.

"I can't tell you how sorry I am that this happe

night here." Senator Kendal Melton's first words w

with heartfelt sincerity.

"I don't think it would have been any more pleasant on any succeeding night," Eve said dryly.

"No, of course not. How do you feel?"

"Lousy. My ribcage is so sore I can hardly breathe." Eve sat up in bed and gazed at him appraisingly. He appeared far more cosmopolitan than Tanzer. Melton's gray-streaked hair sported white sideburns, complementing a tan that looked pure West Palm Beach. "But I'm better than I was this morning. I'll probably be able to work tomorrow."

"I hope so." He came closer to the bed. "Was Paul Tanzer helpful? I told him to give you the VIP treatment."

"He was very kind."

"It's our intention to give you all the support you can possibly want."

"Then tell me what I'm supposed to be working on. I'm getting very tired of all this hush-hush stuff. I took the job; now fill me in."

"I'll tell you all I know, but I'm afraid it won't be as much as you'd like. Hell, I don't know as much as I'd like. I'm asking you to determine the identity of a skeleton discovered quite recently in the swamps south of here."

"Discovered by whom? And why wasn't the skeleton turned over to the local police?"

"Sheriff Bouvier of Jefferson parish got a tip about the possible identity of the skeleton and its location. He was the one who excavated it. The sheriff is a personal friend and notified me. He gave me full permission to try to discreetly discover the identity before he turned in his report. He knew the discovery might present difficulties for me with the media if it wasn't handled correctly."

"Why? Whose skull is this supposed to be?"

He hesitated.

"Senator Melton, remind me to tell you about the Miami drug lord who asked me to do a reconstruction on a skull that—"

"No, no. It's nothing like that. The only reason that we're

trying to keep it under wraps is that we don't want to raise false hopes. We believe he may be Harold Bently." He paused. "You don't remember the press on Bently?"

She shook her head.

"Well, it was over two years ago, but there was a big furor over his disappearance. Bently was a candidate for the senatorial seat I now hold. He was supposed to be a shoo-in, but vanished four months before election day. He was a solid citizen, a man who wouldn't just disappear of his own accord, so foul play was suspected. But no clues were found. His disappearance has hung like a cloud over my career and I want to lay it to rest."

"Because you may want to run for president?"

"That's in the hands of Providence, but I do want to keep climbing. Is that so strange?"

"No."

"Then help me out. The Bently file has remained open, but nothing has surfaced . . . until this skeleton was found."

"Have you told his family?"

Melton shook his head. "Not yet. As I said, I was afraid to raise false hopes. Please believe me. I'm not totally selfish. Sure, I want to protect my career, but I also want to be able to give Bently's wife advance notice before she has to face a media storm again. She's been through enough."

"Why do you need me? What about DNA?"

He grimaced. "Unfortunately, the body of the skeleton seems to have disappeared."

"What?"

"Don't be alarmed. You're perfectly safe."

"Sure I am. Except that someone doesn't want this body identified. What about the teeth?"

"No teeth. And the skull was burned, but we hoped . . ."
Melton shrugged. "Extracting DNA may be very difficult and
time-consuming. We'll naturally pursue that avenue, but there
may be a media leak at any time. I have to have some warning of
the identity."

"So you can put a spin on whatever I find." Eve shook her
head. "It's not worth it to me."

"You're afraid?"

"I'm not dumb. Why should I risk my life for you and your
career?"

"The skull was moved to the church in great secrecy. No one
will suspect it's there, and we'll have people at the church at all
times to protect you."

Eve shook her head.

"I don't blame you for not caring about my problems, but
Bently was a good man." Melton paused. "And he had a wife
and three children. I guess I don't have to tell you what hell
they've been going through for the last two years."

Good move, she thought bitterly. Calculated or not, the
words struck exactly the right note. She knew the agony of going
through years of waiting with no closure.

"Think about it. It's only a few days, a week at most. I'll get
what I want, Mrs. Bently and the children's years of agony may
be over, and you'll have the satisfaction of working on an interesting project. Everybody wins."

"Why didn't you just send me the skull?"

"We were planning on doing that before the skeleton disappeared. After that happened, I thought we should have increased security. I was also concerned about the media, since you
have a greater visibility in your hometown." Melton grimaced.

"I didn't want to stir up the media unless I had something positive to offer them. They'd love to dredge up all that sensational stuff we went through after Bently disappeared." He breathed a sigh of relief. "I'm glad we can have everything out in the open now."

Eve gazed at him skeptically. "Then you won't mind if I check with Sheriff Bouvier about the skeleton."

"I do mind your lack of trust, but I'll call the sheriff and tell him to be entirely open with you." Melton paused. "And now that you realize how fully you're going to have our support, you certainly won't need any outside help."

He was leading up to something. "Meaning?"

"You probably don't realize that Sean Galen has a criminal background and is completely untrustworthy. I'm sure you'll want to send him packing."

"Really? John Logan trusts him."

"Mr. Logan is a respectable businessman and I'd never want to impugn his choice of associates. Perhaps he doesn't realize the extent of Galen's—"

"Logan doesn't wear blinders. He knows more about Galen than you do."

"We won't argue. The crux of my argument is that you have no need of Galen. I'll be glad to dismiss him for you."

"He's not an easy man to dismiss." Eve stared Melton directly in the eyes. "And I've no desire to dismiss him. Galen stays."

"In what capacity? You surely don't think you need a bodyguard just because of this little incident."

"This 'little incident' almost killed me." She waved an impatient hand. "But no, I don't need a bodyguard. Don't you dare suggest that in Marie's hearing. It was an accident. She's going to feel bad enough about my getting ill."

"Then in what capacity?" Melton repeated. "Galen isn't qualified for anything but—"

"You're Melton?" Galen was standing in the doorway. "I'm Sean Galen." He came forward. "And I really think you've overstayed your visit. Eve's looking a little stressed."

"I'm not stressed."

"Will you accept 'pissed off'?" He turned to Melton. "Eve doesn't like to be told what to do. Now, I realize that you only have her well-being at heart, but she can get a little cranky. Suppose you leave."

"You have no right to—" Melton broke off as he met Galen's gaze. He took an involuntary step backward, but recovered quickly. "Ms. Duncan realizes I only want what's best for her." His glance shifted to Eve. "I'll be here to pick you up tomorrow morning."

"I've already claimed that pleasure." Galen made a shooing motion. "Bye."

Melton gave him a cold glance and left the room.

"And what if I hadn't wanted him to go?" Eve asked.

"You were bristling. When a person is as sick as you are, it takes a major annoyance to make her bristle. I overheard quite a bit, including the bit about me. I'm flattered."

"You shouldn't be. You're right; I was only irritated because he was trying to tell me what to do." She thought of something else. "But I'm not pleased you scared him away. I wanted to ask him some more questions about this damn reconstruction."

"To quote one of your fellow southerners, 'Tomorrow is another day.' "

"That's a terrible southern accent."

"It's the best a poor lad from Liverpool can do." He sat in the chair beside her bed. "You didn't know anything about this job when you came here?"

"I knew it was a request from a respected member of the Senate."

"And you wanted to get away from Quinn."

She looked at him.

"Okay, I'm obviously out of line."

"Right." She paused. "And Melton was also right. I don't need you, Galen."

"You're getting hoarse again. You've been talking too much." He took her glass and filled it with ice chips. "I'll stay away from talking about Quinn. But there's the slimmest possibility you may need me, so I'll stick around." He handed her the glass. "I just came from Marie Letaux's house. She's dead."

Shock surged through her. "What?"

"I found her on the kitchen floor. There was a plate on the table with the remains of stew on it." He grimaced. "And also remains all over the floor. She'd evidently been throwing up."

"She took the stew home?" Eve shook her head in horror. "My God, that's terrible."

"You said you assumed she put it in the refrigerator."

"She must have changed her mind. I left before she did." Sad. So incredibly sad. "She had a son. He was studying medicine in New Orleans."

Galen nodded. "She had pictures all over the living room. Nice-looking kid."

"It was clear she adored him." Eve could feel the tears sting her eyes. "Shit. I'd only just met her, but I liked her. I guess I identified with her. She was a woman alone who'd had to make her way in the world. They're sure it was food poisoning?"

"There hasn't been time for an autopsy, but I suspect that will probably be the decision. Particularly since you landed here with the same ailment."

There was something in his tone. . . . "You don't think it was?"

"I didn't say that. I believe it was food poisoning."

"Galen."

"Sorry. It's my suspicious nature. She was in a nightgown and a chenille robe, and her bed had been slept in. That means she probably got up in the middle of the night and ate a huge plate of the stew. Very heavy meal for a midnight snack."

"Maybe she didn't eat dinner and woke up hungry."

"Possibly. Now when you started throwing up, you tried to get help, didn't you? Marie Letaux had a phone, but evidently wasn't able to contact anyone. She lives very close to her neighbors, so wouldn't you think that she'd manage to get one of them to take her to the hospital?"

"It would have been difficult. I was so weak I could barely move."

"But you did move. And you said she was a woman who was accustomed to taking care of herself. Evidently she was so overcome she didn't even make it to the sink or the toilet to throw up. Wasn't that your first instinct?"

She nodded. "What are you getting at, Galen?"

"Oh, I was just playing 'what if.' " He took the glass from her and set it on the table. "What if she didn't get the munchies during the night? What if someone sat across from her at that table and forced her to eat that stew and then waited with her until the poison took effect."

Her eyes widened in shock. "That's crazy. For one thing, I didn't show symptoms for over three hours."

"I agree it would have taken a good deal of patience and tremendous focus. It would have taken even more nerve to sit and watch her die. Particularly if he wasn't sure that someone wouldn't barge in any minute after they figured out Marie might also be at risk for food poisoning."

She shuddered. "The idea's completely macabre."

"I have that kind of mind."

"Why would anyone do that?"

"Well, after I found the body and before I called the police, I went to her desk and checked out her financial records. There was no deposit in her checking or savings account, but she rented a safety-deposit box two days ago. Very convenient. What if she stashed a pile of loot in the box?"

"You think she poisoned me on purpose?"

"I believe there's reason to ask why you contracted food poisoning from a meal produced by an experienced cook."

Eve shook her head. "I can't believe that."

"Because you liked her."

"And why would she have been killed?"

"So that she couldn't talk?" Galen shrugged. "Any number of reasons."

"But you're only guessing."

He smiled. "What if?"

"Did you suggest this to the police?"

"Be for real. I'd be the first one on the suspect list. I had enough trouble explaining why I was the one who found her. They even called the hospital to make sure you'd been checked in with food poisoning." He thought for a moment. "I have a few friends in New Orleans with forensic backgrounds who might be able to go in and scavenge around and see what else they can come up with."

"Official friends?"

"Be for real," Galen repeated as he tilted his head and studied her expression. "You're taking my theory seriously?"

Eve slowly nodded. She had to take it seriously. She didn't want to believe any of it, but she had been exposed to brutality and deception for most of her life and certainly all her career. She shuddered. "To sit there and watch her . . . Jesus, it sounds so . . . cold-blooded."

"No more cold-blooded than trying to kill you."

"And why would anyone want to kill me?"

"Maybe we should ask Mr. Melton."

"You think it's the reconstruction?"

"It's a logical connection. And I'm not sure I buy this story Melton's spinning. I don't like all this secrecy. They know you like working away from the media glare; that knowledge gives them another excuse to bring you here instead of sending you that skull. Don't you think it might be wise for you to pack your bags and head home?"

Eve rejected that suggestion immediately. No way was she going home. "There's no proof that this is anything but food poisoning. Maybe there's no money in that safety-deposit box. Or maybe Marie was saving money for years and just got around to depositing it."

He lifted a skeptical brow.

"I *liked* her, Galen."

"Few people are completely rotten. Some just have a streak or two. But those streaks can be enough to hurt you. And what about that missing skeleton? Doesn't that bother you?"

"Of course it bothers me. It means there's somebody who

doesn't want Melton to identify this man. But most of the skulls I work on are victims, and it's not the first time I've had this problem. If I stopped work every time I thought there was someone out there who didn't want me to do it, I'd never finish any reconstructions."

Galen studied her face. "And you're curious about this reconstruction, aren't you? You really want to do it."

She nodded. "I really do. Harold Bently sounds like a man I'd admire. I hate the idea of him ending up discarded in a swamp like a piece of garbage. I want to know. . . ." She shrugged. "And it's intriguing."

"Maybe a little too intriguing." Galen stood. "Okay, we'll go with it. I know if you want to do it, there's no way I'll be able to talk you out of it. But I'm not going to fade into the background as I'd planned."

"I'm sure that would have been a first."

"I can be unobtrusive." He grinned. "It's just not so much fun." He moved toward the door. "But I'm going with you to the church every day. And I'm your official food taster. I stay with you night and day. Agreed?"

"This may all be for nothing."

"But you feel safer, don't you? How could you not with me on the job?"

Eve made a rude sound.

"That was indelicate." He glanced at her over his shoulder. "You're sure I shouldn't tell Quinn about this?"

"I'm sure."

He gave a mock shiver at her tone. "Just checking. The situation between you two seems to be taking on some heat."

She stared at him challengingly. "What's the matter? Can't you handle it, Galen?"

"That was a low blow. You're a tough lady. I heard you grew up on the streets. I can believe it."

"Takes one to know one. I'm sure Atlanta is no tougher than Liverpool."

"No, it isn't." Galen nodded. "Okay. No Quinn."

She watched the door swing shut behind him.

No Quinn.

The words echoed in her mind. Joe Quinn had been a part of her life for so long, the idea of his not being there was practically incomprehensible. It would take time to understand what it meant.

Could she become accustomed to Joe not being in her life? Eve wasn't sure whether it would hurt more to cut the ties between them or to live with what he had done. She didn't know and she didn't want to think about it right now. She didn't want to think of anything but the work she had come here to do. She would do the reconstruction, and then perhaps send for Jane and go to New Orleans for awhile. She should see something besides her little corner of the world. She didn't have to go home.

And the idea of Marie Letaux making an attempt on her life was as bizarre as the ugly picture Galen had drawn of the way Marie might have died. No one could be that cold-blooded.

Yes, they could. Bonnie's killer had been that kind of monster, and she had known other murderers equally terrible. She just didn't want that kind of horror to touch her now when she was trying to work through a horror of her own. She didn't want it to be true.

Maybe it wasn't. Galen's experience had made him suspect everyone and everything. Well, let him be suspicious. Let him protect her. It wouldn't hurt.

Not if it would allow her the freedom of mind to get her work done.

"I know you didn't want any interference, Jules," Melton said. "I attempted to get her to dismiss him, but she's being very stubborn about it. I wanted you to know that I'm not letting the matter lie. I'm going to call a few people and see what kind of pressure they can put on him to nudge him out of the situation."

"Leave him alone," Hebert said. "He's not going to be a problem for us."

There was a silence on the other end of the line. "Perhaps I should send you a dossier on him?"

"I already have one."

"And you don't think he could be troublesome?"

"I believe he'll be more troublesome if we try to get rid of him. I want her mind at rest when she's working on the skull. Galen's presence will assure that she feels entirely safe and secure."

"Yes, that's important." Melton was silent a moment. "I was uneasy when I heard about the food poisoning. It was an accident?"

"Of course it was." It was a half-truth. It was an accident that Eve Duncan had not died.

"I've just been told that Marie Letaux was found dead of food poisoning a few hours ago."

"Then that should prove it was an accident to you."

"Should it? What about those deaths last month? They were supposed to be accidents, too."

"And probably were." Hebert added mockingly, "You're getting paranoid. Have you started looking over your shoulder lately, Melton?"

"I have a right to be concerned, dammit." A pause. "First Etienne, and now this. Another very curious incident. They seem to be hovering around you like a dark cloud."

Hebert ignored the implication. "Is she hesitating about doing the reconstruction?"

"Yes, but I believe she's still eager to do it. We just have to push the right buttons."

"That's what we need. Eagerness . . . and speed."

"She'll be released tomorrow and I think she'll want to start work at once."

"That's good. I'll make sure that she does. Let me know if there's anything else I can do to help." Hebert hung up.

Melton was suspicious, but not enough to cause Jules any immediate problems. Melton wouldn't make a move until after Boca Raton. The Cabal needed things to go smoothly, and advance preparations took time and effort. They wouldn't want to bring in someone new at this point.

Hebert leaned back in his chair and covered his eyes with his hand. He could feel the panic rising within him and he must crush it down. He'd had to lie to Melton, but things were still under control. Events were escalating, and he had to move fast to keep from being caught and drowned in their wake. God, Eve Duncan was strong. He had *felt* her fighting to live. Too bad that her struggle was for nothing, he thought sadly.

Because the way things were going, there was no way he could let her survive.

————

"You scared me, Mama," Bonnie said.

Eve looked across the hospital room to see Bonnie curled up in a visitor's chair by the window. The nurse had turned out the light forty minutes ago, but the moonlight streaming in the window lit Bonnie's curly red-brown hair. It was too dim to see the freckles marching across her nose. Her small body was dressed in jeans and a Bugs Bunny T-shirt, as it always was when she came to Eve. She smothered the surge of love she felt and said accusingly, "You wouldn't let me go, dammit."

"I told you, it wasn't your time. And you didn't really want to die."

"Don't tell me what I want to do. Who's the mother around here?"

"I think all these years of ghostdom qualify me to have my input." Bonnie sighed. "You've been very challenging, Mama. You still won't admit I'm anything but a dream."

"Because your so-called ghostly powers seem to be rather limited. Ghostdom? What kind of word is that? And if you didn't want me to die, why did you let me eat that stew? It would have saved me a bellyache."

"I've told you I can't stop things happening . . . it doesn't work that way."

"Convenient. That means you're never to blame."

Bonnie giggled. "That's right. It's one of the good things about being a ghost."

"Are there bad things, baby?"

"Look at you. You're tearing up. Yes, the bad thing is trying to keep you from being so unhappy. I thought maybe you were on the right track, but here you are all depressed and hurting and hundreds of miles away from Joe."

"Joe lied to me. About you. Your grave. Why didn't you tell me it wasn't you?"

"If I'm a dream, how could I do that?" She grinned. "Gotcha."

"Why?" Eve insisted.

"You know the answer. It doesn't matter to me where my body is. I'm always with you." She paused. "And you were happier thinking I was there. So why not let you think it?"

"You sound like Joe. It's important to me. I want you home, Bonnie."

"I am home." She sighed. "But you're too stubborn to believe it. You make it very hard for me. And I don't like this depression. You're a fighter, but you weren't fighting last night until I nudged you. That's not to happen again, Mama. Things are very . . . cloudy. You may have to fight hard and I may not be around."

"Is that supposed to make me feel less depressed?"

"I'll always come to you like this, but you can't rely on me, Mama. But you have Joe and Jane and Grandma. Isn't that lucky?" She made a face. "I could feel you freezing up when I mentioned Joe. Get over it, Mama."

"Bullshit."

"Okay, we'll talk about something else. I want you to feel good in the morning."

Eve always felt better after the dreams. They had started two years after Bonnie had died, and at times Eve felt as if they had saved her sanity. A psychiatrist would probably have sent her to the nearest funny farm if she told him that. Well, screw them. There was nothing that wasn't positive about the dreams. "If my ribs are still this sore, there's no way I'll feel good in the morning."

"They'll be a little better." Bonnie leaned back in the chair. "This is a nice place. I like all those bayous. Why didn't we ever come here?"

"I don't know. I guess I never got around to it."

"Well, Panama City was nice, too. I loved the water. . . ."

"I know you did, baby."

"There are lots of things to love. Now tell me about Jane's new puppy. Sarah gave him to her?"

"Yes, and he's a complete rascal. Of course, Jane thinks he's the smartest animal in the universe. She's talking about going out to the coast and having Sarah help her train . . ."

Chapter Five

YOU'RE IN A BETTER MOOD THIS morning." Galen studied Eve's expression as he helped her into his car after they'd left the hospital. "And you look much healthier. Did you sleep well?"

"When I wasn't dreaming."

"Nightmares?"

She shook her head. "No, good dreams." She gazed up at the brilliant blue sky. "It's a pretty day."

He nodded. "You could probably still use a day of rest. Why don't you sit out on the balcony and just watch the world go by?"

The church, dark and looming, filling her entire vision as she lay on the balcony floor.

"I want to get to work. Did you find out any more about Marie's death?"

"Officially food poisoning. Case closed."

"I see."

"I don't. I paid a small bribe to a clerk at the coroner's department to get a look at the provisional report."

"And?"

"Food poisoning." He paused. "The only thing in the least unusual was slight abrasions on her upper arms."

"Caused by what?"

"No conclusions. But I was wondering . . . ropes?"

"But that's not what the coroner said."

"No." Galen shrugged. "At any rate, the body has been released and the funeral is tomorrow."

"Her son is coming here?"

"I assume he will. This is his mother's hometown. Why?"

"I want to see him and express my sympathy."

"What?" He grimaced. "I believe it's very bad form to offer condolences to the family of someone who tried to murder you."

"I don't believe she tried to kill me, and I think her son would like to know what she told me about their relationship. It could help at a time like this. I'd like to go to the funeral."

"Okay. I'll find out when and where. I'm surprised you're willing to delay the start of your work on the skull."

"Support means a good deal to the bereaved. This time is a nightmare. No one knows that better than I do."

"So I've heard." Galen's voice was sober. "Your Bonnie."

"My Bonnie." They had pulled up in front of the house and she got out of the car. "Melton called the hospital and arranged to meet me here at one, then go with me to the church. Are you coming with us?"

"I wouldn't miss it." Galen watched Eve unlock the front door, and then preceded her into the foyer. He glanced around the foyer and then started up the stairs. Eve followed. "Skeletons are my cup of tea. Mind if I take a look around your bedroom? I was here earlier and did a little cleanup job, but I'd feel better if I just checked it again."

"You cleaned up that mess?"

"Well, your housekeeper wasn't able to do it. I didn't want you to have to come home and face it."

"Thank you. That was a very kind thing to do."

"I *am* kind." He threw open the bedroom door and looked around. "My mum always said if you want to get along in the world, you have to do unto others as they do unto you."

"That's not quite the way the quote goes."

"Makes more sense Mum's way." He went onto the balcony and looked out over the bayou. "Seems okay. You rest. I'll just check the bathroom and the downstairs, and then cook you a light lunch."

"I'm not an invalid. I'll do it."

"Are you trying to eliminate my job? How can I be the queen's chief poison taster if you do everything yourself?" He headed for the door. "By the way, I moved into the bedroom next door. I checked and I can hear practically everything that happens in this room through those paper-thin walls. I hope you don't snore. . . ."

Eve heard him running down the steps a few minutes later. She gave one more glance at the church before leaving the balcony. It was difficult to pull her gaze away. She supposed it was natural the ancient structure would command attention, and it was the last thing she'd seen when she'd thought she was going to die. That had guaranteed it would capture her imagination.

Eve forced herself to turn and go back into the bedroom. That wide expanse of bed was very tempting. It was ridiculous to be this sore and tired. She'd thought when she'd left the hospital that she'd spring back much sooner. She should ignore the tiredness and hit the shower. She'd be okay once she got going.

Well, maybe just a short nap . . .

"The shoes were made by the Norton Shoe Company." Carol Dunn tossed the report on Joe's desk. "It's a southeast company with branches in Alabama and Louisiana. Size nine."

"Distribution?" Joe asked.

She shook her head. "Pretty heavy in both states, and to a lesser degree here in Georgia. With this kind of flimsy sole, they're not a high-ticket item so they sell pretty well."

"That's just great." He frowned. "What about the tire tracks?"

"Firestone Affinity HP fifteen-inch. Standard on the new Saturn L-three hundred."

"Thanks, Carol." Joe scanned the report. "I owe you."

"You owe yourself a good night's sleep," she said. "Jane called and told me to send you home early."

"I'm going." He stood up and started for the door. "Will you call and tell her I'm bringing home Chinese, but I have to make one more stop on the way?"

"Coward."

"Right. She's tough." He glanced back over his shoulder. "Did I get a return call from George Capel when I was out today?"

Carol shook her head. "Don't you trust voice mail?"

"I'm an old-fashioned guy. I don't believe in these newfangled gadgets."

"And you were hoping it wasn't working."

"He hasn't shown up at the DNA lab for a week. I went to his house—the mail is piling up and he didn't stop delivery of the newspaper."

"Doesn't sound good, but he could have taken off on a little jaunt. It's happened before."

"Yeah, I know. But I think it's time I talked to his neighbors."

"Okay, I'll call Jane," Carol said. "But you'd better not forget the Chinese."

Joe nodded and waved as he left the office. He called Logan when he reached his car. "Have you heard from Galen?"

"He won't report to me unless he has reason. He runs his own show."

"So you don't know if she's okay."

"We'd have heard if there was a problem. Galen's with her."

And Joe wasn't with her and it was driving him crazy. "Can you ask him to give regular reports?"

"Galen doesn't operate that way."

"Then he should, dammit."

"You asked for Galen, Quinn."

Because he was the best, but that didn't mean Galen's independence didn't annoy the hell out of him. He wanted to *know*.

"How are things going with you?" Logan asked.

"Okay. I'm keeping busy." Not busy enough. Three days had seemed like three hundred since Eve left. "I'm trying to track down Capel. He seems to have disappeared."

"You think he was paid to send that report to Eve and then skipped town?"

"Could be. He didn't try to hit me for more money, so he must have another source."

"Any ideas?"

"Someone who wanted to hurt me or Eve. Probably me. She doesn't have any enemies. I have case files full of them."

"Amazing," Logan murmured.

"And you don't?"

Logan didn't answer. "I'll let you know if I hear from Galen."

"Maybe I should call him. No, never mind."

"Good choice. You wouldn't want Eve to know you're checking up on her. How's Jane?"

"Great. Better than I deserve right now."

"I agree. Good-bye, Quinn."

Joe hung up and started the car. Interview Capel's neighbors and then get home to Jane. Don't think about Eve all those hundreds of miles away in Baton Rouge.

Company branches in Alabama and Louisiana.

Louisiana . . .

Don't jump to conclusions. The defacement could have nothing to do with Eve's reconstruction job in Baton Rouge. But he didn't like the way this investigation was shaping up, dammit.

And he wished to hell he could contact Galen without getting Eve's back up.

Just do your job. Find Capel and the man who bribed him. Do some more checking on the tire. Keep Jane as happy you can. Try to keep yourself from jumping on a plane and flying to Eve in Baton Rouge.

And hope to hell time was healing the rift he'd torn between them.

————

"I fell asleep." Eve came down the stairs, trying to straighten her rumpled hair. "For heaven's sake, it's quarter past five in the evening. Why didn't you wake me?"

"Easy. You needed the sleep." Galen grinned. "And I needed time to prepare a meal par excellence."

"I've got to get over to the church. Didn't Melton show up?"

"He was here right on time. I told him to go away."

"You had no right to do that."

"I told him he could meet us in front of the church at six." He checked his watch. "That gives you forty-five minutes to eat my fine repast." He gestured to the dining room. "I don't like hurried meals; they dull one's appreciation. But I'll accept it this time."

"You should have woken me."

"You're wasting time. You don't want to keep our honorable senator waiting."

She followed him. "I've already kept him waiting for four hours."

Galen grinned. "He deserved it." He seated her at the table and shook out her napkin and put it on her lap. "Now start on the spinach salad."

"No way." She jumped up. "Galen, I want to go to meet Melton. I couldn't eat this meal, anyway. My stomach is still upset."

"What a dunce I am. Of course, you can't. I got carried away with my sheer culinary genius. Okay, maybe I'll make you some soup after we get back from the church tonight."

"I may not come back tonight. I often work at night."

"And then again you may. You still look pale around the gills."

"Galen."

"Don't worry. I'm not trying to bulldoze you. I sometimes take advantage of circumstances to get my own way, but I respect your free will."

"You really like to cook?"

"Eating is one of life's great pleasures. It dulls the roughest edges."

And Galen's life had probably had a multitude of sharp edges. Eve's gaze wandered from the white damask tablecloth to the flickering spring-green candles and then to the delicate bone china. It was as different as night and day from her cozy meal two nights ago in the kitchen.

And that had been his intention, she realized suddenly. He hadn't wanted to remind her of Marie Letaux or that last meal she'd had in this house.

"I'm sure your meal would have been wonderful. Thank you, Galen."

"You're welcome. It's just too bad I have to wait a little longer to be truly appreciated." He took her arm. "Let's get you over to the church so you can stop fretting."

————

To her surprise, Melton was waiting impatiently outside the church when they arrived there. "Good, you're early. You're better? Galen said you weren't feeling well."

"I feel much better." Her gaze went to the door. "I expected you to be inside."

"I don't have a key. I've been waiting for— Here he is." His gaze was on the sandy-haired man hurrying toward them. "This is Rick Vadim. I hired Rick to help you out here. Rick, this is Ms. Duncan."

The young man nodded and smiled at Eve. "How do you do, ma'am. It's my pleasure to meet you."

"Hello. I'm very glad to meet you." She shook his hand. "This is Sean Galen. He's—"

"Ms. Duncan's assistant," Galen supplied. "I make things run smoothly for her."

"Then that makes two of us," Rick said solemnly. "That's also my assignment."

"Rick has been hired to assist Ms. Duncan in any way possible," Melton said.

"You're a forensic anthropologist?" Eve asked.

"No, I have no scientific background. But I'm very good at acquiring things and smoothing the way." He unlocked the door. "You'd like to see the skull?"

"That's why I'm here." Eve glanced around the vestibule. She'd half expected the interior of the church to be covered with dust, but it was spotless. "Where is it?"

"The main chapel." Rick gestured to the arched doorway. "This way, please."

"The chapel?"

"It seemed more respectful," Rick said. "From what I've read about your work, you believe in showing respect for those who have passed on."

"Yes, I do. But I doubt if I'll be able to work in your chapel.

I require a good deal of light, a worktable, and a pedestal for my equipment."

"I've already set up a room for you. I think you'll be satisfied." He threw open the door. "There it is."

A huge black coffin.

She stopped short in the doorway and stared at it. The coffin dominated the small sanctuary.

"I'll wait out here," Melton said.

Eve felt the same strange reluctance to approach the coffin as he obviously did. "I thought you would have already removed the skull from the coffin. I didn't expect to see—It's very . . . big . . ."

"The coffin is designed to protect the remains from further damage or decay. We wanted to make sure the skull was perfectly preserved," Rick said earnestly. "Believe me, I'm very upset that the rest of the skeleton has been misplaced. I wasn't in charge here when that happened."

"Misplaced?" Eve repeated. "I don't believe that's the term I'd use."

"It seems incredible to me, too. This entire affair is bizarre. But that's not my business. My job is to make sure nothing goes wrong from now on." Rick moved forward until he stood beside the coffin. "And I've been told the skull is in very good condition." He opened the lid and stepped aside. "What do you think?"

"I think I need some light. I can hardly see it. It's too dim in here."

"I'm sorry." Rick quickly lit a candle on the altar. "You have wonderful light and heat in the workroom I set up for you. I didn't know you'd want to do a close examination of the skull in here. I should have thought . . ."

He was so upset that Eve smothered the impatience she was

feeling. "It's okay, Rick. If there's a problem, I can take the skull back to the house."

"No, please don't do that. Believe me, I've made your workroom everything you could ask," Rick said. "The senator wants the work done here."

"Why?" Galen asked.

"It's on an island. Senator Melton was very concerned about the missing skeleton. He wants Ms. Duncan to be perfectly safe, and the security people he hired say the church will be much easier to keep protected. I promise I'll do everything I can to make the church comfortable for you."

"That will take some doing." Galen stepped closer, took a penlight out of his pocket, and shone it down into the coffin. "It's damn chilly. It must be damp in every molecule of this place."

"It's very warm in her workroom."

"It's fine," Eve said absently, her gaze on the skull. She still couldn't see worth a damn, but the penlight was better than nothing. Although the skull was blackened by fire, it was intact, except that there were no teeth and the jaw was shattered. But there were no visible punctures or breaks. That was lucky.

"It's a male. Caucasian. The skull is surprisingly well preserved. I'll be able to work with it."

"He's been roughed up a little." Galen pointed to the shattered jawline. "And no teeth. He's been through one hell of a battle. Reminds me of that gladiator movie."

"Shut up, Galen," Eve said. "I have to have an unbiased mind when I do the final stage. I don't want the face to look like Russell Crowe."

"Great movie." Galen glanced at Rick and winked. "You can tell me who you think he is later when she's not around."

Rick smiled and shook his head. "I'm as much in the dark as you are. I can only guess." He turned to Eve. "I've got a pedestal and two worktables in your studio. I understand you'll need a video and computer setup for confirmation. I've been in touch with the Forensic Department at LSU and I think I've got it hooked up right. As soon as you're ready, I'll bring the skull to you."

He was obviously ready to whisk her out of the chapel and set her to work. His eagerness was very appealing, but she wasn't ready to leave the skull yet.

"Galen, why don't you go with Rick and check out the workroom for me while I try to take a better look at the skull?"

"Sure." Galen handed her the penlight. "Not my most interesting assignment, but I live to serve."

"Thanks." She shone the penlight into the nasal cavity. "Definitely Caucasian . . ."

"Come on, Rick. We're not wanted."

Eve was vaguely aware that they were gone and she was alone in the chapel. It didn't matter. Her feelings of unease had completely dissipated the moment she had seen the skull. He was just another one of the lost ones. It didn't matter if this was Bently or some poor vagrant. In the end he had clearly been as much a victim as little Carmelita, whose reconstruction she had just finished. Judging by the condition of the skull and the fact that those teeth had probably been jerked out after death, he might have been more of a victim.

Time to get to know him. Eve gently touched his cheekbone. "What do I call you?" She knew it would seem nuts to anyone on the outside, but she made it a practice to give all her subjects names. Each one had a history and a life. They had laughed and been loved by someone, even this poor beat-up warrior. He'd obviously not won this last battle, but she hoped he'd had his share of victories.

"Victor? Not a bad name." She nodded. "Works for me." She carefully swung down the heavy lid. "I'll see you tomorrow, Victor. And we'll see what we can do about bringing you home."

"Ready?" Galen was standing in the doorway. "Rick's done you proud. Your workroom is wonderfully equipped, lots of light and heat. Clean and shining as a Marine recruits' barracks. Do you want to see it?"

She started to tell him yes, and then stopped. Dammit, the energy she'd thought she'd regained was draining out of her. She came toward him. "No, I trust you. I'll see it tomorrow when I move in."

"Tomorrow?"

"Okay, you were right about my not being up to full speed. I thought I could start tonight, but I'm too tired. I can't begin him when I'm this weak." She grimaced. "I'll be glad when I get back to full strength. I took that long nap this afternoon, but even so, all I want to do is sleep."

"Then that's what you should do. I'm glad you're not going to insist on starting work tonight."

"I've already started work." Eve glanced over her shoulder at the black coffin. "And keen wits and alertness are essential to set up my equipment and start the measuring. Victor can wait a few more hours."

"Victor?"

"The skull."

"Oh." Galen didn't look at her as they started down the hall. "I don't want to be impolite, but do you always talk to skulls?"

"No." She gave him a limpid stare. "I'm very selective."

"It's okay with me. Just thought I'd ask." His gaze went to Rick standing with Melton at the front door. "Rick seems to be a nice guy. Sharp, too. He went to school up north."

"That doesn't surprise me. He sounds like a Yankee. Where did he go?"

"Notre Dame. Big football fan."

"It goes with the territory. He looks like the all-American boy, with that fair hair and those rosy cheeks." She dismissed the subject. "Did you find out when Marie's funeral is tomorrow?"

"Eleven. Are you still going?"

She nodded. "I'll set up early and then break to go to the funeral." As Eve and Galen left the church she held out her hand to Rick, who was still waiting by the front door with Melton. "Thank you for everything. I suppose I'll see you in the morning."

"It will be my pleasure." He shook her hand. "I'll have everything ready for you. I notice the skull is a little dirty, but I left it for you to clean."

"That's exactly right. We don't want to risk any more damage."

He nodded solemnly. "Certainly. Is there anything else I can do?"

Good Lord, he was intense. But that almost childlike earnestness was kind of sweet. "You won't find me very demanding. Just let me do my work."

He smiled. "No one will disturb you. I promise you." He turned to Galen. "An honor, sir."

Galen looked taken aback. "See you, Rick." He said in an undertone as he and Eve left the church, "Sir? Am I getting that old?"

"You don't see that kind of courtesy any more. I think it's refreshing."

"You didn't answer me."

"How old are you, Galen?"

"Thirty-seven."

"That qualifies." She had a sudden thought and glanced back at Rick, who was still talking to Melton. "Rick."

He broke off and looked at her. "You need something? You only have to ask."

"A dragon to kill, a Holy Grail to find," Galen murmured sarcastically.

She ignored him. "Were you here two nights ago when I came to the church, Rick?"

He frowned. "You were here before?"

"The first night I arrived in Baton Rouge. I came and knocked on the door. No one answered."

"Because no one was here. I was at LSU arranging for the video equipment. I just arrived yesterday morning. I would have answered the door if I'd been in the church."

"No one was here?"

He shook his head. "Only the guards patrolling the grounds. And I guess they must have realized you weren't an intruder. You thought there was actually someone inside the church?"

"No, I guess not. I just had a feeling that . . . Never mind. I'll see you in the morning." She turned to Melton. "Good-bye, Senator."

"I take it you're going to accept the job? I wasn't sure you would. I'm very grateful."

"I'm not doing it for you. I'm doing it for that man's family."

He smiled. "I'm still grateful. I'm glad everything is working out well. You have my phone number; please call me if there's any problem."

"You can count on it. Come on, Galen." Eve started toward the bridge.

"Did you see anything that led you to believe someone was here that night?" Galen asked.

"No, it was only a feeling."

He chuckled. "Maybe it was the ghost of our gladiator."

"I don't believe in ghosts."

"That's probably good. Considering how many skeletons you deal with, you could become a basket case."

She glanced away from him. "Do you believe in ghosts?"

"I don't *not* believe in them. I think anything is possible. I just have to be shown." He smiled. "And so far our ghostly friends haven't seen fit to show themselves to me."

"The mind sees what it wants to see. It's all imagination . . . or dreams."

"Dreams?"

She changed the subject. "And stop calling him a gladiator."

"That's right. His name is Victor. Isn't that what you called him?"

She glanced back at the church. Melton and Rick must have gone back inside. The door was shut, and the entrance had regained that air of forbidding secrecy she'd noticed the first time she saw it.

Well, secrets were meant to be solved, and tomorrow she would start. "Yes, his name is Victor."

———

"Will you do it?" Joe asked. "All I'm asking is an afternoon of your time. Just come with me to Capel's neighbors and let them describe the guy to you."

"Don't bullshit me. That's only where it starts." Lenny Tyson penciled in a line beside the flaring nostrils of the woman in his sketch. "Then the real work begins, and I'm swamped right now. You know that, Joe."

"A favor, Lenny."

Tyson glanced up from the sketch. "Why? Is the guy a mass murderer or something?"

Joe shook his head. "This isn't department business, it's personal. I'll pay you twice what the department pays for composite sketches. George Capel was seen by two neighbors the day before he disappeared. He entered his condo with a small, dark-haired man in his late twenties or early thirties. They came out a few hours later and drove off together. He was seen again later that same day at the bank where he has a safety-deposit box. The same man accompanied him. That was almost a week ago."

"And you want me to draw a sketch of Capel's friend?"

"Come on, Lenny. How long could it take?"

"It depends how good a memory the neighbors have." Tyson leaned back in his chair. "Seven days is a long time. It's promising that they remembered the color of his hair and that he wasn't a big man. How close does it have to be?"

"I want to try to compare it to mug files."

"Ouch. That's tough."

"Will you do it?"

"Twice what the department pays?"

"Three times."

Lenny sighed, stood up, and grabbed his art portfolio. "Let's go."

Chapter Six

VICTOR'S SKULL WAS SITTING ON A pedestal when Eve walked into the workroom at seven the next morning.

"I told you I'd have everything ready." Rick beamed as he gestured around the small room. "There are your worktables, and I got the pedestal from a sculptor who lives here in Baton Rouge. Is it okay?"

"Very nice."

"And the video equipment?"

"I'll check it out later. That's the last stage." Eve set her case down on the worktable. "Now, if you'll get me several towels and a bowl of water, I'll be able to start."

"Sounds like you're going to operate or deliver a baby." Galen had appeared in the doorway.

Rick chuckled as he hurried out of the room.

"There are similarities to both." Eve rolled up the sleeves of her loose white shirt. "I was wondering where you were this morning."

"I was on the phone most of the night. I kept an eye on you from my balcony when you left the house."

"Why were you on the phone?"

"Research. Melton is a little too slick for my liking. So I called a few contacts." He made a face. "But Melton seems to be telling the truth on all fronts. Bently did disappear two years ago, and everything you were told about him seems to check out. Model citizen, husband, and father. From all accounts he was a genuinely nice guy. Sheriff Bouvier is a respected law enforcement officer and did release the skeleton to Melton."

"Skeleton?"

"Bouvier knew nothing about the skeleton disappearing. Melton promised him that he'd get an expert to quickly do a DNA test and then quietly return the remains to him. When I told Bouvier that there might be quite a few pieces missing, he was hopping mad. It's his job on the line. When he calmed down, he said he'd contact the senator, and he was sure Melton would use his influence to have the skeleton found and returned to him. He was just brimful of excuses and praise for the senator. He's solidly in Melton's camp."

"You sound disappointed that Melton's story checked out."

He shrugged. "I've got a bad feeling about this."

"If we find out there's a problem, I can always stop and go home." But she didn't want to go home. She didn't intend to go back and face the very situation she'd run away from. She wanted to work until she dropped, and then work some more.

"Are you sure I can't persuade you to bolt out of here? I'll call and see if I can get us tickets to Atlanta."

"Us?"

"My job's not finished. I stay with you until I'm sure there's no more danger."

"I'm not walking around for any extended length of time with a bodyguard, Galen."

"Just until I'm sure. The airport?"

Eve thought about it. She wasn't one to undervalue the power of instinct, but there was no firm reason to think she wouldn't be able to finish this job safely. True, her food poisoning was worrying, but she was well guarded now by both Galen and the men she had seen about the grounds of the church this morning.

And she didn't like the idea of someone killing a man like the one Galen had described and walking away from it without being punished. You couldn't punish a crime without identifying a victim—and that was her job.

"Not until I'm sure that there's a reason to go." She turned back to the skull. "Now go away for a while. I need to get to work."

"He's pretty filthy." Galen touched the mud on Victor's forehead. "Funny-looking dirt, isn't it?"

She shrugged. "Dirt is dirt."

"Are you going to be able to get it all off him?"

"The majority of it. I'm not going to try to get it out of all the cavities. I might cause more breakage." She made a shooing motion. "Go. I want to get a start on cleaning up Victor before it's time for you to take me to Marie's funeral."

"You're still going?"

"Why shouldn't I? One, it could have been an accident. Two, if it wasn't, maybe someone else slipped something into the ingredients Marie brought to the house. If she's innocent, then she was killed to keep her from talking, or to make my attack look more accidental. Not a pretty thought, is it?"

"Murder is even less pretty." Galen smiled. "But you want to believe the best of Marie. So we'll go to the funeral. It can't hurt."

After Galen left, Eve turned back to Victor and began to carefully scrape the dirt from his skull.

It's funny dirt.

She paused and stared at it. It was strange-looking. Minute white chips seemed to be imbedded in rich black mud, making it appear lighter.

Forget it. Maybe all the dirt in Sheriff Bouvier's parish was like this. If it wasn't, then the police must have noticed it. It wasn't her business. Just get it off and do your job.

———

Marie Letaux's son, Pierre, was tall and good-looking and clearly devastated by his mother's death. He was surrounded by friends and relatives when Eve approached him after the ceremony at the small church.

Eve held out her hand. "I'm Eve Duncan. I'd like to express my condolences. I didn't know your mother well, but I may have been the last person to see her. Did she tell you that she was taking a job with me?"

Pierre nodded. "She was excited. She knew you were someone important."

"Not really."

"Mr. Tanzer said that you were famous. She liked the idea of working for a woman who'd made something of her life." His eyes filled with tears. "Mama wanted to be famous. I didn't tell her, but after I get out of medical school and set up practice I was going to set her up with her own restaurant. I should have told her." His voice broke. "I wish I'd told her. It was going to be a surprise."

"She knew you loved her. She was very proud of you." Eve glanced at the flower-draped coffin, which had been placed in a gray hearse. "She wanted so much for you to finish your education."

Pierre nodded jerkily. "She was always thinking of ways to help me. She called me the night before she died and told me not to worry, that she'd worked out a way to get the money for my tuition. That everything was going to be fine."

"She did?"

He nodded, his gaze shifting to the coffin. "I'm sorry, I have to go now."

"Of course. I hope everything goes well for you in the future."

"I can't think of anything but Mama now. It's very difficult for me. I thought my heart would break when I was going through her things last night. So many memories . . ." He tried to smile. "But I go back to school tomorrow, and I'll try very hard to make something of myself that would have made her proud. I thank you for your good wishes." He turned and moved toward the hearse.

"Nice kid." Galen had moved forward to stand beside her.

She watched the hearse move slowly through the cemetery toward the grave where Marie would be buried. "Yes."

He took her elbow. "Ready to go?"

She nodded, her gaze still on the hearse. "Did you hear what he said about the call from his mother?"

"Yes."

"Aren't you going to say anything?"

"You'll make up your own mind. I hate to say I told you so."

"It may not mean anything." Her hands clenched into fists. "Dammit, I didn't want to believe it. I still don't."

"On the other hand, young Letaux may find a pleasant surprise when he opens her safety-deposit box." Galen gently nudged Eve toward his car. "Now how about having lunch and a little tour of the city before I take you back to the house? I think you need to unwind."

"Okay." She took a final glance over her shoulder at the hearse, and Marie's son, who was going to say his final good-bye to the mother he loved. And Marie had loved him, too.

Enough to do this terrible thing for his sake?

"Stop worrying," Galen said. "Never ruin a good meal with bad thoughts. Tell me about your daughter, Jane. I heard she took over my nursing duty last year after I left Sarah Patrick's cabin in Phoenix. Don't deflate my ego by saying she did as good a job as I did."

"Well, Sarah must have thought she did pretty well. Jane got a puppy out of it."

"Do you consider that bad or good?"

Eve smiled. "It's good. The puppy is pure Monty . . . I hope. I haven't seen any signs of anything savage about Toby."

"Too bad. I've never seen anything wrong with a little dash of the tiger. It makes the mix more interesting."

"I don't agree."

"I believe you do. You chose Quinn."

Yes, Joe had more than a little tiger in him, but she'd not seen it in the last year. She had seen nothing but love and companionship and togetherness. It had been magic. No, better than magic, because it had been honest and real.

At least she'd thought it had been honest.

She smothered the ripple of pain. Would she ever be able to think about Joe without that hurt? She changed the subject. "Where are we going to eat? Nothing heavy. My stomach still feels like it's taken a beating from Evander Holyfield."

———————

The safety-deposit box.

Eve sat up straight in bed, her heart pounding. "Galen!"

"I hear you," Galen called from the next room. He was there in seconds. "What's wrong? Did you see any—"

"The safety-deposit box. I was asleep, but I woke up and it was—"

"Slow down. Get your breath." He sat down on the bed beside her and set the revolver he'd carried on the nightstand. "A nightmare?"

"No. It must have been in the back of my mind and it— Marie's safety-deposit box. You thought there was probably a bribe in it, and whoever poisoned me was trying to make sure to make it look like an accident. It was important to him not to draw attention to why it was being done."

"And?"

"Pierre, her son. He was going back to New Orleans tomorrow morning. He wanted to be done with all these details. There's a good chance he would have gone to the bank this afternoon and tried to tie up all her affairs. If there was a huge amount in that safety-deposit box, it would have sent up a red flag, wouldn't it?"

"You're thinking someone might want to stop him from reporting that money."

Eve moistened her lips. "Oh, God, I hope not." She got to her feet. "I want to go to see him. I'm getting dressed. Will you call Marie's house and see if you can reach him?"

"Do you have the number?"

"No."

"I'll call information." Galen reached for the phone on the nightstand and turned on the light.

She blinked. "You're naked."

"You screamed. I wasn't about to take the time to get dressed." He spoke into the phone and then glanced over his shoulder. "Get moving."

She didn't need to be told twice. She hurried out of the bedroom and down the hall to the bathroom.

When she came back five minutes later, Galen was coming out of his room, tucking his shirt into his khakis. "Pierre didn't answer." He glanced at her. "Look, this may be a false alarm, but when we get there, I'm in charge. You don't do anything until I tell you to do it. Okay?"

"I hear you. Just hurry."

No one answered the knock.

"He could have decided to leave early," Galen said. "Or perhaps staying here brought back too many memories."

"I don't like it," Eve said. "Is the door locked?"

"Yes." Galen bent over the knob for a moment. "But if it will make you feel better . . ." The door swung open. "I go in first. You stay out here until I call you. If you see anything, you call me."

"I want to—" Eve nodded impatiently. "Hurry. If he's not here, I need to track him down at a hotel."

"I'll hurry." Galen disappeared into the house.

She didn't want to wait outside. She glanced uneasily over her shoulder at the windows of the houses on either side of the street. Dark, silent.

Watching.

Foolishness. No one was watching.

"Come in." Galen was back. "It's safe."

"Is he here?"

"He's here." He shut the door. "But you may not want to see him. He's not a pretty sight. His head's half blown off."

Shock jolted through her. "What?"

"There at the desk across the room."

The lights were off, but she could dimly see a figure slumped at the desk. "Pierre?"

"As far as I could tell."

"Murdered."

"It's staged to look like a suicide. The gun's still in his hand. He may have actually pulled the trigger."

"Like Marie was forced to eat the stew," she said dully.

"Right."

"I want to see him."

"You're sure?"

"It won't be the first corpse I've seen, Galen."

"I know, but I have to fight my protective instincts." He flicked on the lamp by the door. "Don't touch anything."

Blood and brain matter were splattered everywhere. She forced herself to walk forward until she stood in front of the desk. Several framed pictures of Pierre's mother were spread on the desk in front of him. To one side lay a pile of letters spattered with blood.

"It looks"—she swallowed hard to ease the tightness of her throat—"as if he was going through her things."

And became despondent and took his own life. Everyone at the funeral would testify to how distraught he was. Very nicely staged. Or do you believe he'd actually do this?"

Eve shook her head. "He wanted to make all her hard work worthwhile. He wouldn't—" She had to get out of here. She turned and headed for the door. "It wasn't him—somebody else did this."

"That's what I thought." Galen followed her, stopping only to wipe his prints off the lamp and the doorknob while she waited outside. "But the verdict will probably be suicide."

She drew a deep shaky breath as she reached the street. "We could tell the police about Marie."

"With no real evidence but those bruises? You didn't want to believe Marie Letaux's death wasn't an accident."

"I suppose he did go to the bank today," she said dully.

"I doubt if he'd be dead if he hadn't discovered the safety-deposit box with the money. He must have had time to look through it, or he wouldn't have been a threat."

"He was so young. . . ."

"Yeah, it sucks." Galen took Eve's elbow. "Let's get out of here. If anyone sees us around, they might decide it wasn't suicide and zero in on us as suspects. You might be above suspicion, but I'm not."

———

"Sit down." Galen pushed Eve into one of the kitchen chairs and put on the kettle. "I'll make you some coffee."

"I'm okay." She was lying. She wasn't okay. All she could think about was that beautiful young man who was now no longer beautiful. Pierre, whose years had been cut short in that brutal fashion.

"Then keep me company." He switched on the stove, then took down the instant coffee. "I'm very sensitive. Blood always upsets me."

She tried to smile. "Liar."

"I am sensitive. There's just a layer of scar tissue." He got down two cups from the shelf and spooned in the coffee. "And blood is . . . messy. To be spilled only when necessary. There are so many neater ways." He glanced at her over his shoulder and grinned. "That got you. Did you expect me to soothe you? You're too tough for that."

"Am I?"

"Sure. Of course, Quinn would probably comfort you. But you wouldn't take it from me." He poured boiling water into the cups and sat down across from her. "So take a cup of coffee instead."

In spite of what he said, he was trying to comfort her. She took a sip. "I'm surprised a gourmet like you would tolerate instant coffee."

"It was quick." He leaned back in his chair. "And I can tolerate anything. I'm used to making do."

"It's good." She took another sip. "I . . . did need it. I guess I'm pretty shaky. I *hate* death. We fight and we fight and there's still nothing we can do about it."

"Sometimes there is. Personally, I intend to live until I'm at least a hundred and fifty. I figure with all the research going on I could still be spry at that age."

"Pierre was so young. There's something even more terrible about the young dying."

"Like your Bonnie."

"Yes." Eve looked down into the coffee in her cup. "Like my little girl."

Galen was silent.

Eve drew a shaky breath. "And I hate the monsters who take those youngsters' lives. I want to reach out and get them by the throat. I want to scream at them how unfair it is for them to steal all those bright, wonderful years away. It's cruel and ugly— Shit." Tears were running down her cheeks. "I'm sorry. I didn't mean to—"

Galen was kneeling beside her chair. "Hey, don't do this to me." He took her in his arms and rocked her back and forth. "You're tearing up all my scar tissue." He felt her stiffen against him, and immediately released her and sat back on his heels. "Let's get this straight right now. I'm not trying to take advantage of a bad moment. It's my natural instincts again. A woman weeps and I react." He looked directly in her eyes. "But I know the difference between a vulnerable moment and the real thing. I like you, I respect you, and, if I let myself, I'd find you sexy. But you're not available. It's so clear that you might as well be carrying around a sign. So I'm your protector, your friend, and sometimes a shoulder to lean on. Got it?"

She smiled shakily. "Got it."

He smiled. "At least that little misunderstanding accomplished one thing. You're not crying any more." He breathed a theatrical sigh of relief. "I can't take tears. They lay me low."

"I'll remember that. It may come in handy." She stood up. "I'm going to bed. I have an early start tomorrow."

Galen looked at his watch. "Tomorrow's already here. The airport?"

"Hell, no." She started for the door. "They're not going to get away with killing that boy. They're going to pay for it. I'm going to give Victor a face."

Chapter Seven

MAY I COME IN?" GALEN ASKED.

Eve glanced up from the skull. "If you don't talk to me."

"Just a few words. Where's Rick?"

She shrugged. "Around somewhere. He brought me coffee a couple hours ago. Why?"

"Just checking. He's usually so attentive he makes me worry about losing my job."

"He may be attentive, but he's quiet and unobtrusive. I hardly know he's around."

"I doubt you'd notice if he ran around banging on a drum. I can see you're caught up in the project. I've never seen anyone so obsessed."

"It's what I do." Her work had saved her from the depths of

despair and helped her keep her sanity after Bonnie had been murdered. It was her salvation and her passion.

"I just thought I'd fill you in on a few things I've learned about Bently."

"I thought you'd already told me everything."

"Only the obvious. I decided to probe a little deeper. I don't like to trust the obvious."

"So what did you find out?"

"He was an ardent environmentalist, very passionate about solar energy and cleaning up the rivers."

"And?"

"That would make him a target for any number of energy groups. What if he was planning to run on a platform that would step on some very important toes?"

"You're doing those 'what ifs' again."

"Can't help it. It's a game I have to play. It's my suspicious nature." Galen smiled. "But at least you should be relieved that Bently is turning out to be such a sterling character."

"Why?"

"Because it's obvious you've become so emotionally attached to that skull that it would give you a hell of a lot of satisfaction if Victor turned out to be a good guy."

"Either way, it won't stop me from doing my job."

Galen tilted his head and gazed appraisingly at the skull. "You don't appear very close. He looks like a voodoo doll. What are all those sticks all over his skull?"

"Tissue-depth markers. I cut each marker to the proper measurement and glue it onto its specific area on the face. There are more than twenty points of the skull for which there are known tissue depths." She carefully placed another marker. "There are anthropological charts that give a specific measurement for each point."

"Then your work is mostly measurement?"

"No, that's the donkey work. I take strips of plasticine and apply them between the markers, then build them up to tissue-depth levels. Then I smooth and fill in and work with the skull until I'm satisfied. The last process is the most important. That's why I can't look at photographs of the subject. I can't let even my subconscious be influenced."

"Well, you're safe for now. But I'm planning on going down to the newspaper office and getting a photo."

"Well, keep it 'til I've finished."

"When will that be?"

"As long as it takes. Five or six more days, maybe." She glanced at him. "Any news about Pierre?"

"A story on page five of the newspaper about the suicide of Pierre Letaux, who was apparently despondent about the death of his mother."

"You said the police wouldn't question it."

"I admit I didn't want to be right about this one." He shrugged. "But sometimes the bad guys win."

"Not this time." She placed another marker. "Now go away and let me work."

"I'm on my way." He paused. "You know, we could call Melton and tell him we think Marie's and Pierre's deaths may not be quite what they seem."

"I thought of that. And then he'd assure me that I was mistaken and that the police reports were accurate."

"Could be."

"And I don't need to deal with Melton right now."

"I didn't think so. It might interfere with Victor, and you won't permit anything to do that. Is Rick feeding you?"

"When I let him." She lifted a brow. "It seems my poison tester hasn't been on the job."

"Rick wouldn't let anything happen to you. At least, not until you've finished Victor. I've never seen anyone more intent on making your work easy for you. And I'll cook for you myself tonight."

"That's comforting."

"It should be more than comforting. You should be breathless with anticipation."

"I don't have time."

"Okay, forget about dwelling on my fine cuisine." He turned to leave. "I'd like this job done quickly, too."

He couldn't be more anxious than she was, Eve thought as he left the room. Ever since she had seen Pierre's body the night before last, she had been driven to finish the reconstruction.

Maybe even before that. There were so few truly good people; Bently might have been one of those rare individuals.

She placed another marker. "We're getting there, Victor," she murmured. "Galen thinks you might have been some kind of martyr, but I've got to be very careful not to pay any attention. You might have been just a soldier or a tramp or some other victim. It doesn't matter. You deserve to be brought home, too. . . ."

———

"No identification, Lieutenant." Officer Krakow shrugged. "And we're not going to get anyone to recognize him. The forensic boys say he's been dead for at least four days, facedown in the water in that drain pipe."

"Four days?" Joe's gaze went down the hill to the forensic team gathered around the entrance of the drainage pipe.

"Could be longer. You know it's hard to pin down when a corpse has been out in the weather. We'll have to wait for the medical examiner."

"What kind of clothes is he wearing?"

"Oxford cloth shirt. No tie, but nicely tailored pants. He appears to be very white-collar. He definitely wasn't one of the homeless." Krakow gazed at Joe curiously. "This isn't your case, is it, sir? You looking for someone in particular?"

"Maybe. Thanks, Krakow." Joe started down the hill. He could see the sprawled body, and the size seemed right. Capel had been a big man with receding brown hair, but he couldn't see the hair from here. White-collar described George Capel, and he'd have to see about the time frame. Conditions were everything as far as decomposition was concerned. He'd seen a woman taken out of the trunk of a car after only seven hours; he would have sworn she had been dead for days.

It didn't have to be Capel. He hoped to God it wasn't. If that body was George Capel, it brought this whole mess to a new and dangerous level.

"Hi, Lieutenant." Sam Rowley glanced up as he approached. "Looks like we've got one for you."

Joe looked down at the corpse. The hair was light brown, but he couldn't tell if it was receding from that swollen, disfigured face.

"Homicide?"

"Appears to be knife wound in the back. There are multiple

wounds on the body, but it's hard to determine if they were in-flicted before or after death. He's been out here awhile."

"I need to know who he is. Fingerprints?"

"May be tough to match with the hands so swollen. Prob-ably have to go for the teeth."

"How soon?"

"The lab's pretty backlogged. Two weeks, maybe."

"I need to know now, Sam."

Sam shook his head. "Talk to the lab techs. You know I can't help you."

"I will." Joe turned and strode back up the hill.

A knife wound in the back. Multiple other wounds.

The muscles of his stomach twisted as he got back in the car. Don't panic yet. Get down to headquarters and pull strings to get that ID right away.

Christ, he hoped it wasn't Capel.

————

"How far along are you?" Galen asked as he poured Eve's coffee that evening. "Have you gotten past the voodoo stage?"

"Tomorrow. I have to go very slowly to have an absolutely true foundation." Eve lifted the cup to her lips. "That was a very good meal, Galen."

"It was a magnificent meal. You're too tired to appreciate me."

"No, I'm not." She studied him soberly. What an unusual man he was. Complex, smooth on the surface with depths that were definitely dark and enigmatic. Yet she'd never felt safer with any man except Joe. "You've been very kind to me, Galen."

"Just doing my job."

"No. Ever since I woke up in the hospital, you've given me whatever I needed."

"That's my business. I'm a provider." He leaned back in his chair. "And you've been easy. I haven't had to maul or dispatch anyone lately."

He was joking. Or was he? Maybe not. Those murky depths again . . . "I hope you won't have to do it in the future either." Her hand tightened on the cup. "Death is ugly."

"Yes, it is. And no one should know better than you."

"Not even you?"

He smiled. "Let's say my experience is active and yours is passive."

"Why did you take this bodyguard job, Galen? I got the impression that you played on a much bigger stage."

"I like Louisiana. I even have a house near New Orleans."

"You took the job because you liked the area? I don't think so."

"Okay, Logan is my friend and he asked me to do it as a favor. I move around too much to have many friends, so I try to keep the ones I have." He paused. "And I guess I kind of liked the idea of being cast as a knight to protect a lady. Usually my jobs are much less noble. I'd only met you once, but I wasn't fond of the idea of you jumping into trouble."

She had certainly been in trouble the first time she met him in Arizona two years ago, Eve thought ruefully. Besides taking care of Sarah's wounded wolf, Maggie, she had been trying to sort out her own problems with Jane. "Well, you were very good with Maggie. Sarah was impressed."

"We had a lot in common." He took a sip of coffee. "Quinn must have been really worried about this trip or he wouldn't have called Logan. I got the impression they're not the greatest mates in the world."

She stiffened. "I don't want to talk about Joe." She finished her coffee and stood up. "And in a few days there won't be anything for any of us to worry about. Let's get these dishes done. I want to go upstairs and make my call to Jane before I go to bed. Do you want to wash or dry?"

"I'll do them. I need to expend some excess energy. You go on and call your little girl. I checked out the upstairs when you were taking your shower. It's secure. But don't go out on the balcony."

"You think someone's going to shoot me?"

He shook his head. "It would be too obvious. Everything has been made to look like an accident or suicide so far. But it won't hurt to be careful. Sometimes new elements pop up in these situations."

"You talk as if this is just run-of-the-mill to you. I'm finding it a good deal more stressful."

He started to stack the dishes. "It's certainly interesting."

She looked at him and shook her head. Just when she thought she had made progress getting beyond that smooth exterior, he pulled it firmly back in place. "Good night, Galen."

"Good night. Pleasant dreams."

Don't go out on the balcony or you might get shot.

Don't eat anything Galen didn't cook or you might be poisoned.

Not the stuff of which pleasant dreams were made.

————

Jane looked up from the salad she was tossing when Joe walked in that evening. "Eve called a little while ago."

"How is she?"

"Fine. Tired. She's working on the skull. She calls him Victor. Will you get out the steaks, Joe?"

Joe came into the kitchen and opened the refrigerator. "How soon will she be done?"

"Doesn't know." Jane took out the indoor grill and plugged it in. "You know Eve's never sure. It's going well, though."

"Did she mention Galen?"

"Only that he'd called Victor a gladiator and she was having the devil of a time keeping that out of her mind. Oh, and she said that he was a terrific cook." She chuckled. "Good thing one of them is. Eve's not so hot."

"No, she's not." He handed her the steaks. "Sounds very cozy."

"Yeah." Jane looked at him and her smile faded. "Joe? Is something wrong?"

"No, of course not." He turned away. "I've got to go wash up. I'll be right back."

When he closed the bathroom door, he splashed water on his face and then reached for the towel. Oh, no, nothing was wrong. His grasp tightened on the soft cloth until his knuckles turned white. Only that he was jealous as hell and wanted to kill Sean Galen.

Shit, he'd want to murder everyone Eve looked at on the street or smiled at in a restaurant. Very sane. Very reasonable.

But who said he was ever reasonable when it came to Eve? She'd been the center of his life since he'd met her all those years ago, and he'd had only this short time of her belonging to him. It wasn't enough. It would never be enough.

Joe drew a deep breath. Get control. He had to go out and not let Jane see what a crazy, obsessive son of a bitch he was. She'd been an angel since Eve had left. No, not an angel. She was too earthy and real to be termed angelic. She'd always had that same tough, loving nature that reminded him of Eve.

Eve. Everything came back to her. And she was in Baton Rouge with Galen, who was helping her, making those damn dinners, talking to her, sharing . . . He had sent Galen to be with her and he'd do it again, but that didn't make it any easier.

"Joe, the steaks are done," Jane called.

"Coming." He hung up the towel and opened the door. He forced a smile. "I'm starved. I forgot to eat lunch today."

"You've been working too hard." She carried the steaks over to the table, almost tripping over the puppy. "Toby, get out of my way. You cannot have these steaks."

"I bet he'll get the leftovers."

"Maybe. I shouldn't do it. Sarah said he should have a balanced diet and table scraps aren't really good for him." She shook her head. "But he's such a chow hound. I never saw any dog who loved food like Toby."

"What else did Eve say?"

"Nothing much. She mostly asked about what I was doing and how Toby was. I told her he was fine." She sat down. "I told her you were fine, too."

"But she didn't ask, did she?"

"No, but I figured she probably wanted to know."

"Optimist."

"She's working, and she already seems more cheerful than when she left. Work always helps her."

"I know."

"So you just have to hang on and be patient. Now eat your steak."

He smiled faintly. "Yes, ma'am. Anything else?"

"Yes, don't work so hard." She frowned sternly at Toby who'd rested his head on her knee. "Don't beg. It's impolite."

"You're not going to last until supper's over."

"I will. He's got to learn—"

Joe's phone rang.

Jane sighed. "I was afraid you wouldn't get through the meal."

"I won't answer it. I'll let the voice mail pick it up."

"But then you'd get indigestion worrying. Get it over with."

Joe flipped on his phone. "Quinn."

"It's Carol. The teeth ID came through. It's George Andrew Capel, age forty-two."

Joe's hand tightened on the phone. "Christ. Anything on the autopsy report?"

"I don't know. Let me check. Yeah, here it is. They just tossed it in the in-box. Death caused by knife wound that entered the heart from the back. The other wounds were minor. None of them capable of doing serious damage but would have been extremely painful. Looks like our killer likes to toy with his victims."

"Maybe. Thanks, Carol." He hung up.

"Joe?" Jane whispered.

He was scaring her. "It's okay. It's just that something's come up and I have to deal with it."

"Eve?"

"No. How could it be Eve? You just talked to her. That was Carol at the precinct. It was police business."

"You're never this upset about police business."

She was too sharp, and he was too panicky right now to hide his fear. He got to his feet. "I've got to make a couple of private calls. You go ahead and eat dinner. I'll be back soon."

She frowned, still troubled. "Okay. But your steak will get cold."

"I'll heat it up." He wouldn't be able to eat it anyway. Food was the last thing on his mind. The grave. The report sent to Eve. George Capel. Eve's job in Baton Rouge. All the pieces were falling together.

And the picture they were making was scaring him to death.

"He's still pretty ugly, even without the sticks." Galen tilted his head as he studied the skull on the pedestal. "Maybe it's those empty eye sockets."

"Go away, Galen."

"Nope, it's eight o'clock and you've been here since six this morning. Time to close up shop. I'm going to walk you home and feed you. Rick would let you work all night."

"I'm not ready to go."

"Are you going to be able to finish him tonight?"

"No way. I've still got a good four days' work. Maybe more."

"Then you'll do better with some rest. Since there's no urgency."

"There is urgency."

"Not for you. Melton can wait."

He didn't understand. When she started work, the urgency came from within. It was as if the person she was reconstructing was urging her, whispering to her: Find me. Help me. Bring me home.

"What color?" Galen was still gazing at the eye sockets. "How do you know what color to use for the eyes?"

"I don't. I usually put in brown. It's the most common eye color. Why are those sockets bothering you?"

"I knew a bloke in Mozambique who'd had his eyes cut out by a nasty customer in the drug trade. He got along surprisingly well, but it always gave me the chills."

"I can see why."

"It made me mad. I hate mutilation. No one should do that to anyone."

Eve turned to look at him. "I've never seen you angry."

"You don't want to. I get pretty nasty."

"To that 'nasty customer in the drug trade'?"

Galen didn't answer directly. "No one should be allowed to do that," he repeated. He suddenly smiled. "Now you've done it. You've made me dwell on that unpleasantness and I'm all depressed. You have to come home so that I can fix you a fine meal and forget about it. It's therapy."

"It's manipulation." She draped a towel over the skull. "But I'll let you get away with it. Maybe I am a little tired."

"Right. Now wash your hands and we'll be off." Galen crossed over to the window and looked out at the bayou. "You should really see more of Baton Rouge. It's a great town."

"I had lunch with you the day of Marie's funeral. I saw Baton Rouge for hours and hours that day. And I didn't come here to sightsee."

"Someone needs to take you in hand. There's more to life than skulls with empty sockets."

"They're not empty when I fill them." Eve dried her hands on a towel. "And I'm not a total workaholic."

"You come close. Me, I believe in stopping to smell the roses." Galen opened the door for her. "Though I do know New Orleans better than Baton Rouge. So we'll walk home very slowly, and I'll tell you the history of the Big Easy and maybe a few bits of the history of my stays there. You can decide which is more entertaining."

Galen's stories were definitely more entertaining, and lasted the walk back to the plantation house. They were bawdy, funny, and full of colorful characters and incidents.

"His name was really Marco Polo?" Eve asked. "You've got to be kidding."

"No way. He said his mum named him that because he was destined to be a great explorer. Actually, he fit right in with some of the weirdos who inhabit the French Quarter. He wore thirteenth-century garb whenever he was at home, and he had a particular fondness for Chinese prostitutes. I don't think that was the kind of Oriental exploration his mum had in mind, but who am I— Shit!" He jerked her to one side and stepped in front of her. "Who the hell are you?"

"Quinn." Joe stepped out of the shadows next to the front door. "As Eve'll tell you, if you'll get away from her."

Eve stared at him in shock. "Joe?"

"You remember my name? I guess I should be grateful."

"You shouldn't have come. I don't want you here."

"You've made that clear. Tough. I'm here and I'm staying."

"Where's Jane?"

"She's fine. She's with your mother. Sandra's husband and lit-tle Mike are in Oregon on a fishing trip. The kid's real mother was jailed again for drugs and they thought he should get away for awhile. Your mother was glad to have the company."

Shock was being replaced by anger. "I told you when I left I didn't want you to come with me. Go back to Atlanta, Joe."

"Sorry." He turned to Galen. "What's been going on here?"

"None of your business," Eve said. "Go home."

Joe whirled on her and his words spat out like bullets. "You listen to me. I'm not going to barge in on your cozy little establishment here. I know you wouldn't have me in the same house. But I'm staying. You can't stop me. Now I'm coming in and I'm going to tell you a few things, and then either you or Galen is going to fill me in on what's been happening here."

"I think we'd better invite him in, Eve," Galen said as he unlocked the door. "I do hate scenes in public."

"He's leaving. There's not going to be a scene."

"Yes, there is. At this point I'm ready to burn down the whole damn parish if I don't get my way."

"We wouldn't want that," Galen said. "I've just been telling Eve what a fine little metropolis this is."

"Oh, was that what you were telling her?" Joe murmured. "I would have guessed something entirely different."

"Uh-oh. Is that the way the wind's blowing?" Galen flung open the door. "Come in, Quinn. I can see this is going to be an interesting chat." His gaze shifted to Eve. "Give him twenty minutes, Eve. He obviously has something we might need to hear. From what I've heard about him, he's not stupid enough to have come all this way without a reason."

"I don't want to—" She might as well get it over. She knew that expression on Joe's face. He wasn't budging. "Twenty minutes." She passed Joe and went into the house.

"I'll be right back." Galen was running up the stairs. "I have to check the upstairs. If you want to make yourself useful, you might check the downstairs, Quinn."

"You trust me to do that?" Joe asked sarcastically. "Your faith is—" But Galen was out of hearing. Joe turned and went toward the first door on the left. "Is this the kitchen?"

"Dining room. Kitchen adjoins it."

Joe opened the door. "Stay here."

"The hell I will." Eve followed him through the dining room into the kitchen, and watched him while he checked the two pantries, under the table in the kitchen, and the dining room. "It's not fair for you to do this. I'm not ready to see you, Joe."

"Will you ever be ready?" He went past her into the hall. "Is that a parlor?"

She nodded and watched as he checked the room out.

"Okay?" Galen was coming down the stairs. "Now that we have that out of the way, I don't suppose you'd like a glass of wine or a cup of coffee? No, I didn't think so." He came into the parlor and sat down on the velvet couch. "You'll excuse me for sitting down before you, Eve, but I can tell by your stance that you're in no mood for relaxing." He turned to Joe. "She's bristling. I believe you'd better hurry a bit."

"I don't need your advice. I know Eve better than you'll ever know her." His gaze never left Eve's face. "Don't I?"

"Do you? I thought I knew you."

"You do. You just don't want to accept what you know, what you've always known." He shook his head. "I can't get through to you. Screw it. It doesn't make any difference right now. I have to tell you about Capel."

"Who's Capel?"

"George Capel. He's the doctor I bribed to send you that positive DNA report and bury the real one."

"And the man who sent me the real report."

"It wasn't Capel. It didn't compute that he would do that without trying to get more money out of me first . . . unless someone paid him an enormous amount of cash. So I started digging. Capel hadn't shown up for work in a couple days, so I assumed he'd flown the coop." Joe's lips tightened. "He knew I'd be looking for him. But someone had to have suspected something to have gotten to Capel. I went to the DNA lab and asked questions. I went through a dozen administrative clerks before I found one who remembered a police officer from Forsythe County who'd asked to check Bonnie's records. The clerk was pretty upset because she couldn't find them. The police officer asked who would have been in charge of the case, and she told him George Capel and asked if he'd like to see him. He told her he'd come back when he had more time. Two neighbors saw a small, dark man with Capel later that day. They went to his house and then left again. A man of the same description accompanied Capel to the bank the same day. The bank teller who let him into the vault commented that he looked sick. He told her he had the flu. My guess is that the man who was at the DNA lab suspected some shenanigans when there was no record to be found and decided to check out Capel. He struck pay dirt. Capel was fairly transparent, and wouldn't have been difficult to break for anyone determined enough. He was probably forced to go to his house so the guy could search it. No DNA record. Then it got serious. I believe a good deal of time was spent persuading Capel to reveal where he'd placed the record. Then they went to the bank and got it. It was no wonder he looked sick. He was probably in severe pain."

"All this because of Bonnie's DNA record?" Eve asked skeptically. "It doesn't make sense."

"Does the fact that we found Capel's body two days ago convince you?"

Her eyes widened. "What?"

"Murdered?" Galen asked.

Joe nodded. "Knife wound from the back. Several other cuts on his body."

"The means of persuasion," Galen murmured.

"That's what I figure."

Eve dazedly shook her head. "Why?"

"You," Joe said. "Why did you come here? What drove you?"

"You know why I came."

"Hell, yes, I know. It was very well orchestrated. The deface-ment of the grave to send the first shock wave. Then the arrival of the DNA report. A one-two punch that sent you running as far away from me as possible. And wasn't it convenient that you had a job beckoning here?"

"You're saying that man was murdered to get me here?"

"Do you want more proof? The shoe prints at the hill were made by shoes from a company with heavy distribution in this state. They led to tracks made by tires that are standard issue on the Saturn. I had a composite sketch drawn of the man who went with Capel to his house and the bank. I had the bank secu-rity videos checked, but he was too smart and was looking away from the camera. But both the neighbors and the bank clerk agreed on the face in the sketch, so I played a hunch and took it to the rental car agencies at the airport. Bingo. Avis rented a Saturn to a Karl Stolz from Shreveport, Louisiana. He paid by credit card and was very pleasant to the clerk. He returned the car and boarded a plane for Baton Rouge the day you told Melton you'd take the job."

"You've done a good job of putting it together," Galen said. "I suppose you traced the credit card."

"Billed to the real Karl Stolz at an address in Shreveport. A case of stolen identity. He hasn't left his home for the past six months." His hands clenched into fists at his sides. "Believe me,

Eve. All this was done to draw you to Baton Rouge. Now get the hell out of here."

It was incredible. Yet she did believe him. "You're saying this man tried to ruin my life and killed a man just to get me to take this job?" She tried to think. "Melton?"

"I called him before I got on the plane today. He denies everything, of course, but the entire mess seems to lead toward him—or an associate."

"I'm surprised you didn't squeeze that out of him."

"I didn't have time."

Eve shook her head. "Go home, Joe. I don't want you involved. If there's a problem, I'll handle it."

"You mean you don't want me in your life. Well, that's too bad. You're not the only victim here. Whoever killed Capel did a damn good job of messing up my life, too. Now are you going to tell me what's been going on here?"

"No, I'm not."

"Then I'll find out on my own." He turned on his heel. "If you change your mind, you can reach me at the Westin Hotel."

"Wait." Galen got to his feet. "Could I see you for a few moments in private, Quinn? Why don't you go upstairs and rest, Eve?"

"Galen," she warned.

"You're not involving him. I am. I'll take all the help I can get. He's better occupied in helping than blundering around and getting in my way trying to find out a few simple facts." He smiled. "You can still keep your distance. Let me deal with him."

"I don't want him here."

"I do." Galen smiled. "So unless you're going to pack up

and go home, he stays. Not close. On the edge. But he stays. So go and rest and I'll fix you dinner after Quinn leaves."

"Stop treating me like a child. I'm not hungry and I'll do what I please." Eve strode out of the room and up the stairs. Dammit, she hadn't expected Galen to turn on her. It had come as a surprise—but not as big a shock as the ugly story that Joe had told her. It seemed impossible that anyone would go to such diabolical lengths to get her here. That man had delved into the most painful area of her life and used Bonnie to manipulate her.

A surge of rage tore through her. Son of a bitch. And what about the story that had been told to her by Melton. How much was truth and how much was lies?

Marie and Pierre Letaux? They had been killed to keep her from doing the reconstruction. Where did they fit in?

Oh, she just didn't know. She couldn't think right now. She was confused and angry, and the shock and hurt she'd experienced when she'd seen Joe didn't make it any better. For that first split second she'd felt such soaring joy that it had rocked her, and then she had remembered and the pain had come rushing back.

She had to get Joe to leave Baton Rouge. She couldn't live with this kind of confusion, and she certainly couldn't work.

Work? She felt a sudden icy chill as she realized that maybe she shouldn't be as worried about finishing Victor as about just surviving.

Chapter Eight

EVIDENTLY YOU HAVEN'T GOTTEN TO KNOW Eve as well as I thought," Joe said to Galen as they heard Eve's door slam. "You should never treat her with condescension."

"I hardly think you can qualify as an expert on the subject. You've put your ass on the line with her," Galen said.

Joe stiffened. "She told you about the DNA report?"

"That bothers you, doesn't it? No, Logan told me everything you told him. You took a big chance." He changed the subject. "Now, do you want to know what's been going on here or not?"

Joe was silent a moment. "I want to know."

"That wasn't too painful, was it?" Galen filled him in on the events since Eve had arrived in Baton Rouge.

Joe was cursing by the time he finished. "Why didn't you call me? Why didn't you let me know?"

"Logan hired me, not you. And the only way I could keep Eve willing to accept me here was to agree not to tell you anything. So it was really your fault."

"And you're enjoying telling me that."

"Antagonism always brings out the worst in me. Did you turn over the sketch to the FBI to see if they could track anything down for you?"

"They couldn't. No matches."

"I'd like to see the sketch. The man who took Eve to the hospital that night fits the description. We can run it by the admittance personnel. Do you have it here?"

"I have several copies at the hotel. I'll give you one." Joe looked up the stairs. "She won't listen to me. Can't you talk her out of staying here?"

"I'll try. She'll be absolutely furious with Melton if she thinks he's connected with the things you told her about. On the other hand, she's caught up in the work on Victor. I had to drag her away tonight."

"Dammit, it's clear whoever is behind this isn't playing for small stakes. One false step and she could be—" He broke off and took a deep breath. "I can't take not being here to help her. It's driving me crazy."

"You're not keeping it a secret," Galen said. "I'll do my best. In the meantime, give me your cell phone number and I'll try to keep you informed."

"I want to be more than informed."

"It's the best I can do. You lurk around here and Eve will explode. Trust me, I've taken good care of her. I'll keep on doing it."

"I don't trust you, and I don't want you to—" Joe jammed a

card with his name and cell number at Galen, turned, and moved toward the door. "If you don't let me know what's going on, I'll tear you apart."

"I do hate threats. They offend my genteel nature."

"Bullshit."

"Now what can I do to get my own back? What would rub you raw?" Galen smiled maliciously. "Shall I tell you how well I've gotten to know Eve? We've exchanged viewpoints and past history. We've eaten together, and shared sadness and death. I've protected her and held her in my arms."

"You bastard."

"I thought that would do it." He passed Joe and went toward the kitchen. "Now I have to go and get us a bite to eat."

Joe was tempted to go after him and strangle him.

Galen looked over his shoulder and shook his head. "I'm her safety net, Quinn. Get rid of me and you'll be up shit creek."

Joe muttered a curse and jerked open the front door.

"Oh, I forgot to mention one small thing," Galen said. "I was in her bedroom naked a few nights ago." He disappeared into the kitchen.

Joe could feel the pulse pound in his temple as he started to follow him. He stopped and drew a deep breath. Keep calm. Galen had wanted to score off him. He could have been lying.

And he could have been telling the truth. Okay, accept it. If he'd been telling the truth and Eve had taken Galen as a lover, then he'd just have to take it. His own hands were tied. He needed the bastard to keep Eve alive. He couldn't touch him. Not now.

Later.

"I've brought you a sandwich," Galen said when Eve opened the door to his knock. "I know you said you weren't hungry, but you've got to stoke the furnace if you want to finish Victor."

"I don't like to be overruled, Galen," she said coolly. "Particularly when it concerns my personal affairs."

"But it doesn't only concern your personal affairs. It concerns your life, and that's what I've been hired to preserve. So you do what you please about Quinn, but if I need him, I'll use him." He set the tray down on the bedside table. "Logan tells me he's an ex-SEAL, besides his FBI and police training. He may come in handy."

"No one uses Joe."

"That's why it's so much fun." Galen took a string of silver bells out of his pocket and crossed the room toward the balcony. "That balcony's been bothering me, and I'm tired of checking it a couple times a night."

"I didn't know you did."

"That's because I'm so good." He went out on the balcony and tied the string of bells on one of the wrought-iron spokes. He grasped another spoke a few feet away and pulled at it. Immediately a shower of tinkling sound drifted on the night air. "There we go. Thank God for this shaky ironwork. Not exactly high tech, but it sounds pretty and it's loud enough to alert me if we have a cat burglar." He looked back over his shoulder with a mischievous smile. "Or if Quinn decides to pull a *Romeo and Juliet* scene. 'Once more unto the breach . . .'"

"That last line is from *Henry V*."

"I never let accuracy get in the way if a quote fits."

"And Joe is too pragmatic to play Romeo."

"He didn't impress me as being that pragmatic. He was

seething tonight, and he didn't like me this close to you. It amused me at first, but then my defense mechanisms kicked in and I'm afraid I was a little naughty."

"What did you do?"

"Oh, this and that." Galen jiggled the spoke again, instigating another shower of silver sound. "That *is* pretty." He left the balcony, closed the doors, and locked them. "Eat your sandwich and try to get some sleep. I know what Quinn told you upset you."

"Of course it did." Eve shuddered. "I feel . . . violated. That bastard used my little girl and tried to twist my life to suit himself. And what he did to Capel . . ."

"I'm surprised that bothers you. Capel did some heavy manipulating of you himself."

"No, that was Joe. He manipulated Capel *and* me. When Joe makes a decision, opposing him is like trying to stop a tornado."

"I got that impression." Galen moved toward the door. "But you may be being a little rough on him."

"You don't know anything about it, Galen."

"You're right, but that never stops me from offering an opinion." He smiled back at her as he opened the door. "Good night, Eve. Be sure to eat that fantastic ham sandwich I made so you can praise me in the morning."

She shook her head as the door shut behind him. He was completely impossible. She looked at the sandwich without enthusiasm, but picked it up and started to eat. He was right. She needed strength. Not only to work, but to get through this nightmare that was escalating whenever she turned around. She had to plow through all that Joe had told her and everything that had happened since she got here, and make a decision.

She should probably pack up and go back to Atlanta.

But Victor was waiting. She could feel him calling her. She was getting closer to bringing him home every day.

She had to think, and it was impossible with the emotional upheaval she'd been thrown into when she'd seen Joe again.

Jesus, she wished he hadn't come.

———

The bells on the balcony jingled softly in the darkness.

Eve stiffened in bed, her gaze flying to the French doors.

The bells jingled again.

"Stay put." Galen was at her bedroom door. "We have a visitor." He moved in darkness toward the balcony. "And not too bright a one if he's still trying after he heard that first jingle."

"Be careful," she whispered. She could barely see him in the darkness, but then the door was flung open and he was outside on the balcony. She heard a crash and jumped out of bed and ran after him.

Galen and another man were struggling on the floor of the balcony.

Galen's arm lifted and his fist came down on the jaw of his antagonist.

The man went limp.

"Also not much of an opponent," Galen said as he got off him and dragged the man past Eve into the bedroom. "This job is proving no challenge at all."

She followed him into the room. "I'm sorry you don't believe he's worthy of your talents, but I find men crawling over my balcony threatening enough." The man, who appeared to be in his mid-forties, had heavy Slavic features and dark hair peppered with gray. "Did you hurt him?"

"Nah, he has a glass jaw." Galen squatted beside the man and searched his pockets. "And a potbelly. He's in lousy shape for this kind of—"

"Shit." The man's hazel eyes had opened; he was glaring up at Galen. "I think you broke every bone in my face. What the hell did you do that for?"

"It seemed appropriate." Galen put a knee on the man's chest. "Eve doesn't like second-story men." He opened the man's wallet and checked the driver's license. "Bill Nathan, age forty-seven. Eye color is right, but the weight's wrong. He's a good fifteen pounds heavier than it says here."

"So I gained a little weight when I quit smoking." Nathan's glance shifted to Eve. "Will you call this . . . bastard off me so that I can talk to you?"

"My name is Sean Galen, and you're in no position to call me anything but sir." Galen finished searching him. "He's clean." He handed her a card. "Press ID. He's with the Times Picayune . . . maybe."

Nathan scowled. "Are you going to let me up?"

Galen glanced inquiringly at Eve.

She nodded.

"Maybe I shouldn't—" Galen shrugged. "Oh, well, he's not much threat either way." He stood, pulled Nathan to his feet, and then pushed him into the chair beside the bed. "Talk to me. What are you doing here?"

"I'm on a rescue mission, dammit. And I don't like being tossed around like this."

"Why the balcony?"

"I wasn't sure whether the front door was being watched. Do you think I like crawling up the side of a house like some nutty superhero comic-book character?"

"It's definitely not your area of expertise," Galen said.

"Let him talk, Galen," Eve said. "What do you want from us, Nathan?"

"In the short term, I want to save your necks. In the long term, I'm hoping for a Pulitzer."

"Save us from what?"

"From finishing your reconstruction." Nathan gingerly touched his bruised cheek. "God, I need a cigarette."

"You're saying that finishing the reconstruction is dangerous."

"I think so. If you finish, they don't need you any more, and you may know too much."

Galen lifted his brows. "You *think* so?"

"That's what I said," he said sourly. "I can't look into a crystal ball and know what they'll do. I'm still digging. I don't know what the hell's happening yet."

"You evidently know more than we do," Eve said. "Who are 'they'?"

"The Cabal."

"Sounds like a witch's coven," Galen said.

"It's not funny." Nathan gave him a poisonous glance before turning back to Eve. "Don't you think I was tempted to just let you go on with the reconstruction until I could find out who you were working on? If you don't finish, I risk losing my story."

"Then why didn't you?"

He grimaced. "Ethics. The bane of my existence."

"Inspiring," Galen murmured.

"The truth."

The man's reply was both bad-tempered and defiant, but Eve

thought she could also sense honesty. "How did you know I was working on the skull?"

"I didn't. I followed the skull and staked out the church." He paused. "I'm not the only one. I almost stumbled over two guys near the church."

"Guards. There are four, sometimes five," Galen said. "And much more talented than you."

"I'm a journalist, not a thug."

"From where did you follow the skull?" Eve asked.

"Well, I didn't exactly follow it. Etienne told me it was going to be taken to the church."

"Etienne?"

"Etienne Hebert." He drew a deep breath. "Look, I can't have a cigarette, so will you at least give me a cup of coffee? I need the caffeine."

"This isn't a social occasion," Galen said. "Conversation first."

"Oh, for God's sake. If I hadn't intended to tell you everything I know, I wouldn't have come here tonight. As you've pointed out, I'm no great shakes at this kind of thing."

"True. But it could be a ploy."

Eve made a decision. "We'll go down to the kitchen and get some coffee. He looks like he could use it."

Galen shrugged. "Whatever." He stood aside as Nathan got up and headed for the door. "I hope you don't regret it, Eve."

"A cup of coffee?" She followed them out into the hall. "I don't think that's being particularly soft. I have questions to ask, and he may as well be comfortable while he answers them." She gave Nathan a cool glance. "And I assure you that you will answer them."

Ten minutes later she was pouring steaming coffee into Nathan's cup. "And who is Etienne Hebert?"

"I don't think the present tense applies to Etienne." Nathan took a drink of coffee, and gave a deep sigh of satisfaction. "I think Jules killed him." He held up his hand at Eve's exclamation. "Okay, okay. Let me do this in my own way. I'll start in the beginning. About a month ago I received a phone call at my office from a man named Etienne Hebert. He said he knew what had happened to Harold Bently, and that Bently was the smallest part of the story. He asked me to meet him outside New Orleans, at a little crab shack on the Mississippi."

"Why you?"

"How the hell do I know? Maybe because I covered the Bently disappearance for the newspaper." He took another sip of coffee. "Anyway. I met him. He was a big guy, not over twenty-one or -two, and seemed a little simple at first glance." He shook his head. "But he wasn't that dumb. After I talked to him for awhile, I realized he was smarter than I first thought. He was just troubled, and feeling guilty about talking to me. He had a big brother, Jules, and there was no way he wanted to get him in trouble. It was obvious he had a king-size case of hero worship. Etienne was only a fisherman, but Jules was the smart one in the family. He was the only one who made it to college." He grimaced. "Maybe it would have been better for him if he hadn't. He was a junior at Tulane when the Cabal recruited him."

"What's the Cabal?"

"It's a secret society that's been in existence since the early 1900s."

"Secret society?" Galen said. "Be for real."

"I couldn't be more serious."

"And the society is named the Cabal? For God's sake, that

means secret society. They must be seriously lacking in imagination."

"They're called that because their members are drawn from the top echelon of other organizations." Nathan grimaced. "And they think of themselves as the ultimate secret society."

Galen snorted.

"That was my reaction until I did my homework," Nathan said. "There are hundreds of secret societies around the world, and the U.S. has taken them to its heart. The Freemasons, the Odd Fellows, Skull and Bones." He studied Eve's expression. "I know. They all sound a little ludicrous—unless you study the membership lists. Did you know both George Bush and George W. Bush belong to Skull and Bones, and George W.'s only comment about his membership was that he couldn't talk about it?"

"So what? I assume there's no proof that Skull and Bones is involved in any nefarious activities?"

"No proof. But there are also members in positions of power in the CIA and on Wall Street and practically every level of the business world. It's not only Skull and Bones. The Trilateral Commission and the Council on Foreign Relations have always been influential. The Bilderberg Group is supposed to be so powerful it can influence worldwide politics itself. Margaret Thatcher's career took off like a rocket after she attended a Bilderberg meeting. The same thing happened to Tony Blair after he was invited to a meeting in Vouliagméni, Greece. In 1991, David Rockefeller invited Arkansas governor Bill Clinton to a meeting in Baden-Baden, Germany."

"Now wait a minute. I respect Bill Clinton and Tony Blair."

"So do I. I'm not accusing them. I'm just trying to show you the influence a secret society could wield. Probably the great majority of the members of these societies are totally in the dark about the activities, unaware of the elite groups in their organizations. I don't even know which groups are part of the Cabal. Maybe none of the ones I mentioned. Maybe all of them." He shrugged. "Etienne didn't know how many secret societies were involved. He only knew what Jules had told him, and that was that the Cabal comprised the highest echelon from several organizations, and that these elite members used their societies to influence the world economy."

"How?"

Nathan shrugged. "How the hell do I know? But didn't you find it weird that the gas prices went up so high recently when there was no lack of oil?"

Eve had been as angry as everyone else at that increase at the gas pumps. "And how could they do that?"

"Use your imagination. There are supposed to be members of OPEC, Wall Street shakers, and Japanese computer executives in the Cabal."

"Supposed? That's not good enough. Give me names."

"If I knew who, do you think I'd be here? I'd be back home in New Orleans writing my story." Nathan's gaze searched their faces. "Dammit, it's true. What else can I tell you? I watched the stock market before and after the Greenspan announcements. There was always a flurry of activity from the same banking quarters, and fortunes were made as soon as the announcement came through. They know what's going to happen before it happens. Secret societies pervade our past and our present. They have power in every quarter. Almost every U.S. president of the twentieth century was a Freemason. Hell, George Washington's inauguration ceremony was Masonic. Lyndon Johnson's advisors were in the Council on Foreign Relations when he escalated the Vietnam war. The first peace negotiator for Bosnia was Lord

Carrington, chairman of the Bilderberg Group." Nathan drew a deep breath. "Okay, don't accept what I'm telling you as gospel, just look at the possibility. When men of power get together, it's natural for them to try to combine and push to increase that power. They work in the dark and behind the scenes, because if the public knew they were being manipulated they'd be yelling to the high heavens. It's been that way since the first secret societies in Egypt and Samaria in the B.C.'s. The Cabal's worked for decades to form a spiderweb of tremendous power, and they're not going to let that power be jeopardized."

Galen shrugged. "I don't see how any organization composed of such powerful, renowned figures could even meet without attracting attention."

"They usually don't meet. They communicate by messenger and, more recently, on the Internet. The only exception is when something really big is going down and they have to get together to form a clear-cut majority. When they do meet, they schedule it at a place and time where it seems natural that they would all be present. Like a royal wedding. According to Etienne, the last meeting was at the Summer Olympics. No one suspected that they were there for anything else but to cheer on their national teams."

"And was Etienne recruited by the Cabal?"

"No, his brother tried to persuade the Cabal to accept him, but they didn't believe he was good material. However, they had a gem in Jules. Etienne said Jules was brainwashed until he believed that everything the Cabal said and did was right, that a strong guiding hand was necessary to preserve peace and the status quo. He became their dirty-tricks expert."

"Assassin?"

Nathan nodded. "He was trained in a terrorist school in

Libya, but he developed his own techniques. He became an expert, and worked for the Cabal for ten years before the Bently murder."

"Murder? You're sure he was murdered?"

"Etienne said he was there when it happened, and I have no reason to think he lied to me."

"I thought you said he was refused by the Cabal."

"But Jules trusted him and took him along on a number of jobs. Etienne was no problem to Jules until it came to Bently. Something bothered him about the Bently killing."

"What?"

"He wouldn't tell me. He just said it was wrong, and that why the Cabal was doing it was wrong, too. He didn't like the murder, and he didn't like bringing the skeleton back two years later. It must have worried him seriously to cause him to break with a brother he'd previously always followed blindly."

"But not enough to go into detail."

"He still hoped to change his brother's mind about the Cabal, and he only wanted to use me as a safety net in case he couldn't do it. He said someone had to know about the Cabal and stop them. He said we had to hurry." He paused. "He was worried about something that Jules had been ordered to do in Boca Raton. He kept saying that we had to stop them before October twenty-ninth."

"Why?"

"That's all he'd say. I thought maybe it was a Cabal meeting, but there aren't any scheduled events that would give them an excuse to be in Boca at that time. So maybe it has something to do with Bently." Nathan grimaced. "It's all guesswork. I was frustrated as hell. He told me they were going to bring the skeleton here, but not when or why. He said he'd call me again after the skeleton was in place at the church." He paused. "He didn't call me."

"There was no skeleton," Eve said. "Only a skull."

"Really?" Nathan frowned. "He said skeleton. I wonder what happened to—"

"A skeleton has infinitely more possibilities for DNA," Galen said. "The skull had no teeth, either. Etienne's work?"

"Maybe," Nathan said. "If it was, then I imagine Jules was a tad upset. I warned Etienne to be careful. Stealing a skeleton isn't exactly the most cautious act."

"But you didn't try to stop him."

"I'm a reporter, and this had all the earmarks of a great story. I won't feel guilty about doing my job. Etienne was hardly as pure as the driven snow." He smiled grimly. "But, unfortunately, I do have a conscience where innocent lives are at stake. That's why I'm here."

"It took you long enough to decide to come to warn us," Galen said.

"I had to think about it." He scowled as Galen lifted a brow. "It's the truth." His glance shifted to Eve. "Then I read about Marie Letaux's death, and the article indicated you were struck by the same food poisoning. I tried to tell myself it could be an accident. Hell, it could have been. But when Pierre Letaux died . . . Too much coincidence, considering what Etienne had told me. I chewed on it for awhile, and then decided I couldn't wait until you finished. I'd have to risk my story. So pack up your bags and get the hell out of here."

Galen looked at Eve. "Not a bad idea."

"You believe him?"

"Enough. The evidence is growing, and I don't like it. Added to what Quinn told us tonight, I think we'd be prudent to fold our tents and flit away."

She didn't like it, either. Nathan's story of secret societies with that much control over people's day-to-day lives was both frightening and outlandish. And so was the fact that she'd been lured to this job by Melton, who could be in cahoots with the man who had used her daughter's death as a tool. The thought brought a bolt of pure rage surging through her.

"Eve?"

"I'm thinking." Galen was right. Whether or not the Cabal existed, the evidence for some sort of conspiracy was mounting. Capel's and the Letauxs's deaths should have been enough for her in themselves. It was only her obsession with finishing Victor that had kept her from admitting it.

Victor.

"We're getting out of here," she said. "But I'm not leaving the skull. Victor comes with us."

"What?" Nathan asked. "Why?"

"Because she wants to do it," Galen said. "And I'm beginning to want her to do anything she can to thumb her nose at those bastards. Eve, we can't trust anything Nathan says until I check him out, but if you're not going to be a cat's paw, then you have to be on your own turf."

"And take Victor with us," Eve said flatly. "I'm not giving him up until I make up my mind what we're going to do."

Nathan shook his head. "You're actually stealing him?"

"Just borrowing his skull for a little while. Until I make a decision, he's mine. It's my choice what happens to Victor. Not Hebert's or Melton's or any half-baked secret society. Let them all run around and kill each other. They're not going to use

Victor in their plans." She glanced at Galen. "The church may be locked at this time of night, Galen."

"Are you hinting I should get out of here and do a little breaking and entering?"

"You seemed to do well enough at Marie Letaux's house. Will the church be a problem?"

Galen shook his head. "What do you need from your workroom?"

"Victor. My tools, the leather skull case, the box with the glass eyeballs. Rick is always at the church when I get there in the morning, Galen. If he's there, I don't want him hurt."

"I'll keep that in mind, but he may be part of this, you know."

She didn't want to believe that of Rick. "And maybe he's not. Maybe he doesn't know anything about this. Until we're sure any of this is true, I don't want him hurt."

"Are you going to leave it to me where we're going?"

"You said that your job was to provide what was needed. Provide."

"Taking the skull is a mistake." Nathan's voice was harsh with intensity. "If you go away and hide, they may abandon the search eventually. Take the skull, and they'll come after you. They'll suspect you know something and they'll never give up. Why won't you listen to me?"

"Because we don't have any proof you're anyone more than a second-story man with a glass jaw," Galen said.

But Nathan's desperation was very convincing, and Eve felt a sudden frantic surge of urgency. "We are listening to you . . . within limits. That's why we're leaving Baton Rouge. I'll pack our bags and be ready to leave when you get back, Galen."

Nathan sighed. "If you won't do the sensible thing, then I may as well help you pack."

"No, you're coming with me," Galen said. "I'm not leaving you alone in the house with Eve."

"For God's sake, after all I've told you, I think I deserve a little trust."

"Words aren't worth anything. Trust is earned. You'll have to prove yourself."

"By risking my neck at that church?"

"Good a way as any." Galen glanced back over his shoulder at Eve. "Do you know how to handle a gun?"

"Yes."

"There's one in my duffel. Get it. I don't like leaving you in the house alone."

"Then let me stay, dammit," Nathan said.

Galen ignored him. "Scoot, Eve. Get moving. We may be in a hurry when I get back. I need to get a couple items from the kitchen cabinet, and then Nathan and I will be on the road."

Chapter Nine

WHERE WERE THEY?

Eve's gaze anxiously searched the darkness, but she could see nothing but the shadowy outline of the church.

It had been over thirty minutes. Surely they should be back by now.

Unless something had happened to them.

She wouldn't let herself think that. Galen was too smart to have let himself be caught, and she had heard no sound of conflict while she had been standing here on the balcony.

"Let's go."

She whirled to see Galen coming toward her. At least she thought it was Galen. He was covered in mud and slime, and his wet clothes clung to his body. "What happened to you?"

"Not a tenth of what should have happened to him," Nathan said bitterly as he entered the room. He was also wet and covered in slime. "He's the craziest son of a bitch I've ever met. He made me swim that damn bayou."

"What?"

"We would have been spotted as we crossed the bridge," Galen said. "It seemed the easiest way around the problem."

"Easy?" Nathan sputtered. "He pushed me in the water. What if I didn't know how to swim?"

"The water was almost shallow enough to wade across."

"It was not," Nathan said, outraged. "And what about water moccasins, alligators . . . Anything could have been lurking in that foul mess."

"Stop complaining. You didn't get bitten by anything more dangerous than mosquitoes. You should be glad I let you stay on the bank instead of going into the church with me." He went to the bathroom and got two towels and tossed one to Nathan. "Dry off. We don't have time to shower."

"Did you get Victor?" Eve asked.

He looked at her in surprise. "Of course. Everything you asked me to get is downstairs by the back door. He's fine. I put him in a big Ziploc bag for the swim back, with a couple of inflated trash bags as floats. I took care of him, and I loaded Nathan down with the other stuff you wanted."

"No trouble?"

He shook his head.

"You're lying," Nathan said sourly. "I saw a guard go into the church after you went in. He didn't come out."

"I'm not lying." Galen gave him an annoyed glance. "I was just omitting an incident that might have upset Eve. I told the truth. He was no trouble. I got him before he alerted anyone."

"Got him?"

"Don't worry, it wasn't Rick. Let's go. We have to get out of here before they find out the skull is gone."

"He's crazy," Nathan grumbled to Eve. "The bastard could have gotten us eaten." He looked belligerently at Galen. "And I need a shower."

"No time. Go as you are or not at all. You made your way here; if you want, you can find your own way out of it."

"For this Jules Hebert to find?" Eve asked.

"He has to keep up with the program. My mum always said that what goes around, comes around."

"I'm getting very tired of what your mum said. I think you make it up to suit yourself." She headed for the door. "We're taking him."

He shrugged. "If you insist. But we both smell to high heaven, and two of us packed in that car will be enough to make anyone sick." He passed her and hurried down the stairs in front of her. "We go out the back door and get to the car parked in the cypress grove a few hundred yards from the house." He stopped at the kitchen door. "Stay here for a minute. I'll be right back."

"Where are you going?"

"I've checked the area out. Most of the guards are located across the bayou at the church, but one rascal is a little distance down the bank of the bayou watching the house. I didn't have time to take care of him when I went for the skull." He glanced at Nathan. "And besides, Nathan was making too much noise complaining. We were lucky to get back to the house without anyone seeing us."

"You were trying to drown—"

"Be ready." Galen was out the door and moving to the side

of the house. "And cross your fingers they don't find that guard in the church . . ."

———

"Come on. Move." Galen appeared at the door a few minutes later. "We're on borrowed time."

"The guard?"

"Taken care of." He broke into a trot as they neared the cypress grove. "It's the guard in the church we have to worry about. It's been almost fifteen minutes. Someone will go and look for him."

Eve stopped short. Galen's brown rental car was not parked there as she had expected. Instead, there was a late-model gray Lexus.

Joe Quinn was standing beside it.

Eve whirled on Galen. "What the hell is happening?"

"I'm happening," Joe said curtly. "Get in the car and let's get out of here."

Eve ignored him. "You called him, Galen?"

"Sure. Before I went to the church. I told you I might need him. I'd say the situation is escalating enough to bring him in. I can't be everywhere at once. Pop the trunk, Quinn." He put the cases in the trunk. "This is Bill Nathan. Get in the backseat, Nathan." He turned to Eve. "Your choice where you want to sit, but Quinn is going with us. I've invited him along for the ride."

"Galen, you're taking too much on yourself."

"It's a habit of mine. I'm providing." He opened the back door for her. "And that includes as much protection as I can manage."

"For God's sake, I'm not going to contaminate you," Joe said roughly. "Get in the car."

She hesitated, and then got into the backseat next to Nathan. "I don't like this, Galen."

"Sorry." He looked over his shoulder at the church as he got into the passenger seat. "Nothing stirring yet. God, we're lucky. Let's go, Quinn."

Joe got into the driver's seat. "Where are we going?"

"South. I have a place just a little north of New Orleans. That should be safe for a time."

"They won't look for us there?"

"Well, when you're in my business you don't want the entire world to know where you make your home. The paperwork is buried pretty well."

"Don't be overconfident," Nathan said. "Jules Hebert has the Cabal behind him, and that opens a lot of doors."

"If this so-called Cabal even exists. Anyone can find anyone, given enough time. But we may have enough leeway for Eve to finish Victor."

"Maybe."

"Drive, Quinn," Galen said. "He's depressing me."

————

Joe's shoulders were squared; he hadn't looked back at Eve for the entire journey.

And she had tried her best to keep her gaze off him by looking out the window or trying to chat with Nathan, who was less than communicative. Galen was no help. He'd been uncharacteristically quiet during the trip, only giving Joe an occasional direction. So there had been nothing to distract her from looking at Joe, thinking about Joe, during these hours on the road.

It seemed wrong to be back here, when she was always beside him. All those years when they had been best friends and then lovers . . .

Lovers.

Jesus, how she loved him to touch her. Her body was readying, just thinking about the last time he had entered her, driving deep and hard. And afterward was almost as good, being held as if she was wonderfully precious. She always felt so safe. . . .

She forced herself to look away from him. Life wasn't sex. Life was trust and honesty.

And sex.

She hadn't been away from Joe's bed since they had come back from Arizona two years ago. It was natural that she would become used to his body, used to sex with him. It wasn't as if she couldn't do without it. It would be better once she got out of this damn car.

Okay, block him out. She had to try to decide what to do once she reached Galen's place. There were too many important issues to resolve. What was best for Jane and her mother? Think about them instead of Joe. Hell, what was best for her?

An hour later Galen pointed to a huge wrought-iron gate mounted on an equally huge iron fence. "Turn in there. The house is beyond those cedar trees." He pressed a button on his keychain and the gates swung open. "Thank God, we're here. This wasn't the most relaxing trip I've ever taken. I could have cut the atmosphere with a knife."

"It's all your fault." Eve said her own prayer of thanks that the journey was over as she leaned forward to get a shadowy glimpse of the huge two-story yellow-beige stucco house. "For God's sake, it's a mansion."

"I made the owner an offer he couldn't refuse," Galen said as they drove up the curving driveway to the two carved twelve-foot doors. "I thought it appropriate."

"I hope we're not going to be involved with the Mafia," Eve said. "That's all I'd need at the moment."

"I was joking," Galen said. "My job pays pretty well and I had Logan invest for me. I have a few shekels to rub together."

"Quite a few," Quinn said dryly. "One wonders why you're still working."

"When you grow up in the slums, there's never enough money in the world to make you feel safe." Galen got out of the car and opened the back door. "But I tried to stop about a year ago and I couldn't take it. I was bored to death. As a matter of fact, that statement was pretty close to the truth. I started taking chances. Hell, I even took up mountain climbing. When I sprained my ankle on one of the kiddie slopes, I decided I was a sad case, so I went back to work. I figured it was healthier." He helped Eve out of the car. "You okay?"

"Fine."

"I'm not," Nathan said. "I'm smelly and dirty and I think I have leech bites."

"Really?" Galen's brows rose. "Anywhere interesting? If you were attacked by leeches, then they're probably still attached. Want help pulling them off?"

Nathan glowered at him. "You'd like that, wouldn't you?"

"Don't be surly. You'll survive. I doubt if you have leeches."

"You're such an expert?"

"Sure. Though I'm more knowledgeable about crossing piranha-infested rivers."

Nathan snorted.

"You doubt me? You always cross the river at night when the piranhas are dozing, and you stay away from docks where—"

"I don't want to hear about piranhas. Will you unlock that damn door?"

"Just trying to educate you." Galen turned, climbed the four steps, unlocked the front doors and flipped on the hall lights. "No servants, Eve. I have someone from town come once a week and make a little headway in the dust. Other than that, we're on our own. All the bedrooms are on the second floor. I think there are ten or eleven. Choose any that suits you."

"The only thing I want is a shower." Nathan went past him into the house.

"Wrap yourself in a sheet when you get out of the shower," Galen called after him. "I'll try to find some clothes of mine that are big enough for your rather Olympian frame."

"I'm just a few pounds overweight," Nathan said through his teeth.

"Grumpy, isn't he?" Galen said as Nathan disappeared. "But I agree with him about the shower. However, I'll make the supreme sacrifice and give you a glimpse of the room I think will be perfect for you to work on Victor, Eve. Come on." He went into the house.

"Go on. I'll get the bags." Joe had moved around the car to the trunk. "I'm not all that eager to see Galen's pad. I've had enough of him for the time being."

"Then you shouldn't have come."

"You know why I came." He met her eyes. "And it had

nothing to do with Galen." He opened the trunk. "Apart from the fact that I might get the opportunity to break his neck."

———————

"What about working in here?" Galen threw open the door of a room on the bottom floor. "Lots of light."

"A kitchen?" She looked around at the huge room with stone floors, an ancient AGA range, as well as a fireplace big enough to walk into.

"It used to be a scullery in the last century. The man I bought the place from converted another room to a kitchen on the level above. This was impossible to update, and he liked his comforts. So do I." He gestured to a butcher-block table. "You could put your equipment there. Okay?"

She shivered. "It's a little cold."

"That's what the fireplace is for. I'll keep it stoked for you. So should I bring your stuff down?"

She hesitated, tempted, and then shook her head. "I don't think so. I did some thinking on the way here."

"Second thoughts?"

"Yes."

"And what did you decide?" Joe asked from the top of the stairs.

"That I'm being a damn idealistic idiot to even consider going on with this reconstruction."

"Good." Joe came down the steps. "That's what I've been telling you."

"If I work all my life, I can't get through all the reconstructions for people who really need me. Bently may have been a good man, but there are other good people in the world. People are being killed all around me. How do I know it won't touch my family?" Her lips thinned. "Yes, I'm sorry at the idea of not finishing Victor, but I'm not going to be stupid."

"Well, you seem to have made up your mind," Galen said. "How do you want it handled?"

"I don't trust Melton. He lied to me."

"The FBI?" Joe asked.

"Maybe."

"I know, you don't trust them, either."

"You used to work with them. Do you know anyone who has the reputation of being incorruptible?"

"Incorruptible isn't easy to find. Let me think about it and make a few calls."

"Since I'm not needed, I'm going to see about that shower." Galen turned and started up the stairs. "If you like, I could bring Victor down and you could have one more go at him before you turn him over."

"No!"

He stopped in surprise. "It was just a suggestion. I thought you might like—"

"She's afraid," Joe said. "She thinks if she starts to work on him again, she won't be able to give him up."

Dammit, Joe could always read her. "I'm not stupid. I know what's important." But Victor was important, too. He was lost, and she could find him. If she worked on him just a little longer she might— "Don't set Victor up."

Galen nodded. "Try to get some rest, Eve. It's been a long night."

"Are you giving me orders, Galen?"

He started back up the stairs. "Perish the thought. I know

I'm in your bad books. But I stand by my decision to bring Quinn along."

She hurried after him. The last thing she wanted was to be left alone with Joe. "Are you going to check on Bill Nathan? He seems okay, but nothing has been as it seems since I left Atlanta."

He nodded. "Right after my shower." He smiled slyly. "I wonder if he really does have any of those cunning little leeches . . ."

———

"She's gone?" Melton's tone was controlled, but Jules could detect the anger beneath the smoothness. "With the skull?"

"Yes. But don't worry, I'll find her."

"You should never have lost her, Hebert. Your orders were to see that she finished the skull, and then get rid of her. Where the hell were you tonight? Why weren't you watching her?"

"I had to be in Boca Raton to check on the progress. I thought it was safe. She didn't appear to suspect anything, and I knew she wanted to finish the skull. It seemed a good time to—" He stopped in disgust. He was babbling, making excuses like a fucking amateur to this asshole. "I made a mistake. I'll rectify it."

"You certainly will. If it's not too late. What if she takes the skull to the police?"

"I don't believe she'll do that yet, but I'll have to move fast. My men saw Joe Quinn enter her house earlier tonight. Either he or Galen must have convinced her to run. But she can't know anything for certain. If she took the skull, it's probably because she wants to finish it. We both know how intense she is about her work. That may give me a little time. I'll need your help."

"As long as I'm not compromised."

"She won't go home. If she suspects something, then she'll be hiding out. I need you to tap your sources and find out where Galen may have taken her. Fast."

"It's a big country."

Jules tried to hold onto his temper and spaced each word with precision. "Can you do this?"

"I permitted you to pursue this line with Duncan when you blundered with Etienne, but we can't risk it any more. It's too dangerous for us. You get that skull and then dispose of her and everyone around her quickly. I don't want even a ripple of publicity. Do you understand?"

"I understand. Can you find her?"

"I'll try." He hung up.

And he'd try very hard, Jules thought. Melton might try to lay the entire blame on Jules, but he was responsible for Boca Raton and wanted this Bently problem wrapped up before he had to answer awkward questions.

So did Jules. He was having trouble keeping all the balls in the air. Ever since that night when he had killed Etienne, he had been forced to lie and cheat and make compromises. If he wasn't careful, everything would come crashing down on him.

No, he wouldn't permit it. He had given up too much to be defeated now. He couldn't sit here and trust Melton to find Eve Duncan.

He would take matters into his own hands.

Chapter Ten

CHRIST, SHE WANTED DINNER TO BE OVER.

The meal seemed to go on forever. Nathan's surly attitude had not improved with his shower. Joe had been almost silent, and Eve had been so aware of him sitting across the table that she had only been able to respond stiltedly to Galen's questions and comments.

Galen was the only one who seemed to be unaffected by the atmosphere. He was charged, wired, a one-man show. He alternated between running to the kitchen for a variety of delicious dishes, telling stories, and occasionally jabbing verbally at Joe or Nathan.

"You're all a great disappointment to me." Galen leaned back in his chair after he had served coffee. "If I weren't so socially adept, this meal would have been a disaster. Your performance has been abysmal."

"This isn't a circus, Galen," Joe said. "And you're not the ringmaster."

"Very good comparison, Quinn. Evidently you're not totally lacking in the conversational arts."

"Galen," Eve said.

"She obviously wants to smooth the troubled waters around here." Galen turned to Joe. "Is she afraid for me or you? What do you think?"

"I think I've had a bellyful."

"Crude. Very crude."

Joe turned to Eve. "I did some phoning before dinner. I called a few of my contacts with the FBI, and they all agreed that Bart Jennings is probably our man. He's smart and dedicated, and he's been with the Bureau for the last twenty years."

"Do you know him personally?"

Joe shook his head. "But I heard about him when I was with the Bureau."

"What's happening here?" Nathan asked.

"Eve's decided to turn over the skull."

"Without finishing it?"

Eve nodded.

"Thank God. Smart move. Though you'd have done better to leave the skull and just run for it."

"I'm not giving the skull to Jules Hebert and his crew." She met his gaze. "I don't know how much of your story is true and how much is speculative bullshit, but I don't want to have to deal with it. I'm turning it over to the authorities."

"You can't trust the authorities," Nathan said. "You can't trust anyone."

"You sound like a character in a bad movie," Joe told him. "Eve, I talked to Jennings and he's promised to keep the problem absolutely confidential. But he'd like to come and see you at ten tomorrow morning."

Eve frowned. "You told him where we were?"

"No, I wouldn't do that without checking with you. I told him I'd call him back."

She thought about it. "Tell him I'll see him. Then maybe Victor will be off my hands when Jennings leaves here."

Galen smiled. "You'll be sorry to see him go."

That was an understatement. She was always sorry when she failed to bring a subject home, and Victor had become close to an obsession with her. But she mustn't think about that now. She had fought the battle on the trip here.

"Did you tell him that you got the information about the Cabal from me, Quinn?" Nathan asked.

"No, I thought you'd prefer I didn't. Though he was pushing pretty hard. As you reporters term it, I quoted a confidential source."

"Good. Because you may be making a big mistake." Nathan stood and threw down his napkin. "I'm not going to be there when you meet Jennings. I've kept my neck intact so far by not letting anyone know I'm involved. I intend to keep on doing that."

Galen watched Nathan leave the room before he turned back to Eve. "By the way, I did some checking on Bill Nathan. He's a freelance columnist on the *Times Picayune,* and pretty well known for advocating various environmental reforms." He took a fax out of his pocket and tossed it to her. "The picture in the newspaper isn't great, but it's definitely him."

She glanced at the fax. Galen was right; the photo was bad but recognizable. "Then maybe you should get off his back."

Galen looked at her in surprise. "Why? It's so much fun."

"I've had enough." Joe turned to Eve. "I want to talk to you."

She stiffened.

"Yes, you two run along." Galen stood and started stacking the dishes. "I have to get these in the dishwasher. A housekeeper's job is never done—"

"I don't need your permission, Galen," Joe said.

"It's that ringmaster syndrome I have." Galen started carrying the dishes into the kitchen. "And I believe you can use any help you can get."

Joe watched the door swing closed behind him. "He's pushing it. I wonder if he knows how close I am to—" He turned and moved toward the French doors that led to the veranda. "Let's get out of here." He glanced over his shoulder. "Don't say no to me, Eve. I'm too close to exploding, thanks to that son of a bitch."

"Galen's been very kind to me."

"Yeah, he told me. Are you coming?"

The last thing she wanted was a confrontation with Joe, but she wasn't going to be able to bear any more of this tension. Get it over with. She stood up. "I'm coming."

The autumn night was cold; the breeze from the lake sent a shiver through her.

"Even the weather's against me." Joe took off his jacket and draped it over her shoulders.

The jacket was warm from his body and smelled of his favorite cologne. "I don't want this."

"And I don't want to give you an excuse to run inside and away from me." He leaned against the stone balustrade and looked out at the lake. "I like our lake better. This is too . . . pretty."

She knew what he meant. This place had none of the wildness and rough earthy beauty of the lake cottage terrain. "It doesn't look like Galen's scene either, but he said—"

"We're not talking about Galen," he cut in. "We're talking about us and our life together. Galen doesn't belong in it."

"Joe, this is too soon. I can't—"

"Don't you think I know it's too soon? I was going to give you time. It was killing me, but I would have done it. Then everything blew up. You could get yourself killed. I can't *not* be with you now." He drew a ragged breath. "And I can't stand you flinching away from me. So we have to come to terms."

"What kind of terms?"

"You let me stay with you, protect you, and I won't ask anything else. I won't bother you. I won't back you into a corner. I won't remind you of how damn good we were together." He paused and then said through gritted teeth, "I'll even stand by and let you sleep with Galen if that's what you want."

"What?"

His gaze narrowed on her face. "You're not sleeping with Galen?"

"Are you nuts? After all these years of knowing me, do you believe I could just jump into someone else's bed without a second thought?"

Joe slowly let his breath out. "I'm definitely going to kill him."

"He told you I was sleeping with him?"

"Not exactly." He changed the subject. "Will you go along with me on this? After all this is over, I'll step out of the picture and let you go back to pondering my sins. Since you've called in Jennings, it shouldn't be that long. I just can't leave you now."

Eve didn't answer.

"You listen to me." He grasped her shoulders and shook her. "I deserve this. You may think I'm a bastard, but after all the years and all we've gone through together, you can't close me out. How would you feel if it were me? You care about me. You can't turn it off and on just because you think I did something unforgivable."

"It *was* terrible." And standing here close to him being bombarded by his intensity and her own feelings was terrible, too. "And you're tearing me apart, dammit."

"Answer me. How would you feel if I was the one who might get knifed in the gullet by some scumball?"

A world without Joe? Pain. Agonizing loss. Emptiness.

"You see? Now give me what I want. Be fair to me. Let me stay and help you."

Eve was silent a moment before nodding jerkily. "Okay. But it may only make everything worse."

"I'm prepared for that." Joe's lips twisted. "Though God knows how they could be any worse than they are." His hands moved yearningly on her shoulders before he slowly released her. "Do you know I haven't touched you in days? It hurts. . . ." He turned on his heel. "But I'm not supposed to talk about that. It's against the damn rules." He disappeared inside the house.

Jesus, she was going crazy. She could still feel the weight of his hands on her shoulders although they were no longer there. She was surrounded by his scent and the warmth of his jacket and the sound of his voice, and his words lingered.

What if it was me?

It was the one question that would have broken through any

wall she could erect. She remembered how devastated she'd been when Joe had been shot a few years ago; they had grown still closer since then. Don't think about it. Try to run on automatic when you're around him. She had given in because she had recognized she was being unfair, but to dwell on Joe and their life together would be masochistic.

She took off Joe's jacket. Cold and loneliness immediately assaulted her. It was only a coat, dammit. She carried it inside and laid it on a dining room chair. Let him get it later. She couldn't face him again right now. He had said he would stay out of her way, but just by being in the same house he disturbed her. She would go upstairs and go to bed. She glanced longingly at the scullery door as she passed it. She was too disturbed to sleep well tonight. If she had Victor to work on, it would give her both distraction and release. She could go find the skull and . . .

No, she mustn't fall into that temptation. The decision had been made. Tomorrow that FBI man would be here and both the threat and the emotional upheaval would be over.

***

"Thank you for agreeing to see me." Bart Jennings smiled at Eve. "Logan explained that your attitude toward government agencies isn't entirely cordial." He grimaced. "I have a few problems with bureaucracies myself."

"A man of judgment," Galen murmured. "I think I like him, Eve."

She knew what he meant. From the moment Jennings had appeared at the front door a short time ago, she had been impressed. Jennings was a man in his forties, with salt-and-pepper hair that had an unruly cowlick. His manner was straightforward, his demeanor frank and open. "Logan told you that we didn't want Senator Melton involved in this?"

"I've no problem with that. The senator has some pretty heavy connections in Washington, but I've seen power figures come and go in my years with the Bureau. From now on, he's out of the loop."

"Really?" Joe's gaze narrowed on Jennings's face. "You sound very definite about that."

"Let's say, I don't trust him. He may be a stooge, or he may be up to his neck. Either way, we need to be careful."

"You believe this grand conspiracy theory?"

"I can't dismiss it until I prove it's not true." Jennings paused. "I've heard scraps of information that suggest there's some substance to the story. Some of it's pretty hard to believe, but it could be damn serious if even a tenth of the things we've been told are true. You say this Etienne thought something big was happening in Boca Raton?"

Eve nodded. "At first, he thought it might be a meeting of the Cabal, but there was no event taking place that would give the members an excuse to come. It had to be something else."

"I need the name of your informant."

Joe shook his head. "I told you, I promised to keep it confidential."

"You're making my job harder." Jennings turned to Eve. "Which leads me to you. When do you expect to complete the reconstruction?"

"Three, maybe four more days would finish it." She stiffened. "But I'm not going to finish it. That's why you're here. You're going to take him off my hands. I want out."

He nodded sympathetically. "I understand perfectly. I'd feel the same way. And if I were you I'd want to throw the request I'm going to make back in my face. But I've got to make it anyway: Give us those four days. Finish the reconstruction."

"The hell she will," Joe said.

"No way," Eve said.

"Just listen. Hebert and Melton are obviously desperate to have that skull finished, and they must have a reason. Why?"

"Bently?"

"But why do they need to know he's dead? And what connection does it have to whatever is going to happen in Boca Raton?" He paused. "We need to know, too. We were involved in the investigation of Bently's disappearance, and we uncovered a few intriguing little morsels of information. Bently had some hush-hush dealings with a bank in Grand Cayman right before he disappeared."

"Money laundering?" Galen asked.

Jennings shrugged. "Why? Bently's personal fortune was enormous. His grandfather was in oil—that was one of the reasons Bently became an environmentalist. Payback. But huge transfers were going on in that bank in Grand Cayman. It was a joint account with a Thomas Simmons, who was allowed to withdraw any amount he chose. Then the account was closed, and the money disappeared."

"Who was Thomas Simmons?"

"We questioned Bently's wife and business associates and came up with a blank. No one knew anything about Simmons." He paused. "But another lead surfaced that guided us down a possible path. We ran a nationwide computer search on think tanks and university personnel, and came up with a Professor Thomas Randall Simmons at Cal Tech. He took a sabbatical about the time Bently disappeared. We couldn't find any other link until we checked with Grand Cayman and got a sample of his handwriting. It was a match."

"A con game?" Joe suggested. "Maybe you should look a little harder for the elusive Mr. Simmons. It could be that Bently found out he was being taken, and Simmons decided to get rid of him."

"We have been looking for him, dammit," Jennings said. "We came up with zilch. But Bently was very intelligent. It would have taken someone pretty sharp to put anything over on him."

"Then we go back to whether Bently was a crook himself. Some people never have enough money."

Jennings shook his head. "We don't think so. Bently was an idealist and squeaky clean, but there were signs he might have been channeling his money into a secret project."

"What project?"

"Something he believed in enough to stake his personal fortune on it. That was the lead that sent us scurrying to every think tank in the country to find Simmons. He was up to his eyebrows in some very interesting research." He paused. "What do you know about fuel cells?"

"Not much. It's supposed to be one of the alternatives to using oil and gas to fuel cars. Some of the auto companies have experimented extensively with the cells, but it's never got off the ground. Too expensive."

"Their energy potential goes far beyond the automotive field. Everything from power plants, to homes, to space stations could be operated by fuel cells. At a fraction of the present cost and no environmental side effects. There's hardly a person on the planet that wouldn't benefit if fuel cells became a viable alternative. Scientists are very close to making it a reality. Yet most people have never heard of the technology. Don't you find that curious?"

"What does this have to do with—" Eve stopped. "You think Bently was funding research to develop a workable fuel cell."

Jennings nodded. "Simmons was deep in research on the cells. And we've been able to follow the money trail to a source in Detroit. Bently was being sold several key components for the development of fuel cells. He wasn't a fool. He wouldn't invest that kind of money unless he was pretty sure he was onto something."

"Why keep it secret?" Eve asked. "If this fuel cell is going to be so beneficial, why not go to the government and persuade them to sink a billion or two into the research?"

"Maybe he wanted a finished product, or maybe he didn't trust Congress to pass a bill that wouldn't antagonize every energy lobby in the country," Joe said.

"Or maybe there really is a Cabal," Galen said slowly. "Maybe he knew about it and was afraid that they'd put all their power behind an effort to stop him."

Jennings nodded. "Well, he was stopped cold. Now we need to know what happened, and why it matters to Hebert and Melton."

She gazed at him in frustration. "And I'm supposed to stay involved in this godawful mess?"

"Please. Four days." Jennings's expression was sober. "I'm not going to give you any bullshit about duty. Everyone has to make their own decision about that. But there's a good chance Bently was killed because he was trying to do something good for all of us. I will tell you that you could make a difference. It's important."

"It's important for me and the people I care about to stay safe."

"We'll give you security." He paused. "Only four days."

"You don't have to do this, Eve," Joe said.

"I know that." She went over to the window and stared out at the garden. "How safe are we here, Galen?"

"Pretty safe. I made damn sure we weren't tailed. And, as I said, it will take time to locate us. And neither Quinn nor I is a slouch at this kind of business."

She turned to Joe. "Are my mother and Jane safe?"

"Of course. I called the department and saw to it last night. There will be squad cars cruising by the condo several times a day, and I've asked a detail of several plainclothesmen to keep them under constant surveillance. And I called your mother and told her about the surveillance and not to let Jane go anywhere alone." His gaze narrowed on her face. "That being said, I don't like where this is going."

Neither did Eve. It was difficult enough to fight her desire to finish Victor without Jennings giving her the excuse she needed. She was torn between desperately wanting to be free and clear of all the ugliness connected with this reconstruction and bringing Victor home. She didn't want to be influenced by Jennings. She should tell him to go to hell.

But wouldn't it still be hanging over her? As long as Victor remained unfinished, she would be nagged by both her own desire to finish it and the knowledge that Jennings or some other official might appear and try to pressure her into doing it. There was only one way to put an end to it.

She whirled to face Jennings. "Oh, for God's sake, okay. I'll do it. But I want it out of my hands the minute it's done. I want it over."

"Agreed." Jennings smiled. "Whew. That's a relief." His tone became businesslike. "Is there anything you need? Anything we can do?"

"Just keep my child and my mother safe. And try to be unobtrusive. I don't want them scared."

"No problem."

"There had better not be."

"And I'll send agents up here from New Orleans to protect you and—"

"No," Galen interrupted. "I allowed Quinn to tell you about my little home-away-from-home because you said it would be absolutely confidential. No one else is to know about it. Quinn and I will handle the security here."

Jennings looked at Eve. "You trust them?"

She nodded.

"Well, if you change your mind, let me know." Jennings turned to go. "I'll be in touch. Thank you, Ms. Duncan."

"Don't thank me. Just be on my doorstep the second I've finished him."

He smiled. "Let me know and I'll be here."

She whirled on Joe the minute the door had closed behind Jennings. "No arguments?"

He shook his head. "I don't like it, but I know better than to argue with you once you've made up your mind. I'll have to call the department and tell them that there will be some FBI agents showing up on the scene. They're not going to be happy."

"Shall I set up Victor and your equipment in the scullery?" Galen asked.

"Yes. Right away. If I have to go back to this blasted reconstruction I'm going to get it done as quickly as I can."

"Yeah, sure," Joe said. "Admit it, you've gotten a reprieve. You can't wait to get your hands on Victor again."

He was right. She could feel a tingling in her hands and the familiar eagerness flowing through her. "That doesn't mean I won't get him done quickly."

"I don't doubt it. You'll be working every minute of every day. But then, what's new?"

"It's different this time."

"It's different every time." He smiled. "Go ahead. Get to work. I'll keep the world away."

"I don't want you to—"

He was gone.

Chapter Eleven

Where's Eve?" Joe asked Galen when he came downstairs at ten the next morning.

"You missed breakfast," Galen said. "Actually, your absence made the atmosphere a good deal lighter."

"I've been on the phone with the department. Besides, I couldn't take another dog and pony show like the one you put on two nights ago." He repeated, "Where's Eve?"

"Downstairs, working." Galen glanced at the portfolio Joe was carrying. "The sketch?"

"Yes. The FBI is going to go through its files and try to send me a photo of Hebert for comparison, but it hasn't come in yet. This will have to do for now." Joe was already going down the stairs to the former scullery.

"I'll go with you."

Joe didn't answer. He paused at the bottom of the steps. Eve was working on Victor by the window, the sun shining on her red-brown hair and lighting the absorbed intentness of her expression. How many times had he seen her like that at the cottage. . . .

She glanced up and stiffened.

Dammit. He jerked his gaze away from her and continued down the stairs. "I need your help, Eve."

"Is this what you call staying in the background, Joe?" Eve asked.

"I spared you my presence at breakfast. I'll be out of here as soon as I get a confirmation on this. I've been checking with the department on a possible criminal record for Hebert." He moved across the room and slipped the sketch out of the portfolio. "Have you ever seen this man?"

She took the sketch and looked at it. She frowned. "There's something familiar . . . This is Hebert? Galen, come here."

"What's the—" Galen broke off and gave a low whistle. "Rick."

Eve inhaled sharply. "What?"

"Imagine him with light hair." Galen pointed at the lean cheeks. "Fuller cheeks. Nice, clean-cut look."

"The man helping you at the church?" Joe asked.

My God, Galen was right. Eve nodded. "Rick Vadim. Except his hair wasn't dark. It was light brown, and his cheeks were fuller and sort of . . . rosy."

"Small?"

"Yes, but he looked very athletic, so you hardly noticed."

"Disguises are stock-in-trade for men in Hebert's line of business." Galen studied the sketch. "And this one would have only required dye for the hair, a little rouge, and some cheek pads."

"He seemed almost boyish," Eve said. "And he was very sweet and eager to please."

"Sweet!" Joe whirled on Galen and said sarcastically, "Sharp. Very sharp, Galen."

Galen frowned. "My instincts are usually pretty good. I'd swear he didn't want to hurt her."

Joe frowned. "But why would he think he had to have a disguise? You're sure you never saw him?"

"No, I don't believe I—" Eve stopped. "The man who took me to the hospital. I didn't really see him. It was dim and I was in and out, but the more I think about it, the more it seems like him." Her lips tightened. "This is the man who killed Capel and sent me that report?"

Joe nodded. "It's the composite sketch."

"Bastard." She rubbed her temple. "What the hell is happening? If he didn't hire Marie to poison me, who did?"

"Good question," Galen murmured. "It seems Hebert wanted very much to keep you alive."

"Which doesn't mean a damn thing," Joe said. "Don't think he's your Good Samaritan. Believe me, he's a sadistic son of a bitch. You should have seen what he did to Capel."

"No, thank you," Eve said. "I'm sure he had his reason for keeping me alive: Victor."

"I'd better notify Jennings we may have a wild card in the pack. And, if Hebert's in disguise, he'd better know about that, too. Though he'll probably jettison his Rick Vadim persona since he'll know we're suspicious."

"Jesus, I can't take this," Eve said in frustration. "How the hell do you expect me to finish Victor? I don't want to have to try to figure out whether it was Hebert or one of his cohorts who poisoned me. I don't want to think about Hebert or Rick or Melton or anyone else. Do you understand? Do whatever you have to do." She turned back to the pedestal. "Now, both of you get out of here and let me get back to work."

Joe hesitated, then headed for the stairs.

Galen caught up with him as he reached the foyer. "When you get the photo from the FBI, will you make some copies? I have a few contacts who might be helpful."

Joe nodded. "You'll have them within two hours. It might be a good idea. I'm sure your 'contacts' have a chance of knowing the bastard intimately."

"I know it's hard for you to believe, but I do know a few people who aren't criminals," Galen said. "Look at you and me. We're best buddies, and you've never even pulled a heist."

"You're not going to yank my chain, Galen."

"Hmm." Galen gazed at him speculatively. "That should have irritated you, but you're pretty calm. I'm afraid Eve's told you that we didn't make beautiful music together. Pity, I was having such a great time."

"You came very close to being slaughtered."

Galen grinned. "Served you right for mistaking Galahad for old lecherous Lancelot."

"Galahad?"

"I have references. Of course, some of them are forged." Galen's smile faded. "I guess it's just as well the fun is over. We're going to need to work together to make sure Eve gets through this intact. Pax?"

Joe stared at him for a moment and then reluctantly repeated, "Pax."

"Good. Then get me the photos and I'll get on the fax ma-

chine and get to work. Even though I've buried the paperwork on
this place, it won't take more than five or six days to unearth it if
the search is done by someone with means. Evidently Melton
qualifies. But since Eve's so close to finishing, I doubt if he'll be
willing to wait that long. He'll look for another way to find us."

"And I suppose you have an idea what that will be?"

"No, but I'm working on it." Galen glanced at the sketch.
"He knows a lot about you, and he'll be digging out everything
he can about me. So we start on that basis." His gaze shifted to
the door leading down to the scullery. "And the fact that Eve
won't budge again until Victor is finished. Is she always this
single-minded?"

"Usually more. She's been distracted on this one. But she
won't allow that to continue for long."

"Tough to live with. Is it worth it?"

"It's worth it." Joe added deliberately, "When troublemak-
ing assholes don't get in the way. I'm having enough problems
without you causing more."

Galen chuckled. "I'll try to restrain myself. Most of the pleasure has gone out of it, anyway." His smile faded. "The only
weak link I can see is Jane and her grandmother, and you seem
to have taken precautions there. Are you sure it will be enough?"

"Atlanta police are very good, and they'll be extra careful
since Jane's mine. They're going to call me if there's anything the
slightest suspicious."

"Good, then I reckon you've done pretty well so far. But today is another day." He started up the stairs to the second floor.
"I don't know about you, but I'm going to get to work."

A final jab, Joe thought, as he watched Galen disappear
down the second-floor hall. At least, he hoped it was final. There
was no time for personal duels now. Logan had tremendous

respect for Galen, but Joe would judge for himself. Galen was tottering perilously on the line between the straight and narrow and the criminal underbelly, and Joe wasn't comfortable with that. Not when he was around Eve. Yet Galen seemed to know what he was doing. He'd gotten them out of Baton Rouge and provided Eve with this safe house.

And now it was Quinn's job to keep Eve safe, and he wouldn't do it by standing here worrying about Sean Galen. He strode toward the library to call Jennings at the FBI and light a fire under him.

———————

FBI HEADQUARTERS
WASHINGTON, D.C.

"Interesting." Assistant Special Agent in Charge Robert Rusk leaned back in his chair and gazed thoughtfully at Jennings. "You think the Cabal actually exists?"

Jennings shrugged. "Considering the other information that's been trickling in, I'd say there's a chance. I think we need to dig, and dig deep."

Rusk nodded. "My ass would be on the line if we didn't check everything out thoroughly. Take the next flight to Boca Raton."

"I don't have lead one."

"Then look the town over and see what you can come up with. It can't hurt. Sometimes things jump out at you."

Jennings nodded. "I have to fly to Atlanta first and set up protection for Duncan's daughter."

"Right, I'll send McMillan to head that team. Get in and get out. Boca Raton may be more important."

Jennings grimaced. "Eve Duncan doesn't think so." Neither did he. Boca Raton probably was going to be a blind alley. "I might be of more use in Atlanta. I'll be blundering in the dark in Boca Raton."

"You're a fine agent, Jennings," Rusk said. "And you have damn good instincts. I've seen you pull some amazing rabbits out of the proverbial hat. I want you in Boca."

It was no use arguing with Rusk. He was not only the boss; he was usually on target. Though God knows this might be the exception. Jennings turned and headed for the door. "Whatever you say."

———

ATLANTA

It might have to be the little girl after all, Jules thought sadly.

He watched Jane MacGuire running down the path through Piedmont Park after her puppy. Her grandmother, Sandra Duncan, was helplessly laughing as she ran after them.

The death of the mother might bring Eve Duncan out of hiding, but a threat to a child always had more impact. Particularly in Eve Duncan's case.

His phone rang.

"We've located one of Galen's contacts in New Orleans," Melton said when he picked up. "There's a possibility Galen may have a house near there."

"How near?"

"He doesn't know. He says Galen's a secretive bastard. He thinks within a two-hour drive. I'm working on it. He gave me a solid lead where to start checking paperwork."

"Then put more people on it. Send teams to every city courthouse within that two-hour radius. I have to know—"

A squad car cruised slowly by.

He hung up and ducked deeper in the shadows of the oak tree where he was standing. It was the third time in the last half hour, and it couldn't be a coincidence. He had also spotted that gray-haired jogger in the green sweatshirt outside the child's school. Quinn had called out his old friends at the police department to watch the little girl. It would make Hebert's task more difficult.

But not impossible.

———

NEW ORLEANS

"May I come in?" Bill Nathan stood hesitantly at the bottom of the scullery steps.

Eve didn't look up. "No, I'm busy."

"I'll only be a minute."

Eve breathed an exasperated sigh. "What is it?"

"I've decided I should help you."

"What?"

"Well, I'm here, but Galen and Quinn don't think I'm qualified to help them. The most I've been able to get them to let me do is go to the supermarket and buy groceries." He grimaced. "So I thought I'd stay down here and protect you."

"Protect me? I don't need you."

"You never can tell." Nathan scowled. "I wouldn't get in your way."

"You'd talk to me."

"I can be quiet." He paused and then said grudgingly, "Please."

"Why?" Eve carefully smoothed clay over Victor's mid-therum area. "You obviously disapprove of my doing the reconstruction."

"I don't disapprove. I just think you're taking a big chance. I went to a lot of trouble to try to save you, and I don't want my efforts wasted." His gaze went to Victor. "But I want to know if this is Bently as much as you do."

"Your news story."

"I'm not apologizing for that. It's my job."

"Did Joe tell you about Jennings's fuel-cell theory?"

"Yeah. It makes sense." He paused. "There's another reason I kept pushing for Bently's case to remain open months after his disappearance. He was fighting for something I believed in, and it made me mad as hell that the special interest groups had him taken out. Do you know there's a dead spot in the Gulf of Mexico fifty miles wide, where the Mississippi empties into it? The fertilizer in the river sucks up the oxygen and nothing can live. And do you remember the oil spill in the gulf ten years ago? I covered it for the paper. It made me sick. All the birds and fish that died, smothered by the oil slick. When I was a boy, I used to go fishing in the gulf with my grandfather . . ." He shook his head. "I thought it was a memory that couldn't be spoiled no matter how long I lived. I was wrong." He grimaced. "I want my kids to grow up with clean air and clean water and some of the beauty that I knew. Bently wanted that, too, and was fighting for it. It's not right he ended up like this."

Eve stared at him in surprise. It seemed beneath that surly

façade Nathan had a soft side. It was clear he meant every word he said.

"What are you looking at?" he asked gruffly. "Is it so weird that I don't want the earth to get any crummier than it is now?"

"No, it's not weird," she said gently. "I live on one of the most beautiful lakes you could ever hope to see. I wouldn't want anything to spoil it, either."

"Okay, then, we're kindred spirits." Nathan plopped down in the easy chair by the fire. "So is it all right if I stay and kind of watch out for you? I'm getting bored as hell waiting around for something to happen. I want to *do* something."

"I don't need—" Oh, what the hell. His intentions were good, and he was obviously at loose ends. "If you don't bother me."

"I won't." He took out a paperback from his back pocket. "You work, I read." He opened the book. "Forget I'm here."

"Don't worry, I will." Concentrate. Forget about Nathan and Jules and Joe and everything else troubling.

Think only about Victor and the task of bringing him home.

"I brought you coffee and a sandwich." Galen set the tray on the worktable. He glanced at Nathan, sound asleep in the big chair by the fire. "If I'd known you had company, I'd have brought more food."

"He's protecting me." Eve grinned as she glanced at Nathan. "He was very insistent, but he got bored after about four hours and dropped off. He meant well."

"Hmm." Galen poured Eve's coffee before turning away from Nathan. "How are you coming on Victor?"

"I'd be better if I didn't keep being interrupted."

"Ouch. Well, you won't have to worry about me for much longer. I'll be out of your hair. I'm going to snoop around and see what I can find out about our friend Jules."

"Where are you going?"

"New Orleans, first."

"How long will you be gone?"

"Not long, I hope. I'll be in touch."

"So much for my poison taster."

"I'm designating Quinn as my temporary replacement." He held up his hand as he saw her stiffen. "I knew that would be your reaction. That's why I decided to come and talk to you before I left. It's important that I go, and I wouldn't have the option if Quinn weren't here. You're evidently resigned to his presence, but that's not enough." He paused. "He knows what he's doing, Eve. You have to cooperate. You have to listen to him."

"Do I?"

"You're not thinking straight. Do you believe there's a threat to your life?"

"I'd be stupid not to consider the possibility."

"Do you believe Joe Quinn is competent?"

"Of course."

"Then, dammit, stop being stubborn and let him help you. He's not going to take advantage of the situation. I'll feel better about being away if you'll promise me you'll cooperate with him."

She didn't want Galen to go away. He had been a buffer between Joe and her. Now he was tearing down the barrier and leaving her exposed.

Okay, be adult. It was a life-and-death situation, and she couldn't expect to have everything her own way. She was the one who had chosen to take Victor from the church. Face the consequences. "I'll cooperate."

"Good. I'll be back as soon as I can. You should be okay with Quinn protecting you." He glanced at Nathan. "Though I doubt if Nathan is going to be of any use." He started for the stairs. "I have to see Quinn before I go. I'll be back as soon as I can."

"Where are you going?" Nathan's eyes were suddenly open, and he was sitting upright in the chair.

"Ah, good to see you with us again. I was afraid I'd have to get a frog to kiss you to wake you up. Or is that the right fairy tale?"

"Where the hell are you going?"

"To track down Hebert. But I feel very confident that Eve will be safe with you as long as you take your No-Doz."

"Smartass." Nathan glowered at Galen. "At least, I don't willingly jump into bayous with alligators and . . ."

He was talking to air. Galen had already disappeared up the stairs.

Nathan muttered an oath, and his glance shifted to Eve. "Quinn's staying?"

"Yes." She turned back to the reconstruction. With all these interruptions, it would be incredible if she ever finished Victor. "Now I have to get back to work."

"Sorry." He didn't speak for a moment, and then he grumbled, "I wasn't really sleeping. I was just resting my eyes . . ."

"Anything from the FBI?" Galen stood in the doorway of the library.

"I have your photos. The sketch and the photo were two peas in a pod." Joe nodded at the four faxes on the desk. "Hebert must be very smart. He's been picked up on suspicion of murder once, but he's never gone to trial. Lack of evidence."

"Or pull in very high places."

"I'm not going to believe that until I get proof."

"That's the problem with being a cop. I have the advantage of being able to make guesses out of the blue." Galen folded one of the faxes and put it in his jacket pocket. "But this could come in handy. I'm heading into New Orleans and I have to take the car. I'll stop and have another car dropped off for you. Any preference? Another Lexus?"

"Why are you going to New Orleans?"

Galen didn't answer for a moment. "To catch a plane to Atlanta. I'm not really needed here, and I thought I might as well join the legion you have looking out for your Jane and her grandmother."

Joe stiffened. "You think something's going to happen in Atlanta?"

"I don't know. It shouldn't. You have enough protection for them." He shrugged. "My problem is that I never trust anyone but myself. Since you're here, I thought I might as well go scout out the area." He paused. "Unless you object?"

Joe thought about it and then slowly shook his head. "Not if you call me every day and keep me informed. I think you're wrong. Eve will be the target. But I'd never turn down any help to protect Jane, even yours."

"I'm touched by your confidence. I'll call you." Galen turned and headed for the front door.

Joe followed him and watched as Galen walked toward the Lexus. "Did you tell Eve?"

"Not that I was going to Atlanta. I didn't want her to worry when I didn't really have any solid reason to question your security arrangements." He opened the car door. "The car being delivered here isn't a rental car. I have a few contacts in New Orleans who managed to find a car to borrow."

"Borrow?"

Galen grinned. "It's not hot. I'll drive over to Mobile and drop this car off there. It may lay a false trail for Hebert if he manages to trace it." He started the car. "Nathan seems to be determined to keep Eve safe. He could prove helpful to you on a limited basis, but don't trust him too far. He wouldn't measure up to Hebert."

"I can make my own judgments, dammit."

Galen studied him. "You're uneasy about me leaving. I'd be flattered, but I know it's only because you're afraid Eve will prove difficult. You'll be relieved to know I got her to promise to cooperate with you." He smiled slyly. "That struck a sour note, didn't it? You don't like having anyone act as an intermediary between you and Eve. Well, you won't have to worry for a little while. You're on your own, Quinn." He lifted his hand in farewell as he pressed the accelerator.

Joe watched the Lexus rolling down the long driveway. He was glad to see Galen go and to know that he was now in sole control of the situation. And he couldn't deny he felt a little relieved that Galen would be one of the team looking out for Jane. A heavyweight like him on the job almost guaranteed her safety.

Now he had his own job to do. He straightened his shoulders as he turned back to the house and went inside.

———

"You've turned Victor around on the pedestal," Nathan said. "Why?"

"I'm getting to the final stage and I don't want you to see me working on him."

"Why not?"

"You know Bently. Your expression might tell me something. If I see your approval or disapproval as I do the final sculpting, it might influence me. I might zig when I should zag and spoil the reconstruction."

"You're very careful."

"I have to be. Victor deserves it. They all deserve it."

"Bently deserves it. I'm not sure about the other skulls you work on. Some of them probably deserve to be tossed in the ground and forgotten about."

"But I don't know that."

"What would you do if this skull belonged to the man who killed your daughter?"

Eve stopped in mid-stroke. "I'd finish it." She finished the stroke. "And then when I was sure, I'd stomp on it, crush it, and then incinerate it. I might even hire a voodoo priest to put a curse on it." She glanced at Nathan. "Is that what you wanted to know?"

"Yes." Nathan smiled. "I didn't want to be insensitive, but I feel much better now. You were a little too noble for me."

"Noble? Nonsense. I didn't have much of a home life as a kid, and I guess home became something of an obsession to me. I believe everyone should have their own home, their own place, even in death. Maybe even more in death, if their life was tortured and troubled. If I bring them home, it validates their life, it shows the world they weren't disposable, that they had value." She glanced at Nathan. "Does that make sense to you?"

He nodded slowly. "Knowledge of your own value is important. We all have to realize what's important to us."

"What's important to you?"

"My kids, my job."

"How old are your children?"

"Henry, twelve, and Carolyn, seven. Great kids." He made a face. "I wish I were as great a father. I haven't seen them for over four months."

"Why not?"

"I'm divorced and she has custody. It was the fair thing to do. I'm freelance and I specialize in environmental stories, so I travel all over the state. I couldn't make a stable home for them. My ex-wife lets me see them when I can. She's a nice woman. She put up with my job for longer than she should have before she bailed." He made a face. "In a way, I'm like you. I'm kind of obsessive about my work. I wish I could have put her and the kids first. You know, journalists get a bad rap. But often we're the guards who keep the public safe from the bad guys."

"My experience hasn't been too positive, but I've known a few reporters I respect." Eve had a sudden thought. "And what I've just said is strictly off the record. I don't like hearing myself quoted by the press."

"You won't. You have my promise."

She believed him. "Thank you."

"Thank you for letting me come down and keep you company." He grimaced. "It's pretty obvious that all of you are pretty skeptical where the Cabal is concerned."

"Jennings seems to put some stock in it."

"But you don't."

"I think there's a possibility."

"It's more than a possibility; it exists. Etienne was telling me the truth. I know it in my gut. These days, every time I hear about another Bosnia or Sarajevo, I wonder if the Cabal decided it was politically to their advantage to use a war to move their agenda forward."

"Now that I have trouble believing. Starting wars is on a different scale from manipulating economic policies."

"Wars are economic tools. Look beyond the rhetoric and idealism, and you find the money pot. War scares me. The Cabal scares me." His lips tightened grimly. "And not knowing what's going to happen in Boca Raton scares me most of all. It must be something pretty nasty to shake Etienne enough to make him bring me into this."

He believed what he was saying, and he was making her believe it, too. And belief brought her the same uneasiness Nathan must be feeling. Jesus, she didn't need this disturbance. She instinctively pushed it away, her gaze fixed on the skull before her. "Maybe Etienne was telling the truth. Maybe the Cabal is everything he says it is. But dealing with them is the FBI's job. Mine is to reconstruct Victor. I know Hebert is out there killing people and that Melton is probably in it up to his neck. That's as much as I need to know right now."

"It must be comforting to be so focused." Nathan stood and arched his back. "God, I'm stiff. I must be getting old. Oh, well, it's time I took a look around the grounds and stretched my legs, anyway." He headed for the stairs. "I'll be back in thirty minutes with coffee." A moment later the door at the top of the stairs slammed behind him.

He was a strange and complicated man, she thought as she turned back to Victor. At first, she had been torn between exasperation and amusement at his interchanges with Galen, but since he had parked himself in her workroom, she had begun to like and respect him. He was smart and perceptive, and his rueful honesty was appealing.

"Nathan asked me to come down and stay with you." It was Joe at the top of the stairs. "No, he didn't ask, he ordered me to come. He didn't want you to be left alone."

Eve tensed and then forced herself to relax. "He's being overprotective. He seems to think I'm helpless. But I can take care of myself."

"I know. I taught you."

Yes, he had. He'd taught her self-defense in those first years after Bonnie had been killed. She had felt helpless and angry, and he had empowered her. She looked away from him at Victor. "Then you shouldn't have paid any attention to Nathan."

"Give me a break. I'm overprotective, too. You know that." He paused. "If you don't want me to come down there, I'll just stay here."

She didn't want him to stand there at the top of the steps. She didn't want him anywhere near her. She was acutely conscious of him whenever he was in the same room. All the comfort of their relationship had vanished. Well, she'd have to get used to it. She had promised Galen to cooperate because it had made sense. She wasn't a child who hid her head under the bedclothes.

"You might as well come on down." She kept her gaze fixed on Victor. "You'll be less distracting sitting by the fire than hovering up there like a gargoyle."

"Heaven forbid," he said as he came down the steps. "After that comparison, I guarantee I won't hover." He settled down in the chair. "I know the routine."

Yes, he had sat on the couch in the lake cottage for hundreds of hours, reading, doing paperwork, helping Jane with her homework while she worked on her reconstructions. He had rubbed her neck and shoulders when she was tired and stiff. He had forced her outside for walks when she had become so obsessed she wouldn't leave the cottage.

"Those times weren't so bad, were they?" Joe asked softly.

Dammit, he knew the memories that last sentence had brought to mind.

She didn't answer, and continued to work on Victor. How the devil could she close him out when he was only ten feet away and she was aware of every breath he took? He wouldn't be here long. Nathan would soon be coming in that door with coffee, and Joe would leave.

Just keep working.

————

"Good to see you, Mr. Galen." The red-haired young man was at the gate when Galen's flight arrived from New Orleans. He shook Galen's hand. "David Hughes. Welcome to Atlanta. I've heard a lot about you. Bob Parks gave me a picture of you and asked me to meet you and extend all courtesies. Do you have any more luggage?"

Galen shook his head. "I'm traveling light. Have you put the kid under surveillance?"

"As soon as you called last night." Hughes walked down the corridor with him. "The police squad cars Quinn arranged for surveillance are on the job, and he has at least two plainclothes officers hovering over her. The cops and the FBI guys you called us about seem to be working together. My guys have had a few problems avoiding them."

"They're not there to check out the squad cars. Have you seen any sign of Jules Hebert?"

"Not yet. I made copies of the photo you sent us and distributed them. Maybe he's not here."

"And maybe he is. It's where I'd be if I wanted to flush out someone. You always try to hit them where they hurt the most. What's the kid's routine?"

"Her grandmother takes her to school every day and picks her up. The kid takes the dog for a walk in the morning, and they all go for a run in the park after school. The kid doesn't leave the condo after she gets back." He checked his wristwatch. "They should be in the park in about fifteen minutes. Do you want to go there?"

"Yes." He wanted to see the child and her grandmother and make sure he'd be able to recognize them. "Let's go."

"I'm surprised Quinn isn't with you."

"He has another priority." Massive understatement. Eve was clearly an obsession with Quinn. "And he thinks the kid is safe. He trusts his police buddies."

"But he knows you're here?"

Galen nodded. "He thinks I'm wasting my time." Maybe Quinn was right. Everything seemed to be fine on the surface, but he was uneasy and he'd always trusted his instincts. "Let's hurry, okay?"

Chapter Twelve

HE WAS LEAVING, THANK GOD.

Eve watched Joe walk up the staircase. She had always loved the way he moved. There was a sort of sensual grace, an alertness so different from the stillness of Joe at rest. Yet even that stillness was never passive. She could always sense the intelligence, the emotions that were going on behind that almost expressionless face.

"I didn't bring cream," Nathan said from across the room. "You take your coffee black, don't you?"

"What?" She quickly picked up the cup Nathan had put on the worktable beside her. "Yes, I take it black."

She heard the door at the head of the stairs close behind Joe.

"I thought I remembered right."

"It will be fine." Everything was fine. Joe was gone now. She could work.

She pulled her gaze back to Victor. Concentrate, dammit.

"Go to bed," Eve ordered Nathan. "It's almost midnight, and you've been sitting there all day."

"When you go to bed, I'll go to bed. I haven't disturbed you, have I?"

"No, you've been very quiet." Eve took off her glasses and rubbed her eyes. "But it's nonsense for you to hover over me. I'm beginning to feel guilty every time I look over there at you."

Nathan smiled faintly. "You've been so absorbed, you haven't even known I was here for the last six hours. How's it going?"

"Okay." Eve's glance shifted back to Victor. "He's coming along."

"You're excited. Will you finish tonight?"

"I'd like to, but I'm too tired. I should stop." Her fingers longingly touched the cheek of the reconstruction. "But I'm so *close*, dammit."

"May I look at it now?"

"No, you couldn't recognize anything yet. It's the final stage that tells the tale." She wiped her hands on a towel. "But by the end of tomorrow, he'll be done."

"Good." Nathan's gaze was fixed on the back of the skull. "Why are those last hours so important?"

"It's the time when instinct takes over. Sometimes I feel as if the subject is guiding me, telling me." She made a face. "Weird, huh?"

Nathan shrugged. "I've heard crazier things. The whole process is a mystery to me. I don't understand how you do it."

Eve smiled. "First, you have to want to do it with your whole being. After that, it's a piece of cake."

"Yes, sure. That's why you work your ass off. Because it's so easy."

"No career is easy if you want to be the best. You're pretty driven yourself, or you wouldn't be going after that Pulitzer."

"It's the peak of a journalist's career. I've never wanted to be anything else but a reporter. Maybe someday I'll write a book or two. I'm a simple soul."

"Yeah, sure."

"You're the one who chose a career that's considered macabre at best."

"Everyone believed I should have had enough of death after Bonnie died. But you go where you're led." She cast a final glance at Victor before turning away. "And I'm being led to bed so that I can get up early tomorrow."

"What time?" Nathan got to his feet. "I want to be here for the great unveiling."

"Whenever I wake up. But he'll still take several more hours' work."

"I'll be down at six." Nathan moved toward the staircase. He paused at the top of the stairs to gaze back at Victor. "Are you sure I wouldn't recognize him now?"

"I'm sure." Eve followed him up the stairs. "Now forget about him and get some sleep."

"Have you heard from Galen?"

Eve shook her head. "But it's only been two days. He'll let us know if he finds out anything." She flipped the wall switch that controlled the lights in the scullery. "And we'll call him tomorrow if I finish Victor."

She took one last look at the dim shape of the skull on the worktable below.

We're nearly there, Victor. You're almost home.

———

BOCA RATON, FLORIDA
October 23

"It's a waste of time, sir," Jennings told Rusk. "I've checked in with the agents in our Miami office, and there's not even a hint of anything happening down here except drugs, confidence schemes, and money laundering. I might as well come back."

"If you're sure." Rusk's voice was disappointed. "I was hoping you'd get lucky." He hung up the phone.

It would have taken more than luck, Jennings thought. He leaned back in his chair and gazed out the hotel window at the gray-blue Atlantic. Everything on the surface in this city was all small-time. Maybe below the surface, too. There was nothing like the ugliness of that anthrax scare.

As he had told Rusk, it had been a waste of time. He hadn't accomplished anything here; he should go back and try another path.

Yet why did he have this nagging sense that he had missed something?

What the hell? One more try.

He flipped open his portfolio to the notes on Bently and the Cabal that Joe Quinn had given him that first night he had called him. Beside it, he placed the notes he'd made since he'd arrived in Boca Raton.

It was fifteen minutes later that he suddenly stiffened in his chair.

Holy shit.

———————

The little girl looked a little like Eve Duncan, Galen thought as he watched her running through the park after the pup. Strange. He knew the two were not related, but that red-brown hair was almost the same shade. She didn't have Eve's wariness, though. This was Galen's second afternoon of watching her, and she was blissfully unaware of anything but that dog.

"She reminds me a little of my daughter. My Cindy's that age." Hughes sat down beside Galen on the bench. "Cute kid."

"Yes." Galen watched Jane pick up a stick and toss it for Toby. "No sign at all of Hebert?"

"No. Maybe you're barking up the wrong tree." He suddenly chuckled. "Like that dog of hers. He doesn't seem to know that you have to concentrate on one tree and not the whole park when you're on the hunt."

"Maybe I am wrong." But Galen didn't think so. "No one hanging around the condo?"

"Nope. We checked out all the vehicles and questioned a few people who seemed to be loitering. Everyone on the street belongs there." He grinned. "Here she comes, running after the pup again. Better open your newspaper."

Jane was careening toward them after Toby. Galen lifted his copy of the *Atlanta Journal Constitution* in front of his face.

"Who are you?"

He lowered the paper to see that Jane had stopped, and was standing in front of them.

"I beg your pardon."

"What's happening?" The child was staring him belligerently in the eye. "Why are you watching me?"

"I don't know what you mean."

"Don't lie to me. You've been here for two days. Are you a plainclothes detective like Joe? If you are, I want to see your ID."

"No, I'm not a detective like Quinn. And you shouldn't confront strangers in the park."

"The squad car will be driving by any minute, and a plainclothes detective is trailing behind Grandma. I'm not supposed to know about them, either." Her lips tightened. "I'm not supposed to know about anything. What's your name and why are you here?"

And he'd thought this kid was lacking Eve's wariness, Galen thought ruefully. "My name is Sean Galen. This is David Hughes. We're here to make sure you're safe."

"You're Logan's friend. I've heard about you. You're supposed to be with Eve now." She glanced at Hughes. "But I don't know anything about him. Send him away."

Hughes hurriedly got to his feet. "I'm out of here. See you later, Galen."

She turned back to Galen. "Let me see your ID."

"Yes, ma'am." He handed her his driver's license.

She glanced at it and then handed it back to him. "If you're Galen, you must know my dog Toby's mother's name."

"The beautiful, bad-tempered Maggie. Satisfied?"

Jane relaxed. "No." She glanced over her shoulder. "Here comes Grandma. We have to be quick. Why are you here?"

"I'm sure that if you ask your grandmother, she'll tell you anything you should know."

"Don't give me that bull. Grandma doesn't want to worry me. If I asked her anything, she'd only lie to make me feel better. It's something to do with Eve, isn't it? Is she in trouble?"

"We're trying to keep her out of trouble."

"I could tell something was wrong when I talked to her on the phone a few nights ago. She said everything was fine with her, and that Joe was with her."

"He is."

"But you're here. Why?"

"Jane!" her grandmother called, running toward her.

Jane turned and waved before telling Galen, "Hurry."

He decided to level with her. The kid was sharp, and it wouldn't hurt to warn her. "We think there's a possibility the people who are trying to hurt Eve may attempt to get at her through you. Have you seen anyone suspicious?"

"You mean besides you? You're not very good at this, are you?"

"I can be. I didn't try to be this time. I didn't expect you to be suspicious, and the sight of me could have been a deterrent to anyone else."

"Who? The other creep?"

Galen stiffened. "Creep? You noticed somebody else watching you?"

"Two days ago. He followed me to school, and then he was here in the park. He was much better than you."

"Did you get a good look at him?"

She nodded. "I made sure I did. I'd already noticed the squad cars. I knew something was happening."

He took out the photo of Hebert. "Look anything like this?"

She glanced at it. "That's him."

"Why didn't you tell your grandmother?"

"I couldn't be sure he was a creep. He might have been one of Joe's friends, and it would just have worried her. Or he might have been just your ordinary run-of-the-mill pervert. I've seen plenty of those."

"Oh, have you?"

"I haven't seen him since. I have to go, or Grandma will call the cops on you." Her lips tightened. "I don't like not knowing what's happening. You tell Eve and Joe that."

He shook his head. "I'll tell Joe what you said, but I won't tell him about your 'creep' yet. It would be a sure way to make them drop everything and come running. They're much safer if they stay in hiding."

"Hiding? Eve never mentioned anything about that. Why are they in hiding?"

"It's complicated. Eve wanted to finish the job she started."

"Then why are you here? You go back and make sure Joe and Eve are safe," she said fiercely. "You do your job. Don't you dare let anything happen to them. I'll take care of Grandma." She whirled and ran back toward her grandmother. "It's okay," she called. "He only wanted directions, Grandma. Just another lost Yankee. They get so confused with all these Peachtree Streets."

"I told you not to talk to strangers." Her grandmother whisked her up the path. "Now you call that idiot dog and we'll go home to supper."

"Wow," Hughes said softly as he strolled back to Galen.

"Correction: She's not at all like my kid. If I needed some muscle, I might decide to hire her."

"Eve told me she grew up on the streets." He watched Jane and Sandra Duncan walk down the path. "She didn't tell me she was twelve going on fifty."

"You showed her the photo?"

"She saw him. Hebert is here in Atlanta. Or at least he was two days ago." He stood up. "But where the hell is he? If he was hanging around, you should have been able to spot him."

"Maybe he was scared off."

That scenario didn't fit with the picture of Jules Hebert Galen had been building up. "Or maybe he went underground and is only waiting for his chance." The idea of Hebert stalking that bright kid, hovering over her like a dark cloud, turned his stomach. "We're not going to give it to him, Hughes."

Jules watched as the black pickup truck sank below the waters of Lake Lanier with scarcely a ripple. There was so much water here in Atlanta. He had found it very convenient.

He had chosen a deep part of the lake so the man would not be found too quickly. There should be no outcry for at least three days. Leonard Smythe was divorced and lived alone in his mobile home, and from Jules's brief surveillance he appeared a solitary man.

Jules glanced down at the treasure for which Smythe had died. If he'd been given a choice, Smythe would have given it up in a heartbeat, but Jules couldn't risk giving him that option.

It was sad when a man had to die for a clipboard and a few scraps of paper.

NEW ORLEANS

Victor's skull was dimly lit by the moonlight streaming through the window.

Nathan didn't flip the switch that would have lit the steps to the scullery. He knew Joe Quinn made several trips around the grounds at night, but he had no idea what time.

He moved carefully, quietly down the steps. It should be safe. He had checked on Eve and she was sound asleep. But both Eve and Joe Quinn were still unknown quantities to him, and the unknown was always dangerous.

He reached the bottom of the stairs and glided silently across the scullery toward Victor's pedestal. He knew the back of that skull so well, and nothing about his features. He had only been able to watch Eve's intent expression as she worked.

He took out the flashlight he had found in the kitchen cabinet and moved closer to the pedestal. He took a deep breath, his thumb pressing on the flashlight switch.

The scullery was suddenly flooded with light.

"Would you like to tell me what you're doing?" Joe Quinn said from the top of the stairs.

Dammit.

He stiffened defensively. "I wasn't going to hurt it."

"You didn't answer me." Joe came down the stairs. "What are you doing creeping down the stairs in the middle of the night?"

"I just wanted to see it."

"But Eve didn't want you to see it until she finished. Is she done?"

Nathan shook his head. "Not until tomorrow. She said I wouldn't be able to tell anything until then. But I thought maybe I could tell where it was going." He scowled. "I'm going to look."

"Go ahead. I'm not going to stop you."

Nathan moved around the pedestal to stand before Victor. Disappointment surged through him. The visage had form, but no definition. No one could recognize the features at this point.

"You should have believed her," Joe said. "Eve doesn't lie."

"I didn't think she'd lied. I just thought I might be able—" His hands clenched at his sides. "Dammit, it's hard to wait. I want to *know*."

"And you didn't trust her."

"In my business you learn not to trust many people." Nathan started toward the stairs, and then stopped to stare at Joe. "Are you going to tell her I was here?"

"I should. Eve likes you, and she has a habit of trusting people she likes. She doesn't appreciate people sneaking around behind her back."

"I didn't do anything to hurt her. If I'm guilty of anything, it's of caring too much." Nathan's gaze went back to Victor. "It's important to me to know who he is. God, I hope it's not Bently. I hope he's still around, maybe gone underground and ready to come out swinging against those bastards."

Joe studied him. "I believe you." He shrugged. "I'll hold my peace for now. There was no harm done. But you made a mistake."

"Everyone makes mistakes. You must have made a big one, or Eve wouldn't be angry with you." Nathan moved quickly up the stairs, and then stopped and glanced over his shoulder at Joe.

"I must have made another mistake. How did you know I was down here?"

"I was outside patrolling, and I saw movement in the kitchen through that bank of windows. It aroused my curiosity when I saw it was you rifling through the cabinets. Particularly when you only took that flashlight."

"I checked outside the kitchen, but I should have been more careful."

"Like you said, we all make mistakes."

And Quinn wasn't making him pay for this one. "Thanks. I owe you." Nathan hurried up the rest of the stairs. It could have been much worse. He had done what he felt he had to, and no real harm had been done. He had hoped to get a jump on the situation, but he would just have to wait.

Damn, it was hard to be patient.

———————

The basement was well lit, the heating and air-conditioning mechanisms gleaming and powerful. The best of American technology, Jules thought, as he moved down the aisle.

"Hey, what are you doing down here?"

He glanced over his shoulder. A uniformed security guard was coming out of the elevator.

"Don't you guys ever talk to each other?" Jules waved his clipboard. "I just went through this with the guard at the front door." He glanced at the man's badge. "Phillips. I'm from the supe's office. I'm supposed to do the yearly service check."

"I've been out on a coffee break," the guard said defensively.

Jules knew that. He hadn't expected Phillips to be back

this soon, but you always had to be ready to make adjustments. "I'm almost through here. Have you noticed any problems on your rounds? Puddles beside the air conditioners? Excess steam?"

Phillips shook his head.

"Since you're here, would you mind coming with me to that furnace room and holding my flashlight? I have to crawl in back of the units and it's damn hard to see."

Phillips frowned. "If it doesn't take too long. I have to get back to the front door and relieve Charley."

"Like I said, I'm almost done." Jules picked up his toolbox and started down the aisle. "It won't take a minute."

Phillips followed him. "If you're sure."

"Oh, I'm sure." Jules smiled at him over his shoulder. "I know my job."

———————

"Ready, Victor?" Eve murmured. "It's almost time."

"Did you say something, Eve?" Nathan asked from across the room.

"Hush. I don't want to hear a word from you until I'm done."

The clay was soft, cool beneath her fingers. She touched it delicately, tentatively.

Smooth.

Don't think.

Instinct.

She was moving quickly; her fingers were tingling.

Who are you, Victor? Tell me, help me.

Smooth. Mold. Fill in.

She had no idea how to shape the ears. Make them generic.

The mouth. God, the mouth was hard. She only knew the width. . . .

Instinct. Close out what she didn't know, and let her hands flow.

Smooth. Mold. Fill in.

She was going too fast.

Stop for a minute and study the eyes, the angle of the orbits, the bony ridge above . . .

Okay, go for it.

Smooth. Mold. Fill in.

Check that lip height . . . 12mm. That was right. Nose projection 18mm. It should be 19. Change it.

Smooth. Mold. Fill in.

Be aware of the measurements, but let instinct dominate now.

Tell me, Victor. Let me bring you home.

Her hands flew over the visage. Her fingertips seemed to have a life, a mind of their own.

Smooth.

Mold.

Fill in.

———

Galen stepped out of his car and strode over to Hughes, who was standing under a streetlight. "Anything?"

Hughes shook his head. "Everything's quiet. The kid went into the condo with her grandmother at the usual time. A squad car cruised by five minutes ago. They must have put more plainclothesmen on the job. I saw one guy I didn't recognize talking to the front-door guard." He held up his hand as Galen opened his lips. "It's okay, I watched him and he got into the squad car twenty minutes later. The cops knew him."

"Inside?"

"I have a guy on the same floor as the kid, and he reports no activity. What have you been doing?"

"Scouting. There's a telephone truck five blocks from here. What's it doing here at this time of night? Have you checked it out?"

Hughes shook his head.

"Why not?"

"It wasn't there today. I'll get on it."

"Now."

"Why are you so edgy? It's five blocks away."

"It could be a surveillance van. Eve calls Jane regularly."

"I told you we'd checked out the high-rise. The condo's too high and there's too much interference for the phones to be bugged."

"Just check the truck, okay?"

"Whatever you say." Hughes reached for his phone.

Galen stared up at the condo while Hughes was telling one of his men to check out the vehicle. Damn, he felt uneasy.

Hughes hung up. "He's trying to get through to the telephone company. Satisfied?"

"No. Something's happening. He's got to be around here. He knows he doesn't have much time."

"What do you mean?"

"Never mind." He glanced at the cars parked along the street. There were no new vehicles, and all of these had already been checked out. "It just feels wrong."

"If Hebert's gone underground, he's buried himself pretty deep," Hughes said.

Galen stiffened. "What?"

"You said that Hebert must have gone underground, or we would have been able to—"

Underground.

"Shit!" Galen moved toward the canopied entrance of the condo. "Come on."

Hughes got out of the car and hurried after him. "Where are we going?"

"You're going to distract the security guard and find out from him if anything unusual has happened today." He opened the glass door. "And I'm going to see how far Hebert is willing to go to get that kid."

———

Galen found a uniformed guard in the furnace room behind the massive units that heated the high-rise. His throat had been cut.

He found the plastic explosive and the timer that controlled it behind the furnace unit beside the dead man.

Twenty-two minutes.

Shit.

It wasn't a simple timer, and was probably booby-trapped. No time to disarm it.

He turned off his telephone as he ran toward the elevator. A ringing phone could set off a bomb. He turned the phone back on as he reached the street.

It rang at once.

"Nothing much unusual," Hughes said. "A building inspection. One of the guards got sick and had to go home. Want me to—"

"Forget it." It would take more time for him to go get Jane himself than to delegate. "Get out of the building. Call your man on the twelfth floor to get Jane MacGuire and her grandmother out of there. Now. He has about twenty minutes. Then call the bomb squad and get them here. I think it will be too late, but I could be wrong."

"Right." Hughes rang off.

Galen checked his watch.

Nineteen minutes.

Jane MacGuire was on the twelfth floor. Not much time.

And no time at all for the rest of the people who lived in the building. Galen wouldn't get past the first few condos before the bomb went off.

Christ, what the hell could he do?

———

"It's done." Eve leaned back against the worktable and wiped her face. God, she was exhausted. The adrenaline was draining out of her, and she felt limp as a dishrag. "It's the best I can do."

"I thought you'd never get done. It's almost three in the morning." Nathan leaned forward, his body tense with eagerness. "May I look at it now?"

"Not yet. I have to put the glass eyes in the sockets." She smiled faintly as she turned to the eye case on the worktable. "Galen would be glad of that. He has a thing about empty eye sockets."

"Hurry!" Nathan moistened his lips. "I'm sorry. I didn't mean to—I'm just . . . anxious."

"I know." Eve opened the case and took out a pair of brown eyes and turned back to Victor. Only it might not be Victor now. He might soon have a real name. "It will only take a few minutes."

It took less than that before she stepped back and turned to Nathan. "You can look now."

Nathan jumped up from the chair and moved quickly across the room. He stopped, took a deep breath, and then moved around to stand beside Eve.

He stared at the features of the reconstruction.

Eve's gaze searched his face. "Well, say something. Is it Bently?"

"It's him." Nathan's lips thinned. "It's Harold Bently."

"You're sure?"

"I'm sure." His voice was uneven. "You did a good job. That's him." He turned away and moved quickly toward the staircase. "Excuse me. I'm so mad I want to choke someone. I can't look at him. I was hoping—"

Nathan flew up the stairs and almost ran into Joe coming down. "I'm sorry. I didn't mean—" He brushed past him and was out the door.

"What's wrong with him?" Joe asked as he came the rest of the way down the stairs. Then he saw Eve's face and said, "Oh, the moment of truth?"

"It's Bently." Eve rubbed the back of her aching neck. "You always have hope until you actually see the proof."

Joe came to stand beside her, and looked at the face. "You evidently did a good job if he's so certain."

"I was hoping as much as he was that it wouldn't be Bently," Eve said. "From what I've heard of him, he was a very good man. I didn't want him to have died like this." Her eyes were filling with tears, too. She blinked them back. "But it never does any good. So many more of the good die than the bad. They trust. They have no defenses. Like Bonnie . . ."

"Shh." He pulled her into his arms. "Jesus, you're so tired you can hardly stand up. Listen to me, you did a good job. You brought this poor guy home. Isn't that what's important?"

"Yes." Comfort surrounded her, keeping out the cold and the loneliness as it always did when she was close to Joe. "That's important. But not right now."

"It will come." He rubbed the exact spot between her shoulders that always bothered her. Her knees went weak with relief. "Your muscles are all knotted. Go on to bed and try to sleep. I don't guess you'd let me give you a massage?"

"No." She shouldn't even be standing here like this. There were reasons, good reasons, why she should be pushing him away, but they didn't seem to matter right now. "I'll be okay."

"You'd be better than okay with me. I'd make sure you were." He shrugged. "But that's not in the cards. Come on, I'll help you up to bed and tuck you in."

"I'm fine."

"Stop arguing. You're about to fall over. I know you're vulnerable right now, and I'd love to take advantage of you. But I won't." He slid his arm around her waist and half led, half carried her toward the stairs. "Why are you fighting it? It's no big deal. How many times have I done this after you've finished a job?"

So many times she couldn't remember. Sometimes it seemed as if they'd been together all her life. Ten, twelve years? She couldn't think. Everything was a blur right now. "Now that Victor's done, I guess it's time to call Jennings. The FBI should probably . . ."

"I'll take care of it."

"I really didn't want it to be Bently, Joe."

"I know. Never mind. It will seem better in the morning."

Eve was barely aware of Joe helping her up to her room and pushing her down on the bed. He took off her shoes and pulled up the coverlet. "I'll be right back." He went into the bathroom and came back with a damp washcloth. He carefully wiped the clay off her hands. "That'll do for now. You can hit the shower when you wake up."

"Thanks, Joe."

"I've always liked doing things for you. It makes you more mine. Next to sex, I liked it better than anything. Didn't you know that?"

She shouldn't be listening to this. It was . . . intimate, and everything was wrong between them. It was hard to remember why. She didn't want to remember why. Not now. "No, I didn't know. . . ."

"And you don't want to think about it. That's okay. I'll settle for you not scuttling away from me." He sat down beside her and took her hand. "That's good enough."

Her hand tightened around his. "It shouldn't be . . ."

"Shh. Go to sleep."

She was already half asleep. She curled up on the bed and closed her eyes. "It's . . . so sad. . . . Poor man . . ."

Chapter Thirteen

EVE WAS ASLEEP.

Joe stared down at her face. Christ, he wanted to ease her pain. Fat chance. Ever since Bonnie's death, Eve had been dealing with this pain. Giving her mind and skill and heart to bringing both the living and the dead home. Well, she had found another lost one and, as usual, he could only stand on the sidelines and help when she would let him.

Hell, he felt pretty lost himself right now. Stop feeling sorry for yourself. She doesn't need that, too. He released Eve's hand and bent down to press his lips to her forehead. "Sleep well, love," he whispered.

He didn't want to leave her, but he forced himself to stand up and head for the door. When she woke, they'd probably be back to square one, but maybe he'd made a tiny inroad tonight. He hoped to hell he had.

His phone rang as he reached the hall.

———

The side of the high-rise had exploded in a ball of flame and concrete.

Galen gazed up at the flames erupting out of the windows. It could have been worse. The bomb had been placed so that it only affected the west side. Jane MacGuire's grandmother's condo was on the west side of the building.

"Grandma's scared. You get that creep." Jane MacGuire took a step closer to Galen. "A lot of people could have been hurt if those sprinklers hadn't gone off. Did you do that?"

"It was the only thing I could think of that would get everyone up and out of the apartments in time. I disconnected the fire alarm bell that might have set off the bomb, and sent Hughes's men to knock on doors as long as it was safe. The water flooding their apartments saved a lot of arguments." His glance wandered over the dimly lit street filled with men, women, and children in all stages of dress huddled together. Dogs ran around barking at cats held tightly in their owners' arms. "I hope they all got out."

"Me, too." Jane pulled at Toby's leash to keep him at her side. "Grandma didn't want to go when that man came to the door. It was only when the sprinklers went off that she ran out."

He could hear the sirens of fire trucks in the distance. "Where's your grandmother?"

"Over there trying to calm down Mrs. Benson. She just had a baby and she's pretty shook up."

"I'm surprised she's letting you talk to me."

"I just told her who you were. Maybe I should have done it before. Grandma's usually pretty cool." She looked back at the fire. "He did all this to kill us?"

Galen nodded.

"And he did it to get Eve out of hiding?"

"Yes."

"Then you tell her to stay put." She moistened her lips. "And you'd better do it fast. The first thing Grandma did when she got down to the street was call Joe."

"What?"

"Joe told her to call him if there was a problem." She looked at the burning high-rise. "He's going to think this is a big problem."

"How long ago?" He'd wanted to call Quinn himself.

"Five minutes. He told her to stay with me and he'd send a black-and-white." She glanced at a squad car careening around the corner. "There it is."

"Maybe." A police car appears and whisks Jane and her grandmother away? No way. Not until he'd checked it out. He moved toward the car. "Stay here."

"What the hell is happening?" Joe demanded when Galen answered his phone ten minutes later. "I just got a hysterical call from Eve's mother, and she was talking about you and the condo blowing up and the sprinkler—"

"Jane's safe. The squad car you sent picked her and her grandmother up and took them to a safe house. That's what's most important."

"You went there to protect Jane. How did that bastard get so close to her?"

"She's safe. That's all that's important." Galen looked at the high-rise, which was still in flames. "I'll tell you about the rest of it later."

"The hell you will. I need to know what—"

"Wait a minute." Hughes was trying to get Galen's attention. "There's something going on."

"Sorry," Hughes said. "I just heard about that telephone truck. Bell South says they sent no truck to that area." He paused. "And the truck is gone now."

"Jesus." Galen's hand tightened on his phone.

"What's happening?" Joe demanded. "Is Jane okay?"

"Jane's fine." Galen was thinking, going over the possibilities. He didn't like any of them. "But Hebert may have gotten what he wanted."

"Then what do you mean Jane's okay?"

"Calm down. I think Hebert hedged his bet. There's a good chance he had a surveillance truck parked a few blocks from here tonight. There was no question of him intercepting phone calls from the high-rise, but once Eve's mother was out of the building he'd have no trouble."

"And she called me right away."

"If the bomb killed them, you'd come out of hiding. If the bomb didn't kill them, she'd call you and give him a chance for a trace. Get out of there, Quinn."

"You're guessing."

"Do you want to risk proving me wrong? Hebert may prefer to do his dirty work personally, but he wouldn't risk losing you because he wasn't on site. He'd send someone else to do the job. If he got the fix, you don't have much time." Galen repeated, "Get the hell out of there."

Silence. "Where?"

Thank God Quinn was listening. "Just get on the road. Call me when you're clear. I'll be working to find you somewhere safe."

"Wherever that is." Quinn hung up.

———————

Joe hesitated for a moment, thinking. Eve was exhausted. She'd been barely coherent. So he'd let her sleep as long as possible while he made preparations for departure.

He moved down the hall to Nathan's room, threw open the door, and turned on the light. "Get up. I need your help."

Nathan sat up in bed. "What's wrong?"

"We have to get out of here. Go down and pack up all Eve's equipment and the reconstruction. I'll go and bring the car around to the front door."

"Why?" Nathan swung out of bed and pulled on his pants. "What's wrong? Why do we have to go?"

"Galen says we may have visitors any minute."

"Hebert?"

"No, Hebert's in Atlanta. So is Galen." Joe turned away. "Get moving. I have to get Eve out of here."

"Have the trunk open so I can put the equipment in." Nathan was tying his shoes. "You'd better pack Eve's clothes when you get her up. She was pretty tired."

"I'll take care of Eve." Joe was already moving down the hall. "Hurry."

———————

"Wake up, Eve."

Joe was shaking her, Eve realized dimly. So tired . . .

"Wake up. We have to get out of here."

She opened her eyes. "Sleepy . . ."

"Sorry. You can sleep in the car. We may have visitors."

At the lake cottage? They seldom had visitors. It was always an oasis of peace and quiet. Joe made sure of that.

But they weren't at the lake cottage, she realized suddenly. New Orleans. Victor. No, it wasn't Victor. It was Bently. She sat up and rubbed her eyes. "What are you talking about?"

"I've got your bag packed." Joe pulled her to her feet. "Nathan's already in the car." He half carried her from the room and down the stairs. "He packed up all your equipment. All we have to do is get on the road."

"Why?"

"Galen called. We have a problem." He pulled her out the front door. "It's not safe here any longer."

"Why not?"

"Later." He pushed her into the passenger's seat of the Lexus that Galen had sent and ran around to the driver's seat. "Did you get everything, Nathan?"

"The equipment's in the trunk. I have the reconstruction back here with me." Nathan fixed his gaze on the road. "Headlights. They'll be at the gates in no time."

"They're locked, aren't they?" Eve asked.

"They'll have the equipment to get them open," Nathan said. "It will only take a few minutes."

"Then let's use those few minutes." Joe didn't put on the headlights, but drove slowly, silently down the driveway. When he got to the small wood surrounding the house, he left the driveway and drove into the trees.

The car that stopped at the gates was a dark-colored Volvo.

Two men got out of the backseat and went up to the gates. It took less than three minutes before the gates swung open. The men piled back into the car.

Eve held her breath as the car glided by them and up the driveway to the house. The Volvo's lights were out now, too, and the car appeared sleek and menacing in the darkness.

"Now," Nathan whispered.

"Not yet. Let them get inside." Three men entered the front door. Two others went around the back. "Close enough." He let out the brake and pressed down on the accelerator.

The sound of the engine couldn't have been as loud as it sounded to Eve, but it was loud enough. One man ran around the side of the house.

"Gun it," Eve said.

Joe was already gunning it. He tore through the open gates and hit the road at sixty miles an hour.

Damn those trees surrounding the house, Eve thought. She couldn't see anything. What was she thinking? Those trees might well have saved them.

Now she could see. Headlights racing down the driveway toward the gates.

Then they were gone as Joe went around the corner of the road and stomped on the accelerator.

"There's a gas station up ahead. It's closed, but I can see the pumps," Nathan said. "You could pull behind it and let them go by."

"It worked back at the house." Joe pulled off the road and came to a stop behind the gas station. "Maybe they won't expect it a second time. We'll have to see. . . ."

He cut the lights.

Or maybe they would expect it, Eve thought. Joe's hand was sliding beneath his jacket. She knew that gesture. He was loosening his gun in his holster.

"Get out," Joe said. "Now."

"What?"

"Don't argue. Both of you. Get out," he snapped.

Eve instinctively obeyed and found Nathan beside her.

"Take care of her, Nathan." The Lexus roared away from them and back on the road.

Shit. Eve's hands clenched into fists as she watched the taillights disappear around the curve. Everything had happened so fast she hadn't realized what Joe was doing. But she should have realized. She knew him, dammit.

The Volvo screamed around the turn and barreled toward them.

Closer.

Almost on top of them.

And then passed them.

It was out of sight seconds later.

"It worked," Nathan said. "We should leave now."

"What do you mean, leave? They're going after Joe."

"But that's what he wanted them to do. We have no way to help him. We'll call him once we're clear of this place. You'll ruin his plan if you stay here. If he loses them, they could double back to check out the area."

"You give him a little time to shake those men, and then call him and tell him we're not going anywhere. I'm not moving until Joe comes back."

Nathan gazed at her expression and then shrugged. "Okay, but it's not good tactics."

"I don't care about tactics." She leaned against the wall of the gas station, her gaze on the curve where Joe had disappeared. Jesus, she was scared.

"He'll probably make it," Nathan said. "He's been well trained, hasn't he?"

"Just because he was a SEAL doesn't mean that he's a champion race car driver. And he shouldn't have left us here, damn him."

"It was a good tact—" Nathan broke off as he met Eve's gaze. "Sorry." He quickly pulled out his phone and in a moment was talking to Joe. "He's not happy," he said when he hung up.

"Too bad. He had no right to take off like a bat out of hell. He's not the only one involved here."

"There wasn't much time for discussion."

Eve knew that, but it didn't make her feel any less angry and helpless . . . and terrified.

Joe.

"He seemed to be able to drive pretty well," Nathan offered.

He was trying to comfort her, Eve realized. "Yes."

"And I think the Lexus was faster than that Volvo."

"Let's not talk about it, okay?" she said jerkily.

Nathan nodded and fell silent.

Ten minutes passed.

Where the hell was he?

Fifteen minutes.

It was forty-five minutes before Joe appeared around the curve and glided to a stop behind the gas station. He reached over and opened the passenger door. "Get in. I think I lost them five miles back, but we should get out of here."

Nathan scrambled into the backseat. "You didn't do bad at all, Quinn."

"Thank you," he said ironically as he pulled back onto the road. "I'm glad I met with your approval."

"I tried to get her to leave, but she was worried."

"Was she?" Joe glanced sideways at Eve's set face.

"I *wasn't* worried. You were stupid. You could have stayed with us and we'd have given them the slip, but you probably enjoyed playing Keystone Kops." Her voice shook. "It was . . . stupid."

"It seemed the most reasonable thing to—"

"It was good tactics, right? Just shut up and get us out of here."

Joe gave a soundless whistle. "Yes, ma'am. Right away, ma'am." Joe went back in the direction they had come from.

"Where are we going?"

"I have no idea. I'll worry about that when I'm sure we don't have anyone tailing us."

———

Joe didn't stop until he was fifty miles away from Galen's house and he'd changed roads and directions twice. He finally pulled over at a supermarket lot in a small town on the east side of New Orleans.

He pulled out his phone and dialed Galen. "We're clear. We did have visitors."

"I was afraid of that. No one was hurt?"

"No, but we're in a Podunk town in the middle of nowhere. Find me a place to put Eve."

"I'm working on it," Galen said. "I'll get back to you." He hung up.

"Now can I find out what the devil is happening?" Eve asked.

He got out of the car. "Come on, let's take a walk."

"I do have a stake in this, too, you know," Nathan said.

"Later," Joe said. "Stay here and take care of the skull."

It was chilly, and Eve jammed her cold hands into the pockets of her jacket as she fell into step with Joe. "Talk to me."

"You're not going to like it."

"So what's new. I haven't liked anything to do with this reconstruction," Eve said.

"This strikes close to home."

She stiffened. "Jane?"

"Don't panic. She's okay. So is your mother." He quickly filled her in on what her mother and Galen had told him.

"And you say she's okay?" Eve's hands clenched into fists in her pockets. "For God's sake, that crazy bastard blew up the condo. It's a miracle they're still alive."

"But they are alive."

"I should never have left her. You should never have left her."

"Don't you know that's what I've been telling myself ever since I got that call from your mother? I thought Hebert would concentrate on you, but I still tried to give them enough protection."

"You didn't do it. She almost died. You should have—" She shook her head. "Why am I blaming you? It's just as much my fault as it is yours. I'm the one who took this job. I'm the one who chose to steal the damn skull. I thought he'd go after me, too. I'm the one who's to blame."

"Shh. Stop shaking. Nothing happened."

"What do you mean? Something did happen. He almost killed them. I was so worried about Victor and so busy thumbing my nose at Hebert that I—"

"Hush." He took her in his arms and pressed her head into his shoulder. "Jane and your mother are fine, and we're going to keep them that way."

Oh, God, she needed him. An anchor in a rough sea. A rock that never moved. "Joe . . ." Without thinking, she slid her arms around him. "Jane's never been sure that I really loved her. She's always thought Bonnie came first. I do love her. It's just . . . different."

"She knows you love her."

"She's not sure. I want to tell her again. What if she'd died and I didn't get the chance to tell her how much she means to me?"

"But she didn't."

"There are so many things I didn't tell Bonnie before she was taken from me. I'm not going to make that mistake again." Tears were flowing down her cheeks. "But I almost did. *Shit.*"

"Okay, you're not perfect. Who is? But Jane's not one of your lost children. She's strong and smart, and she's a survivor. She'll only take so much from you. We're lucky she lets us as close to her as she does." His hands cupped her face and he looked down into her eyes. "Are you listening to me, Eve? Jane doesn't want a mother. She loves you, but you came together too late for all the maternal folderol. She doesn't expect it. You're a damn good friend, and that's great with her."

"Is it?" Eve smiled with quivering lips. "I never realized you'd made such a study of our relationship."

"I had to. Anyone who touches you touches me."

She couldn't look away from him. His eyes . . .

Joe's hands dropped away from her and he stepped back. "That's the way it's always been; that's the way it is. I'm just very fortunate that I love Jane, too."

She drew a deep breath. "Well, neither of us has been very good at showing her we love her by keeping her safe." She turned back toward the car. "Well, it's not too late, thank God. It's time I thought about Jane and Mom instead of my damn job."

"And that means?"

"I'm going back to Atlanta. I'm not going to let Jane and my mother take the punishment for my actions while I'm hundreds of miles away."

"Galen said that was what you'd do. He thinks you'll walk right into Hebert's hands."

"Screw Galen. Jane needs me."

"She needs *us*." Joe smiled faintly and nodded. "Screw Galen."

––––––––––

Eve's phone rang as she reached the car. It was Bart Jennings. "I need to tell you that there was—"

"Damn you," Eve's voice was shaking with anger. "You promised me they'd be safe. That's all I asked, and you fouled up."

"You have every right to be angry. Galen called you? My men would have appreciated it if he'd been working with us. He didn't even identify himself to them until they were taking away your daughter."

"It was a good thing he was there. You screwed up."

"I'm not making excuses. If it will make you feel any better, we're working hand in hand with the Atlanta police, and we have the safe house completely covered."

"You had the condo covered."

"Hebert's ID was perfect, and he was in disguise. There was supposed to be an inspection today—the guard at the desk verified it with the superintendent's office when Hebert arrived. We can't locate Leonard Smythe, the man who was to do the inspection. We have to assume Hebert got to him."

"I don't want to hear it."

"I'm sorry. I said I wouldn't make excuses. I'm sending two agents to pick you up and bring you—"

"Too late. You blew it." She hung up. "He's sorry. He had the nerve to say he was sorry. My mother and Jane were almost blown up, and he's—"

"Easy. He's a decent guy. What else could he say?" Joe's lips tightened. "Not that I don't want to take a poke at him right now myself. He should have—" His phone rang, and he didn't wait for Galen to speak. "We're going back to Atlanta. Don't argue, Galen. Just find us a way to get home." He took out his pen and wrote down a name and phone number. "Okay, I'll see you in Georgia." Joe hung up and turned to Eve. "He said he knew it would come down to this. He gave me the phone number of a Philip Jordan. He said to call him and he'd pick us up and take us to a very private airport in Metairie, Louisiana."

"Just so it's soon."

"You're going to Atlanta?" Nathan asked.

"Yes."

"I want to go with you."

"What a surprise," Joe said. "It wouldn't have anything to do with the fact that Hebert may be there? He could be on his way here, you know."

He shook his head. "Not when he finds out they didn't get us at Galen's. Jules Hebert is smart. Take me with you."

"You've become something of an albatross, Nathan."

Nathan turned to Eve. "I want to come. We're in this together."

Eve gazed at him a moment and finally nodded.

"I thought as much." Joe began dialing his phone. "I'll tell Jordan there'll be one more to pick up."

———

The plane landed at an airport north of Gainesville, Georgia in the rosy dawn light. Galen met them as the plane drew up before the hangar. "Welcome home." His brows lifted as his gaze went beyond them to Nathan. "I see you brought your bodyguard."

"Be quiet, Galen." Eve moved toward the car on the tarmac. "I'm mad enough at you for not telling me you thought Hebert would go after Jane."

"Ingratitude, thy name is woman."

"I am grateful. I just wish I'd known . . ." She turned to face him. "I'm a bitch. You saved their lives. I'll owe you a debt for the rest of my life."

"That's better." He looked pointedly at Joe. "Now, do you have something to say to me?"

"Yes." Joe pushed the leather case he was carrying at him. "Stop playing around and put Bently in the trunk."

"I'm not playing around. I'm trying to garner what's due me." He looked down at the box. "It's really Bently?"

Eve nodded. "Nathan's certain, but I'll have to do the usual photo and video comparisons. I'll get on that as soon as we get settled." She got into the car. "Where's Jane?"

"She and her grandmother are in a safe house in Gwinnett."

"I want to go get them."

"What a surprise." He turned to Joe. "I've set up security around your lake cottage. I thought you'd want to go there. I've hired Bill Jackson and his team to patrol the area around the cottage. I've used him before and he's very good."

Joe looked at Eve.

She nodded wearily. "I want to take Jane home. She's been bounced around enough."

"She's not going to be pleased," Galen said. "She wanted you to stay in hiding. She told me to tell you not to be dumb and come home."

Eve smiled. "That sounds like Jane."

"And you're going to ignore her." Galen put the case with the skull in the trunk. "I can guarantee the safety of the cottage and the immediate area around it, but the hills and the lake are vulnerable. You have a hell of a lot of private acreage. Which means you can't go outside, and being cooped up nonstop with that dog may be worse than facing Hebert."

"We'll confront that problem when we come to it."

"May I make a suggestion? Hebert has gotten what he wants. You're out in the open, and you brought him the skull. You're the target now, not Jane. The danger to her will only increase the closer she is to you. We can have the police switch the safe house to Markum, a town within a five-minute drive to the lake cottage, but she shouldn't be with you."

"Don't tell me that. I want her close to me. I can't stand the thought of—"

"He's right, Eve," Joe said.

She knew he was right. It didn't make the prospect of being separated from Jane and her mother any easier. She drew a deep breath. "Okay. But you'd damn well better make sure they're safe."

"I will," Galen said. "With the help of Quinn's friends and four very sheepish FBI agents. I'd never take chances. But as I said, Hebert's got what he wants. There's no longer a reason for him to go to the trouble of going after Jane when he can concentrate on going after you. After all, you have the skull."

"Okay, okay, you've made your point." Eve got into the passenger seat. "But I want you to take me to see Jane right now. I'm not going to have her know I'm in the same city and staying away from her. You can take us to the cottage later."

"She won't like it," Galen said. "But I'll drive you there."

Nathan made a face. "Can you drop me off at a rental car agency? I'm tired of being without wheels, and I don't want to butt in on a tender family moment. I'll meet you at this lake cottage."

"Why, Nathan. How sensitive," Galen said. "I'm touched."

"Only in that convoluted brain," Nathan said dryly as he got in the car. "Did I tell you how pleasant these last days have been without you?"

"All good things must come to an end."

As the car started, Eve gazed blindly out the window. "This is such a damn mess. There has to be some way out of it that's safe for Jane. I just have to think about it."

"What do you mean?" Joe asked.

"I mean I may be mad as hell at Jennings, but he could still take this skull off my hands. It was the smart thing to do before, and it's the smart thing to do now."

"Does that mean you're going to hand it over to him?"

"I don't know what I'm going to do. I can't even think straight right now. I just want to keep Mom and Jane safe."

Chapter Fourteen

THE HOUSE IN GWINNETT WAS A small brick bungalow with a wide front porch. Jane came out on the porch when she saw Eve get out of the car. "What are you doing here?" She stared accusingly at Galen. "Can't you do anything right? I told you to keep them away from here."

"I tried. I had to make a compromise," Galen said. "She's almost as tough as you."

"Yes, she is." Jane was still frowning. "Joe, you know this isn't a good idea— Oh, what the hell." She ran down the steps and into Eve's arms. "I've been so worried," she whispered as she gave Eve a bear hug. "I've missed you."

Eve blinked back the tears. "Me, too. I'm so sorry you've been put through all this."

"No big deal. But you still shouldn't be here." She released her and gave Joe a hug. "You tell her, Joe."

"We're only going to be here for a little while," Joe said. "A few hours maybe. Where's Sandra?"

"Inside feeding Toby. I'll be glad when I can get him away from her. She feeds him every time he begs. He's going to be fat as a polar bear."

"And where are the detectives that are supposed to be protecting you?"

"Playing cards." Jane wrinkled her nose. "I like them better than those two FBI guys in the house across the street. They follow me wherever I go."

"Good. But they shouldn't have let you come out on the porch."

"They looked out the window and saw who it was. Detective Brady said he knew you. Come on, let's go inside." Jane turned away. "I've got to stop Grandma from stuffing Toby."

"And I'll take on the job of stuffing us," Galen said. "I hope you've got a well-stocked kitchen?"

"Frozen food. Grandma's a lousy cook."

Galen flinched. "Frozen? I'll improvise. I'm sure I can still provide a superb lunch."

Jane opened the screen door. "I hope you manage to do *something* without bungling it."

There was a sound from Joe that might have been a chuckle.

Galen darted him a baleful glance. "Not a word."

Joe gazed at him innocently. "From the mouths of babes."

Eve's mother, Sandra, looked up from the dog bowl she was washing.

"It's about time you got here." She hugged Eve. "The only person who doesn't complain about my cooking is Toby."

"She actually fed him pancakes this morning," Jane said. "Come on, Toby. I'll take you in the backyard to run it off."

Eve turned from watching Jane leave the room. It was obvious Jane wanted to give Eve and her mother a chance to mend some fences, but it wasn't necessary. Eve's relationship with her mother was complicated, but their affection had overcome a multitude of hurdles and still survived. "I'm sorry about all this. How bad has it been?"

"Well, other than having the condo blow up—" Sandra smiled as she saw Eve flinch. "Really. It's okay, Eve."

"It's not okay. I dumped a responsibility on you that should have been mine."

"Shit happens." Sandra shook her head. "You're feeling guilty. Maybe you should. Or maybe it was my turn to be the responsible citizen. I didn't do a very good job of it when you were growing up. It's a wonder you're not serving a sentence in some prison. It's time I paid my dues."

"That's bullshit."

"Okay, then maybe I like taking care of Jane and that idiot dog. They keep me on my toes." Sandra's gaze went to Jane in the backyard. "She calls me Grandma. No one has called me that since Bonnie . . . I thought it was odd, since she calls you and Joe by your given names. But then I realized she sensed that I'd like it. She's a very smart girl. Like you, Eve."

"Probably much smarter."

"No way. You got through a childhood with a mother like me. That qualifies you for Einstein status." She took Eve's arm. "Now shut up and let's go get Jane. She won't come in until she thinks we've had enough time together."

Eve gazed at her in loving exasperation. "Will you at least let me say thank you?"

"You've said it. Or something pretty close. Now you're getting boring."

"Heaven forbid." Eve smiled. "By all means, let's go get Jane."

———

"Someone else has to wash and dry the dishes," Galen announced after lunch. "I've done the creative part and provided you all with a meal par excellence. It's only fair that you do the drudgery."

"I'll wash them," Jane said. "Galen would probably mess it up."

"Another blow to my self-esteem." Galen sighed. "She has great aim, Eve." He moved toward the living room. "I've got to go out on the porch and fill your cop friends in on the relocating change."

"I'll help Jane," Sandra said. "I've grown to be an expert over the years. People always rather I do the cleanup than the cooking."

Eve stood and started stacking the dishes.

Jane shook her head. "You and Joe go sit in the living room with a cup of coffee and let us do the work. You'll just get in the way."

Eve hesitated.

"Go," Sandra said. "And after I finish here, I'll take Toby for a turn round the yard. He's been a little lazy today."

"Because you feed him too much, Grandma," Jane said as she went over to the sink. "How am I ever going to make him a search-and-rescue dog if he weighs five hundred pounds?"

"You're exaggerating . . ."

"Come on. We've been evicted." Joe picked up his coffee and Eve's. "The living room."

Eve followed him into the living room and sank down on the couch. Lord, she was tired, and Galen's meal hadn't made her any less sluggish.

Joe handed Eve the coffee cup and sat beside her. "I'm glad we came to see her. I've missed her like the devil."

"Me, too." The arched doorway allowed a clear view to the kitchen and Sandra and Jane standing working at the sink. "You're right, there's no one like her."

"Well, maybe one person like her." Joe's gaze followed hers. "You."

Eve shook her head. "Just because we both grew up on the streets doesn't make us twins."

"Close enough for me."

"You said something like that before."

"Oh, I'm not saying I love her because she's like you. She deserves better than that. But every now and then I get a glimpse of something that reminds me of you." Joe smiled. "And I melt."

"Melt?" Eve quickly looked down into the coffee in her cup. "Not you, Joe."

"Oh, yes. 'Melt' is a good word." He finished his coffee and stood up. "And now I think I'll go out on the porch and see if I can help Galen set up that new safe house."

She watched him until the screen door closed behind him. Those few minutes had been so comfortable and warm that she had almost forgotten the distance between them.

Or was time making the distance lessen?

She didn't know, but she had felt a closeness that was both

familiar and perilously sweet. The events of the last few days had thrust them together and blurred the jagged lines of the break between them. Yet she knew the break was still there. . . .

Stop staring after him. It only disturbed her.

Jesus, it disturbed her.

She jumped to her feet and went into the kitchen to help her mother and Jane with the dishes.

———————

"You should never have come. But I'm glad you did." Jane gave Eve a final hug after walking her to the car. "Now you know I'm fine and that I'll take care of Grandma."

"I know you will. I'm sorry I let you in for all this, Jane."

"Hey, maybe Toby needed to put on a little weight."

"Don't joke."

"It's okay. Stop worrying." Jane paused. "What are you going to do about that creep who blew up the condo?"

"Don't worry. He won't get near you again."

"That's not what I asked. You're not going to let him get away with it, are you? You're going to go after him."

Eve stared at her. "I'm going to do what's best for you and my mother."

"I thought that was the problem." Jane frowned. "It's not like you to hide out and let that bastard run around and do a lousy thing like that. He could have killed a lot of people in the condo."

"He could have killed you."

"But he didn't, and now you're trying to find a place to hide me again. You're going to crawl into a cave and try to protect all of us. Don't do it, Eve."

"What?"

"I've been thinking about it. I want you to be safe. But you can't run away from creeps like that. You've got to slug away toe-to-toe. So go after him and nail the asshole."

"That's not a wise thing—"

"Oh, for heaven's sake, I'm tripping over all the protection you've set up for me. Don't you dare use me as an excuse. If I could do it, I'd go after him myself. It sucks to be a kid."

"It's not an excuse. It's the right thing to do."

Jane shook her head. "Hiding isn't like you. Maybe you've forgotten who you are, what you do. It's partly my fault, and I don't like it. Promise me you'll think about it."

"I promise." Eve hesitated. "I love you very much, Jane."

Jane nodded. "Don't get mushy."

"I just wanted to make sure you knew."

"I know. Just get that SOB and take care of yourself." Jane took a step back and watched Eve get into the car before leaning forward to whisper, "And take care of Joe. He needs it more than he'll let you know."

How the hell could Eve answer that? "I'll call you tonight, Jane."

———

Nathan met them as they drove up to the cottage. "Everything okay?"

Eve nodded as she got out of the car. "Okay. Not perfect."

"Not many things are." Nathan's gaze shifted to the lake. "But this place comes pretty close. You were right; your lake is beautiful, Eve. It soothes the soul."

"We like it."

"It reminds me that there are still some battles worth fighting."

"Galen tells us you're quite a crusader," Joe said.

Nathan shrugged. "I try. Most of the time it's a losing battle. I get really tired of going up against the big companies who pollute our lakes and streams. They have money. I have only words."

"I don't see how a man who feels so passionately for water can have such a dislike for alligators and snakes." Galen started to unload the car. "You need to rethink and include our companions in the wild. I bet you never wrote an article about the virtues of the preservation of leeches."

"No bet," Nathan said. "I ran into Hughes, the head of your security team, when I showed up here. He said he wanted to see you."

Galen nodded. "I want to see him, too." He handed Nathan two suitcases. "So you can play the beast of burden and take these inside." He pulled out his phone as he started down the path.

Nathan gazed after him. "One of these days . . ." He turned and carried the bags into the cottage.

Eve picked up the leather skull case, but hesitated before following Nathan, gazing out at the lake.

It soothes the soul.

Beauty did soothe the soul, she thought. She could feel some of the rawness and pain of the past few days ebbing away.

"Home," Joe said quietly.

She looked at him, and then quickly looked away.

But the word lingered with her as she walked up the steps. Home.

———

"Where's Galen?" Eve asked Joe as she came out of the bedroom after talking to Jane on the phone that evening.

"Out on the grounds talking to the security team. He's complaining the area is one big headache to secure. Nathan is out on the porch communing with nature. How's Jane?"

"Disapproving." She made a face. "And making her displeasure known at every opportunity."

"And that means?"

"She wants us to go after Hebert and try to nail him."

"That sounds like Jane." He smiled. "Not a bad idea. I've been thinking the same thing."

"So have I." She shook her head. "I get so angry when I think of that condo, I want to murder the bastard. But it's not a responsible thing to do when Jane—"

"It may be the most responsible thing we could do. Get rid of the bastard before he does any more damage. Maybe if we had a lead . . ."

She didn't answer for a moment. "We may have a lead."

He looked at her inquiringly.

She emphatically shook her head. "I don't even want to think about it. It's not—"

"Okay. Okay. We'll talk about it when you're not so upset." He paused. "Jennings called on my cell phone while you were talking to Jane. He wants to come and pick up the skull."

"He'll get it when I decide I want to give it to him. I'm still pissed at him."

"He was very persistent. Just thought I'd relay the message." He stood up and moved over to the window. "The sun's going down. Pretty. I always like autumn sunsets. They seem to be sharper, more defined."

Like Joe. He was silhouetted against the dim light streaming through the window, and he seemed made of edges and angles. How many times had she watched him at this window? She crossed the room to stand beside him. "It's beautiful." Her gaze went to the lake glittering mirrored gold in the twilight. "I've always loved it here."

"I know." His glance shifted to her face. "But I'm surprised you're admitting it now. You couldn't wait to run away from here."

"I was hurting." Eve's gaze went to the hill where she'd thought she'd buried her daughter. "Everything reminded me of what you did."

He stiffened. "Was?"

She hadn't realized she'd spoken in the past tense. "I don't know, Joe. I still feel— It's not over. I'm not sure if it will ever be over."

"I don't know if I want it to be."

"What?"

"That surprises you." Joe's gaze shifted back to the lake. "Do I want to live with you for the rest of my life? Hell, yes. Am I sorry I hurt you? You know I am. Do I want to go back to what we had before? I'd take it, but I think we can do better."

"Do you?"

"I asked you to marry me two years ago. You said you loved me. Why didn't you do it?"

"We were both busy. We just didn't get around to it."

Joe turned to look at her.

"You never pushed it, dammit."

"Because I was scared. I was always the supplicant in our relationship."

"The hell you were."

"It took me ten years to get you to admit you loved me and

agree to live with me. Do you think I'd rock the boat by trying to nudge you anywhere you didn't want to go?"

"I *did* want to marry you."

"Then why didn't you do it?"

"What are you trying to say?"

"I'm saying that I've made some giant strides, but I'm still second banana to Bonnie."

"And I suppose that's why you lied to me?"

"No way. I would have done the same thing even if I thought I was number one on your hit parade. I wanted your search for her to end."

"By lying to me."

"It was a mistake. But it wouldn't have been a tragedy if you'd fought your way back to the land of the living before it happened."

"You don't know what you're talking about," she said shakily.

"No one knows better how far you've come. I watched you battle your way back from pain and depression and madness. Why do you think I love you so much?" He gently touched her cheek. "You just have to come a few more steps."

"I'm . . . confused. You're trying to turn this all around." She blinked back tears. "And you were never a supplicant, blast you."

"Yes, I am. I'm asking you to let me stay. Let me help you take those final steps. It's all out in the open now. We can make a fresh start."

"Joe . . ."

"You love me. You were happy here. You can be happy again."

She stared at him helplessly.

"Okay." He took a step back. "I'm not pushing you." Then he took a step forward and kissed her, hard. "The hell I'm not. I'm tired of being patient. We need each other, and I'm not going to let you blow it." He headed for the front door. "I'll see you in the morning."

She flinched as the door slammed behind him. The air seemed to vibrate with the passion he had emitted. And not only Joe's passion. She was shaking from emotion. All the barriers she had erected between them seemed to be toppling. She lifted her hand to her lips. She could still feel the pressure of his lips.

Joe . . .

Why didn't you marry me?

Why hadn't she? Why had she shied away from that final commitment? Joe thought he knew, and had still been willing to accept second best.

He wasn't second best. He'd never be second best to anyone.

She was being defensive, trying to protect him, she realized. But she was the only one who could hurt him. How much had she hurt him during these past two years?

He was walking down the path, every movement suggesting pent-up emotion ready to explode. His attitude was so different from the last time she had watched him and Jane together just a few weeks ago.

But then, nothing was the same now.

She turned away from the window. She was too upset and confused to sort out her emotions now. So stop staring after Joe and think about something else.

Yeah, sure.

"Jennings is coming." Joe had thrown open the door again and was striding into the room. "Galen just called from the checkpoint at the main road. Jennings is alone in one car, but he's accompanied by a police vehicle."

"What?"

Joe shrugged. "I don't know what the hell is happening. This isn't Jennings's style."

Eve went past him out on the porch.

Headlights were coming down the road.

Nathan got up from the porch swing. "What's happening?"

"Jennings. He probably wants Victor."

He frowned. "Why the police car?"

Joe didn't answer. "If you don't want anyone to know you're involved, you'd better disappear, Nathan."

Nathan hesitated, and then slowly shook his head. "I'm tired of skulking around. You came out in the open. It's time I did, too."

"Suit yourself."

A few minutes later Jennings's car was pulling up before the cottage. He got out of the car and started up the steps. "Sorry to do it this way," Jennings said quietly. "But I have to have that reconstruction, Ms. Duncan."

She bristled. "I don't like to be pushed, Jennings. You'll get it when I'm ready to give it to you."

"I know you're angry with me, but don't let that get in the way of your good judgment. You did your job; now let us do ours."

"Or you'll break down the doors and take it?" She glanced at the patrol car. "Do you have a search warrant?"

"Oh, yes." He pulled it out of his pocket and handed it to Joe. "I couldn't take the chance of your refusing me again. Since the condo was blown up, my superior, Agent Rusk, has been on my ass about finding Hebert."

"I'm not done. I've finished the reconstruction, but I haven't done photo and video confirmations."

"I'll do it. I have photos of Bently in the car. Rusk wants me to check it out right away. I have to get on the horn and call him as soon as I leave here."

"It's not the same. I want to do it myself." Eve's lips firmed. "Did it ever occur to you that Hebert might come after it? Why don't you stake out the cottage instead of taking the skull away from me?" My God, she had just suggested she be used as bait. What the hell was wrong with her?

"Actually, we may set up a similar situation to lure Hebert. That's one of the reasons we have to have the skull."

"But I'm out of it?"

Jennings nodded. "I don't see why you're objecting. You couldn't wait for me to take the skull when I came to see you."

"I don't like to have my work taken away from me by force. If you'd waited, I'd have probably called you."

"We don't have time." He paused. "I just got off a plane from Boca Raton. I've been there scouting around for the past few days."

"And?"

"Nothing concrete, but something occurred to me when I was down there. I went over what you told me, and the answer just came out of the blue. It was all there right in front of me, but I didn't see it. I may be wrong, but I have a hunch . . ." He shook his head. "I need to talk it over with Rusk and see if he thinks I'm nuts. If not, we'll have to move fast to put everything together."

Eve sensed an undercurrent of excitement. There was tenseness, an alertness in his manner that was unmistakable. "What hunch?"

Jennings shook his head. "Will you please go get the skull for me? Don't make me take it."

Joe took a step forward. "No way."

"I wonder how this kind of harassment would play in the press," Nathan said softly from his seat on the swing.

Jennings glanced at Nathan sitting in the shadows. "Who the hell are you?"

"Just a friend," Joe said.

Jennings looked back at Eve. "Quinn is a policeman. Do you want to make him disobey a legal writ in front of men from his own department?"

So that was why he'd brought the police car. Smart. Very smart.

Joe never took his gaze from the FBI man. "I don't give a damn about your writ. Eve?"

"No." She turned on her heel. "I would have eventually given it to him anyway. I just don't like the use of force, and I wanted to do the finish work myself. It's not worth causing you trouble."

"I can handle any trouble he's dishing out."

"No, Joe." She went into the cottage and got the leather case with Victor's skull from her bedroom. She took it back out on the porch and thrust it at Jennings.

"Thank you." He unfastened the snap, glanced inside, and then fastened it again. He looked up and said soberly, "I apologize for causing you this disturbance. It wasn't my choice. I would have been glad to give you a little more time, but the matter is too urgent."

"Don't you think I'm feeling a sense of urgency? My daughter almost died in that condo."

"You can safely leave the matter in our hands now."

"I left my daughter's safety in your hands and you fouled up. Why should I believe you'll be any more effective in finding Hebert?"

He flinched. "I deserved that." He turned and went down the stairs. "I'll try to keep you informed."

"Not likely," Joe said. "I was an agent. I know the drill."

Jennings got in the car. "I'll do what I can. That's all I can promise."

Eve watched the two cars wind down the road and around the bend. She should have felt relieved, she told herself. Victor was out of her hands, and the responsibility was entirely with Jennings. But she didn't feel relieved. She felt strangely flat and . . . cheated.

"He was hard for you to give up," Nathan said.

"I hadn't completed the work. I needed to do the video overlay and the final comparison."

"The Bureau will do it."

"But Victor was *mine*."

"You didn't have to give him up," Joe said. "I would have backed you."

"Yes, you would have fought them all and probably lost your job."

"Maybe."

"And you love that damn job."

"Yes, but it's way down on my list. Shall I tell you what's at the top?"

"No," she said unevenly.

"I didn't think so." He started down the stairs. "Then I'll go try to find Galen and tell him what's happened."

"I'm sorry, Eve," Nathan said. "I tried to help."

"I know. You should have kept quiet. Jennings may have

been too absorbed to follow up on what Joe said, but later he's going to remember you being here."

"So what? It won't kill me." He grimaced. "I hope."

Eve felt a chill go through her.

"Hey, it's a joke."

"Yeah." She nodded jerkily and went into the cottage.

Chapter Fifteen

JENNINGS WAVED THE POLICE CAR ON past him and pulled over to the side of the road. He speed-dialed Robert Rusk in Washington. "I've got it, sir. It wasn't pleasant. I *like* that woman, and if we'd given her another day she'd probably have turned it over without a protest."

"You didn't have time to be diplomatic," Agent Rusk said. "We've got to know if this is Harold Bently. You brought the photos of him with you?"

"Sure." Jennings turned on the overhead light before taking the three pictures out of the briefcase and spreading them on the passenger seat. Then he opened the leather case and carefully pulled out the skull. "I'm doing a comparison now."

"And?"

He studied the features of the skull and then carefully did the same to the photographs. He gave a low whistle. "Duncan's really good."

"Is it Bently?"

"No doubt about it." Jennings studied the skull again. "It's definitely Harold Bently."

"You're positive?"

"Yes."

"Good."

"Shall I bring it to the office right away? And I need to talk to you about Boca Raton. I may have found the—"

He never finished the sentence.

———————

Eve heard the explosion first. The sound was so loud it shook the cottage.

She ran out onto the porch.

"What the hell?" Nathan was running down the porch steps.

Then the night sky lit up with a red glow.

"I don't know what—" Eve stared in horror at the tops of the pine trees flaming on the horizon. She ran down the steps and up the path, followed closely by Nathan.

"Come on, we'll get the car." Joe was beside her, taking her arm and pulling her toward the jeep. "I think it's on the road. But it's got to be a couple miles away."

Eve and Nathan jumped into the jeep and Joe stomped on the accelerator.

She moistened her dry lips as they raced down the road. "What is it?"

Joe didn't answer.

The sky was still lit by a baleful red glow.

Fire.

But what had caused it?

As they turned a corner in the road, she saw billowing black smoke and a roaring inferno. At first she couldn't tell what was at the heart of the flames.

Joe took a deep breath as he stopped the car. "Christ."

A car, or pieces of a car.

"My God." Nathan jumped out of the jeep.

Eve's eyes widened in shock. "Jennings?"

Joe nodded. "That's my guess."

"Could he still be alive?"

She knew the answer before Joe said, "No chance. Whatever device blew that car was damn powerful. There's not much left of the metal."

And human flesh was so much more fragile. "It was a bomb? How?"

"It may take days of lab work to determine that. Somebody didn't want any pieces left to put together."

"Hebert," Eve said dully. "He seems to be very good with explosives. The condo was—"

"I'm getting the hell out of here." Galen was running toward them. "My guy at the highway phoned to say the police car is turning around and coming back. They must have heard the explosion."

"I'll talk to them," Joe said.

"Fine. But that won't help me. You two may be fairly above suspicion, but I'm not." Galen glanced at the burning car. "And you may have a few things to explain yourselves. You tell me you're hostile to Jennings, and a few minutes later his car blows up. Jennings was FBI. The least that could happen is that you'll be grilled about your involvement. I'll call you later tonight after all the hoopla dies down."

"I'll go with you." Nathan got out of the car.

"Then you'd better move fast." Galen turned and disappeared into the forest.

Nathan muttered an oath and trotted after him. "Wait, dammit, I'm carrying a lot more weight than you are."

Eve turned and looked back at the burning car. Poor Jennings . . .

"Listen," Joe said. "Galen's right; there are going to be all kinds of questions. I'll handle as much as I can, but I can't keep you out of it entirely."

Eve nodded numbly. She was so stunned, it was difficult to think what was best to do. She didn't want to end up at either the police department or FBI headquarters answering interminable questions. On the other hand, taking off and running was not an option, either. "I don't expect you to keep me out of it. I'll be okay."

"Tell me that after we get through this night." He flipped open his phone. "I'm calling the chief and telling him to get a forensic crew out here right away. I want any evidence to be channeled first through our labs. There's no guarantee that the Bureau won't step in, since Jennings was one of their own, but if they do barge in and take over, at least they'll be obligated to share results with the ATLPD."

"Will your chief bow to pressure?"

"Probably. Like I said, if the tests are already underway before the FBI steps into the picture, the chief will have a legitimate gripe if the information isn't shared. The Bureau is always saying that everything's peaches and cream between the Feds and local police departments, but the antagonism is still there.

It would be a bad public relations move for them to refuse access."

Eve continued to look at the flames as he spoke quickly into his phone, and felt her stomach clench. At first, she'd only been aware of the smell of gasoline and burning pine, but now she realized there was another scent. . . .

"You okay?" Joe's gaze was on her face.

She took a deep breath and nodded. "But let's go back to the cottage."

"Sorry." His gaze was on the road. "Here comes the patrol car. I'll get you out of here as soon as I can."

———————

They didn't get back to the cottage until after the forensic team arrived at the wreckage fifteen minutes later. Special Agent Hal Lindman from the FBI Atlanta field office arrived an hour later, followed closely by two detectives from Joe's precinct. It was several hours after that when the questioning ended and the final statements were taken.

"It's not over," Joe said as they watched the police cars drive down the road away from the cottage. "The FBI is going to come down on this case like gangbusters as soon as the man Rusk is sending down from his office gets here. They'll take over the investigation and be on our doorstep tomorrow morning at the latest."

"We won't be here."

"What?"

"Call Galen and get him and Nathan to come back right away. I want to talk to them."

Joe studied Eve's expression, and nodded. "I'll get them."

She crossed her arms over her chest as she gazed out at the pine trees. The sky was no longer red, but the trees were scorched and bare.

Jennings was dead. Blown to bits. She closed her eyes, sick, as the memory of that blazing car came back to her. She had been angry with him for arbitrarily taking the skull, but she had genuinely liked the man. He didn't deserve to have that monster kill him.

"They'll be here within an hour," Joe said. "They'll have to take a speedboat from the opposite end of the lake to avoid the guards around the crime scene."

The crime scene. It was an ugly phrase for an ugly act.

"Eve?"

Rage was beginning to supplant the horror. "I'm mad as hell, Joe. Hebert killed him because of Victor. When Hebert thought that he might not be able to find out who Victor was, he wanted to make sure no one else would know, either. He didn't care that a decent man was blown up, too."

"It may have been more than that," Joe said. "Jennings was on the track of something in Boca Raton."

Yes, Jennings had been excited. What had he said?

It was there in front of me all the time. I didn't see it.

What had been there in front of Jennings?

She rubbed her aching temple. She couldn't think. She was in too much of a rage for cool reason. She wanted to strike out again and again and again.

You have to stand toe-to-toe and slug it out.

Jane had said that, but Eve had backed away. Now there was another death, and once more Hebert had gotten away with it.

Damn him to hell.

She wasn't going to crawl into a cave and hide again.

————————

Galen cut the motor of the speedboat as he reached the pier. "You called, we came."

"Come into the cottage," Eve said as she walked back up the pier. "We may not have much time. Joe's not sure when the FBI will show up again."

"Yes, ma'am." Galen gave a low whistle as he got out of the boat and followed her toward the cottage. "Whatever you say."

Joe was sitting in the easy chair by the window. "Any trouble getting here?"

Nathan shook his head. "No problem. God, I need some coffee." He moved toward the kitchen. "You talk, I'll listen while I'm making a pot."

His face was pale and pinched, Eve noticed. "You don't look well."

"I'll be okay. I'm not used to this kind of thing." He scowled. "I once thought I'd like to be a police reporter, but I never made it past the first gang shooting." He poured water into the coffeemaker. "I hate violence. It makes me sick."

"Join the club." Eve shivered as she remembered Jennings's burning funeral pyre. "It shouldn't happen. We shouldn't let it happen."

Joe's gaze narrowed on her face. "And do we have a way to stop it?"

"We've got to try." Her hands clenched at her sides. "We can't let him keep on with this. He almost killed Jane and my mother. He did kill Jennings and Capel and—" She stopped and drew a deep shaky breath. "Jane told me that I should 'slug it out toe-to-toe,' but I was too scared of what he'd do. That was a mistake. I have to stop him before he does anything else. No one is safe as long as he's alive and free. I can't let him go on like this."

"To stop him, we have to find him," Joe said.

She was silent a moment. "Or he has to find me."

"He's already destroyed the skull," Nathan said. "He may not target you now. Particularly if he has other fish to fry in Boca Raton."

"Oh, I think he'll target me. I know too much, and he evidently likes to keep everything tidy for the Cabal." She paused. "But it will add a little impetus if he thinks I'm going after evidence he doesn't want to be discovered."

"And that is?"

"Bently's grave. I don't have to have the entire skeleton. In this day of DNA technology, if I discover hair, a bone, even a tooth, I may have a chance of spoiling whatever game Hebert and the Cabal are playing."

"How?"

"I'm not sure yet. But they don't want him identified, or they wouldn't have blown up Jennings's car tonight."

"And how are you going to find the grave?"

"I may not be able to. But if Hebert thinks I'm getting near it, he may be drawn in." She opened her handbag. "On the other hand, I may be able to find it." She took out a letter-size manila envelope and opened it. "If I can find out where this came from."

Joe took the envelope and looked inside. "Dirt."

"Galen called it 'funny dirt,' " Eve said. "It's a light color, and it has a large amount of tiny bones or shell chips. Victor had this caked mud in all his orifices."

Nathan made a face as he poured coffee into his cup. "Pleasant."

Galen smiled. "Isn't it nice I'm so observant? You were so obsessed with Victor, I didn't think you were paying attention when I made the comment."

"I didn't want to. It got in the way of my work. But after you left, it kept nagging at me. So I scraped some of the mud into an envelope and put it in my purse."

"Why didn't you tell me?" Joe asked.

"I forgot about it."

He raised his brows. "Forgot?"

"Okay, I blocked it out," she said defiantly. "I told you, it was getting in my way with Victor."

Galen shook his head. "Obsession."

"And what are you going to do with the mud?" Nathan asked.

"Take it to Louisiana State University. They have one of the best geology schools in the South there. I'll see if they can give me a lead as to where dirt like this can be found."

"And then?"

"I go there and Hebert follows me."

"No," Joe said flatly.

"Yes." Eve looked him directly in the eye. "Toe-to-toe, Joe. I'm going to get the son of a bitch."

He was silent a moment. "I wasn't objecting to that. You said I, not we. I'm going with you."

She opened her mouth to protest, and then slowly nodded her head. It was no time to worry about their personal conflict.

They had worked together before, and there was no one she trusted as she did Joe.

Trust . . .

Galen nodded. "I think I'll tag along, too."

"No," Eve said. "I want you to stay and watch over Jane. I need you here."

"That wasn't what I was hired to do."

"I want her safe."

Galen grimaced. "Okay, but Jane will have my head if she finds out that I'm not dogging your footsteps."

She smiled faintly. "You'll survive."

"I'm not so sure. She's a tough customer."

Eve turned to Nathan. "Are you coming with us?"

He shook his head. "I'm heading for Boca Raton. If Jennings found out something down there, I might be able to do the same. I'll be in touch." He poured more coffee into his cup. "We don't have much time. It's already the twenty-fifth, and the twenty-ninth was the date Etienne was so concerned about."

The ticking clock. She wouldn't think about it. She would move as quickly as she could, but there was no sense in panicking. "Then we need to get going." She turned to Joe. "Can you call your chief and get them to keep the FBI off our backs for a few days?"

He shook his head. "But I can try to get the chief to keep his mouth shut about where we are."

"Good." Eve turned to Galen. "I need Hebert to know what we're up to."

"He already seems to know a hell of a lot more than I'm comfortable with."

"I have to be sure."

"Any ideas?"

"I believe what Melton knows, Hebert will know." She frowned, thinking. "Tanzer. He bragged that nothing went on in Baton Rouge that he didn't know about. Can you finesse someone at the college to filter information to Tanzer after we leave there?"

"And Tanzer will call Melton." Galen nodded. "I might be able to get one of my contacts to work it." He smiled faintly. "After all, Tanzer is a *trou du cul*."

Jesus, it seemed a long time since Marie Letaux had used that phrase. So much had happened, so many deaths . . .

"Be careful," Nathan said soberly. "I wouldn't want you to be caught in the trap you're setting for Hebert. The man gives me the willies."

She had a sudden memory of the chill she had felt when talking to Nathan earlier in the evening. "You be careful, too."

"I'm always careful." He finished his coffee. "I have to live to get my Pulitzer." He started for the door. "Come on, Galen. Get off your ass and take me to the airport."

Chapter Sixteen

IT'S TERREBONNE PARISH." PROFESSOR GERALD CASSIDY straightened his bifocal glasses on his nose before looking up at Eve and Joe. "I'd bet on it."

"You haven't even tested it," Joe said. "How can you be sure?"

"I'll take it to the lab and run some tests, but I've seen this dirt before. It's unusual. I did a paper on the area for my doctorate."

Which couldn't have been too long ago, Eve thought. Cassidy didn't look a day over twenty-five. "Why is it unusual?"

"High concentration of calcium." Cassidy pointed to the minute white chips embedded in the dirt. "Shells. Hundreds of years ago, the entire area was flooded and the shells were deposited all over." He frowned. "But I've never run across this heavy a percentage of shells in the soil samples I took. I'd be interested to know where it's located. . . ."

"We need to be absolutely sure we can start at Terrebonne," Joe said. "Will you run some tests?"

Cassidy shrugged. "Sure. Come back this afternoon." He paused. "Why do you want to know? What are you looking for?"

Eve hesitated. "A grave."

Cassidy made a face. "Good luck. That's bayou country. Hundreds of waterways, and the Cajuns aren't all that communicative. They don't like strangers. It took me months to gather enough information for my thesis."

"But you must have made a few contacts. Can you put us in touch with anyone who might be able to pinpoint the area where this might be found?"

"Jacques Dufour. If he needs money and wants to cooperate, he knows the bayous better than anyone else I was able to hire. I'll give you his phone number in Houma." He opened a desk drawer, took out a black leather address book, and flipped through it. "I wouldn't use me as a reference. He made no bones about showing his contempt for me."

"Why?"

"I was twenty-four years old, a little bookish, and not Cajun. All sins in his eyes." He studied Joe. "Somehow I don't think you'll have a problem with him."

"I won't." Eve wrote down the phone number and stood up. "When will you know for certain?"

"It should be about four this afternoon. Are you coming back here?"

Eve shook her head as she went toward the door. "Joe will give you our cell number. We're leaving for Houma right away."

"They're going to Terrebonne parish," Melton said as soon as Hebert answered the phone. "They're after the grave. For God's sake, can you screw up any worse than you've been doing?"

Hebert smothered the surge of anger. "They won't find anything."

"I'm not so sure. You've screwed up everything about this business from the beginning."

"It will be all right. Maybe better than all right. I know those swamps, and the people who live there. Etienne and I grew up near those bayous."

"Listen to me. I want no disruption. Get rid of them quickly, quietly, and then get your ass back to Boca Raton. Christ, I can't believe you've cut it this close. You're sure that everything's on schedule down there?"

"It's all in motion. I'm sure your informants have already told you that the plan's working beautifully."

"Yes, there was an article in the newspaper this morning. Security?"

"In place. As soon as I finish, I'll get back and tie up any loose ends."

"Then do it, damn you." Melton hung up.

Arrogant son of a bitch. Hebert didn't need Melton to tell him how tight the time frame was getting. His gut twisted every time he let himself think about it. Every move he had made lately had been either threatened or checkmated. It was as if there were some force keeping him from succeeding.

Etienne.

He closed his eyes. Ridiculous superstitious nonsense. He mustn't panic. All he had to do was remove Duncan and Quinn, and he'd be free to concentrate on his job in Boca Raton. It would be easy to do.

Unless it was a trap.

But even if it was a trap, he'd have the advantage. Every year people disappeared into those swamps and never came out. There was death waiting for the careless around every bend of the bayou. But he was experienced enough to spring any trap— or set a deadly one of his own.

A two-hour flight and he'd be in New Orleans.

An hour later and he'd be deep in the swamp.

Waiting.

———————

HOUMA
4:05 P.M.
October 25

"Shells?" Jacques Dufour shrugged. "There are shells all over the parish."

"But this place has a very high concentration of them," Eve said. "Professor Cassidy said you might know where it was located."

"I might. I'll have to think about it."

Eve gritted her teeth. The man was as arrogant as Cassidy had told them. "Then think about it."

"Maybe we should just go looking. My swamp tour is the best in the bayou."

"I don't want a tour. I want to find a place with—"

"How much?" Joe asked curtly.

"I didn't say—" Dufour stopped as he met Joe's gaze. "I have an idea where it might be. My cousin, Jean Pierdu, lives in an area where there are many shells."

"Then give me his telephone number. I want to talk to him."

Dufour smiled. "He has no telephone. People are very poor here. You'll have to go to him. Five hundred."

"Three hundred. And you'd better be right about the shells. I wouldn't want you to waste your time." Joe's voice lowered to silky softness. "Or mine."

"Too cheap. It's deep in the bayou, and I might have to—"

"Maybe I didn't make myself clear." Joe took a step closer. "Three hundred, and you might come out of that bayou with your skin intact. Annoy me with this bullshit and you may end up alligator bait."

Dufour's lips tightened. "You should remember that a bayou can be a dangerous place for someone who isn't familiar with it."

"Three hundred."

Dufour hesitated, then shrugged. "Three hundred." He turned away. "We leave tomorrow morning."

"Now."

"I have a swamp tour in forty minutes, and after that it will be too dark to see." He smiled maliciously. "We go very close to the trees. I think you'd want to be able to see a coral snake before it dropped in the lady's lap."

Joe muttered a curse as he watched Dufour swagger away from them.

"It might have gone a little better if you'd been more patient and not threatened him with the alligator," Eve said.

"I'm tired of being patient."

That was evident to Eve. Ever since they'd arrived at Houma, she'd been aware that Joe had gone into battle mode. She had seen that side of him only a few times since she had known him. He tried to keep the violence of both past and present apart from her. Yet she still recognized the tension, the alertness, the barely contained eagerness. Yes, eager was the word. He was eager, wanting to break loose, wanting to strike out. No wonder Dufour had backed down. "We might as well find a hotel to check into for the night," she said. "I need to call Galen and make sure Jane's safe."

———

"Of course, she's safe," Galen said. "I believe I'm insulted."

"Insulted? May I remind you that she and my mother were almost blown up?"

"Good point. But now I have them surrounded by so many of Hughes's security men that it would take an army to get near them. Even if Hebert could breach the FBI and police guards, it would—" He stopped. "But Hebert is going to be too busy to make an attempt, isn't he? Any sign of him?"

"Not yet. But we have a lead on the grave site. We're at Houma and we go into the swamp tomorrow."

"I'm very good in swamps. I think you need me. Hughes could do my job here, and I—"

"We don't need you. Stay with Jane. Have you heard from Nathan?"

"No, but he'd more likely contact you. For some reason, he finds me a little annoying."

"I wonder why. I'll call you tomorrow." She hung up.

Eve was relieved. The odds that Hebert would strike again at Jane were slim, but that hadn't stopped her from worrying. Galen's attitude might have seemed light, but she knew him well enough now to know that he was dead serious about his job. Jane was safe in his hands.

She stood up and moved over to the window. It had started to rain; the distant swamp looked gloomy and menacing in the early dusk.

"Did you reach Galen?"

Eve turned to see Joe standing in the doorway. "Yes, Jane's fine." She smiled faintly. "He wanted to come and help us. He says he's good in swamps. I told him we didn't need him."

"Thank God. In my present mood I don't think I could handle Galen's humor. As it is, I may have to drown Dufour before this is over."

"Did you find out anything from the department about Jennings?"

He shook his head. "Not yet. The FBI took the forensic testing away from them, but the chief is pushing hard to get all the reports as soon as they come out of the FBI labs. I asked Carol to call me as soon as the reports hit any desk in the precinct." He made a face. "And Rusk isn't at all pleased about our disappearing before his team got down to Georgia. He's raising hell."

"Tough."

"That's what I said." Joe paused. "I don't suppose you'd let me go alone to see Dufour's cousin?"

"No."

"I'm pretty good in the swamps myself. I learned a lot on assignment in Nicaragua when I was a SEAL."

"I bet you did. And you can't wait to use it."

"No." He held her gaze with a searing intensity that caused her eyes to widen with shock. "You're not the only one who's mad as hell. I almost lost you. He's got to pay."

Jesus.

She finally managed to tear her gaze away. "I'm going."

"Just thought I'd try." He turned away. "I'll see you in the morning. I've got the room next door. If you need me, call."

Eve stood staring at the door that had closed behind Joe before finally forcing herself to turn back to the window.

If you need me, call.

Her hand clenched on the drape. She did not need him.

But, God, she wanted him.

Chapter Seventeen

1:10 P.M.
October 26

HOW CLOSE ARE WE?" EVE ASKED. "It seems as if we've been in this boat for days."

"Only four hours." Dufour maneuvered the motorboat around a huge mangrove branch jutting out of the water. "These bayous wind around like eels. You're lucky you have me to guide you." He darted a glance at Joe. "Maybe you pay me more money to take you back."

Joe didn't look at him. "You're pushing it."

"It's a terrible thing to be lost in the swamp."

"I'm not lost." Joe's gaze shifted to Dufour's face. "I memorized every turn you've taken from the time we left the dock. Do you want me to repeat them back to you?"

Dufour blinked, disconcerted. "No." He quickly looked

back at the muddy water ahead. "Can't you take a joke? A deal is a deal."

Joe smiled without mirth. "That's my philosophy."

Eve didn't doubt that Joe had told the truth about knowing where they were, but she didn't see how. The weather was chilly and damp, and ever since they had left the dock, it had been like being in an alien world. Scraggly cypress trees formed a dark canopy over the narrow, muddy waterway. Brown-black snakes occasionally glided by the boat, and skeletal trees clung with desperation to the bottom of the bayou, fighting for life in this hostile environment. And the vegetation was not the only thing fighting for life.

"What are those shacks on those little islands? Do people actually live there?" Eve asked.

"My cousin, Jean, would not be pleased to hear you call his home a shack. His place is very like those houses. Though most of the places we've passed are used primarily as camps by hunters and fishermen," Dufour said. "But as you go deeper you find Cajuns who live as well as hunt in the swamps and marshes. I told you the people were poor here; they don't have the guts to get out and earn real money like I do. So they're lucky to have a roof over their head."

"Sometimes overcoming poverty isn't a matter of guts."

He shrugged. "Guts or stupidity."

"Why are the houses built on stilts? The ground comes up to the front door."

"That's not the ground, it's mud. This area is close to the ocean and, when the tide comes in, it brings the mud with it. When the tide goes out, the houses would sink below the water if they weren't on pilings."

"What a precarious way to live," Eve murmured. Precarious and sad. "How deep is that mud?"

"Sometimes five or six feet." Dufour grinned. "Not good if you're a sleepwalker. You drop off the porch and you have a mouthful of slime." He pointed to a shack several yards ahead. "That's Jean's place."

It was another small cypress shack, built on stilts and linked to the bayou by a narrow pier. A woman came out onto the porch and stood staring unsmilingly at them. She was small, thin, and very pregnant. Two small boys garbed only in dirty T-shirts and underpants were clinging to her skirts.

"Don't stand there gawping at us, Marguerite," Dufour said as he guided the boat close to the makeshift pier. "Tell Jean he has guests."

"We don't want the kind of guests you bring us. We've no use for tourists." She glanced at Eve. "If you want to see how we Cajuns live, then go somewhere else. Leave us alone."

"Such rudeness." Dufour clucked reprovingly. "I'll have to tell Jean to beat you more often." He tied the boat and jumped out on the pier. "Is he here?"

She nodded. "He won't want to see you."

"Yes, he will. There's money to be had." He glanced at the woman's swollen belly. "And you can obviously use money right now. Two children under five years and another mouth to feed on the way?"

She hesitated, then turned on her heel. "Bring them."

"Stay here, Eve." Joe jumped out of the boat and strode toward the shack. "I'll just take a little look around."

Eve stiffened as he disappeared into the house. Joe was obviously in protective mode. The hell she'd stay here.

She scrambled out of the boat, but was only halfway up the wooden dock when Joe came to the door and waved for her to come in. She breathed a sigh of relief.

They were safe.

For now.

————

"I might know of such a place," Jean Pierdu said slowly. "How much?"

"Five hundred to take us there," Joe said. "And another five hundred if you can tell us anything that might be of interest to us about it."

Jean gazed at him impassively. "I know nothing about shells."

"What do you know about graves?" Eve asked.

His expression didn't change. "We keep to ourselves here."

"But that doesn't mean you don't know exactly what's going on," Dufour said. "I heard rumors there were outsiders here a few years ago. We don't care about outsiders, Jean. Why not get a little money for yourself?"

"We need it, Jean," Marguerite said quietly. "He's right, why should we care about outsiders?"

"Don't interfere, Marguerite." Jean was silent a moment, and then slowly nodded. "A thousand."

"I can tell you and Dufour are related," Joe said dryly. "Seven hundred."

"Give him the thousand, Joe." Eve's gaze was fixed on Marguerite and the two children.

Joe smiled faintly. "Okay." He turned back to Jean. "Where is it?"

"The money."

Joe reached for his wallet and counted out the cash. "Satisfied?"

Jean nodded and stuffed the money in his pocket. "There are two islands about four miles from here. They're in a little natural pocket of the swamp, and they caught the bulk of the shells when the floods came. That might be what you're looking for."

"They're little mud islands like this one?" Eve asked.

Jean nodded. "I've lived here all my life and I've never run across anywhere else that had that many shells."

"Are the islands close together?"

"Yes." He paused. "But you'll only be interested in the second one. There's nothing on the other."

Joe stiffened. "And what's on the second one?"

"You won't find your grave. It's not there any more."

"But it was there?"

"Get more money," Marguerite said.

Jean gave her an annoyed glance. "I was going to do that."

Joe peeled off another five hundred. "Was there a grave?"

Jean nodded. "Two. Not marked. But they were there. I saw Etienne digging them. He was having a hard time. He said he had to anchor the bodies to the pilings because he didn't want to chance the bodies being washed out and found."

"Etienne Hebert? You knew him?"

Jean nodded again. "He came about the time the other two came. But he wasn't like them. He was Cajun like us."

"What other two? When?"

"About two years ago. Two men came and hired some of us to build them a house on the island and then forget they were there." He shrugged. "The money was good. Why should we care what they were doing? As long as they didn't sell their drugs to our children, they could make all the powders they wanted. It wasn't our business."

"You thought they were into drugs?"

"We knew they were. Etienne told us. He would come and bring a bottle of wine and sit in that very chair and tell us about all the supplies that he brought down the bayou from Houma to the island."

"He was a nice man," Marguerite said. "You're not going to get him into trouble? He wasn't to blame."

"No, I promise Etienne won't get into trouble," Eve said.

"He always said that those crazy men would blow themselves up with all those chemicals they had him bring," Marguerite said. "He was sad. I think he liked them."

"And what happened to them?"

"What Etienne said would happen. One night there was a big explosion. When we went to see what happened, we found Etienne digging two graves. He told us to go away and forget what had happened. He said the police mustn't know, or they would think we were all criminals, too."

"And that's what you did?"

"We're not fools. The police think we're scum. Etienne was right."

"And what were the two men's names?" Joe asked.

"What do you think?" Jean's tone dripped sarcasm. "Smith and Jones. Do you think they'd give us their real names?"

"How long were they on the island before the explosion?" Eve asked.

"Four months, maybe. They came to us two months before that, but we wasted a little time because we started building on the first island. Then they decided it would be better to go a little deeper into the swamp, and we had to start again on the second."

"How far apart are they?"

"About a mile. But a mile can make a big difference in the swamp."

"You said you knew the grave wasn't there any more. How do you know that?"

"Etienne came back. He told us that the police were asking questions and he had to get rid of the skeletons." Jean grimaced. "Trust the police to worry about dirt like that and try to cause us trouble. It wasn't our fault they blew themselves up."

"What do you know about Etienne's brother?"

Jean frowned. "He has a brother?"

"He didn't talk about him?"

Jean shook his head.

"That's enough," Dufour said. "Don't tell them anything else unless they give you more money, Jean." He smiled. "And a little bonus for me for bringing them to you."

"You've probably squeezed enough out of them without dipping into my pockets," Jean said. "And I'll need all my money if me and my family have to disappear for awhile."

"Why do you have to do that?"

"You think I trust you or these people?" He looked at Joe. "We did nothing. We're not responsible for how those crackheads died. They did it to themselves."

"We're not blaming you," Eve said. "You don't have to run away."

Jean ignored her. "Pack up, Marguerite."

"We need you to take us to this island," Joe said.

"Why? I told you, there's nothing there."

"There may be more than you think."

Jean gave an exasperated exclamation. "Waste of time." He stood up and headed for the door. "You want to see the place? You have a guide. I'm through with this." He motioned to Dufour. "Come on, Jacques. I'll walk you to the boat and tell you where it is."

Joe moved after them. "I think I'll tag along and listen in. I want to make sure we're heading in the right direction."

Eve was about to follow Joe out of the house, but stopped beside Marguerite, who was pulling out clothes from a scratched, shabby pine bureau. "Where will you go?"

"That's none of your business."

"We really mean you no harm."

"Go away."

Eve started for the door.

"Wait." Marguerite was silent a moment. "We'll be all right. We'll go stay with friends for awhile until we're sure it's safe to come back. No one can find us in this swamp unless we want to be found."

"If you knew you'd have to run away like this, why did you take the money?"

Marguerite looked at her in wonder. "We needed it. It may not seem like a lot to you, but that much money will keep my children fed for months." She pulled out a faded duffel bag from beneath the bed. "It's worth the risk."

"Eve," Joe called from outside.

"Coming."

Joe's gaze raked her face as she came down the pier. "Did you convince her that we don't mean to toss her family in jail?"

"No, she wouldn't believe me. But she said the money was

worth the risk. Those two little boys . . . I wonder if they get enough to eat. Poverty *sucks*, Joe."

Joe nodded, his gaze on Jean. "That's not all it does."

She went still. "What do you mean?"

"It was a little too easy. It should have been harder to dig that information out of him."

She nodded thoughtfully. "And it was a little odd that they didn't know Etienne had a brother. From what we've heard, Etienne wasn't the most discreet person in the world."

He smiled. "I thought you were so concerned about those two little kids that you weren't paying attention."

"I'm sympathetic, not blind. You think Hebert got to Jean and set up a trap?"

"It's possible."

"Then his story is all a lie?"

"Not necessarily. The best lies are always the ones founded on truth." He gazed thoughtfully out at the bayou. "Etienne probably did spin them a tale about a drug lab, and Jean and his neighbors did turn a blind eye. That doesn't mean that Jules Hebert didn't pop in last night and offer them enough money to make our bribe seem piddling."

A chill went through her. "Then he'll be waiting at the island."

"That's my guess."

She drew a deep breath. "Good. Now how do we find a—"

"Later." He turned and helped her into the boat. "Leave it to me."

Like she'd left it to him when he'd dumped her by the road outside New Orleans?

No way.

Chapter Eighteen

HERE'S THE FIRST ISLAND." DUFOUR POINTED to the mound of mud looming ahead. "The one that your drug-dealing friends were afraid was too out in the open and decided to abandon. My cousin didn't get much done on it, did he?" A narrow pier weathered by water and time led to an equally weathered platform that must have been meant to be the foundation of the research facility. "According to Jean, the next island should be the one where you'll find your grave." He grinned. "Or lack of one. You sure you want to go on?"

"We want to go on," Joe said. "But pull over to this island first. I want to make sure cousin Jean wasn't lying about the shell content."

Eve looked at him in surprise.

Dufour shrugged. "Why not wait until you get to the right island?"

"Pull over."

Dufour hesitated and then guided the boat close to the pier. "You're wasting time."

"It's our time, and you've been well paid for it." Joe jumped out of the boat before helping Eve. "We'll be back in a minute, Dufour."

"What the hell are you doing?" Eve asked in a low voice as she followed him onto the platform.

"I saw Dufour press a button on his cell phone right before we turned the last bend in the bayou. It was probably a signal to Hebert. I'd bet he's waiting for us up ahead."

"And why are we here?"

"I'm getting rid of an encumbrance." Joe stood gazing out at the bayou. "You."

Eve stiffened. "Encumbrance?"

"You don't like the word. But I'm not going to be polite. You'll be in my way. You're staying here."

"The hell I am. You pushed me out of that car in New Orleans. You're not going to do it again."

"Yes, I am." He turned to face her and a ripple of shock went through her. His expression was colder and harder than she had ever seen it. "I'm not going to let either one of us die because you don't want to be left out. This is my job, not yours. I don't interfere when you're doing the work on your skulls. Don't interfere with me now."

"I'm just supposed to let you go out and maybe get yourself killed?"

"I'd be more likely to be killed if I had to worry about you getting in my way. That's not going to happen."

"And how are you going to stop me from going with you?"

"I'll put you down for a little nap if I have to. Don't make me do it, Eve."

And he would do it. She could see it in his expression. Joe had been heading in this direction since they had entered the swamp. The subdued excitement she had sensed had now broken free. Eve had never seen him more alive . . . or more dangerous. He was the hunter, the stalker, the warrior. "You can't wait to dive in and go after him."

He nodded. "I'm not like you. You want Hebert to be taken out because he's a danger, because it's necessary."

"And you're happy as hell to get the opportunity."

"You're learning a lot about me that you didn't know before." He smiled crookedly. "For instance, I never told you why I left the SEALs. You didn't want to know about that part of my life. It was too violent for you."

"Why did you leave the SEALs?"

"Because I liked it too much," he said simply. "And I was getting too close to the line no one should cross. I was a killing machine."

"That's not true. That's not you."

"It was me. It could be me again. It could be me now."

"No way. You couldn't—"

"Hey, Quinn," Dufour shouted from the boat. "Are you going to be all day?"

"He's getting impatient." Joe smiled. "Or maybe Hebert is impatient. We mustn't keep him waiting." He reached in his jacket pocket and handed her his gun. "Just in case."

"Are you crazy? You're going after Hebert without a gun?"

"I won't need it." He glanced down at the machete holstered on his belt. "In the swamp, guns aren't my weapon of choice." He turned and crossed the platform. "Keep cool until I get back."

"Joe, dammit."

He glanced over his shoulder at her. "You know I'm right. You know you'll be an albatross and could get me killed. You know you'd have to shoot me to keep me from going after him."

"I might do it."

He shook his head as he jumped into the boat. "Move, Dufour."

"*Joe.*"

"You shouldn't leave the lady alone," Dufour said. "What if a snake—"

"Go," Joe said.

Eve's hand clenched on the butt of the gun as she watched the boat glide away from the island. Joe's head was lifted as if he was scenting the wind. Maybe he was. Nothing would have surprised her in this strange, fierce Joe.

She shouldn't have let him go. She should have found a way to stop him.

Yet he was right. Joe knew what he was doing, and she could have put him in terrible danger if she'd gotten in his way. No matter how much she wanted to help, logic told her that going with him would have been a mistake.

Screw logic. She *hated* feeling this helpless.

She crossed to the edge of the platform, her gaze straining to get a last glimpse of Joe. Too late. The boat had already turned the bend of the bayou and was out of sight.

Come back.

Be safe, Joe.

Come back.

———

"It should be right around the next bend, Quinn," Dufour said without turning around. "A few minutes. No more." Where was that bastard Hebert? Dufour didn't want to be the one to take out Quinn. He didn't like the vibes the man was sending out.

Hebert had promised him things would go smoothly, and yet Quinn had already taken the woman out of the situation. He'd tell Hebert that he wasn't to blame, that it wasn't his fault.

Another moment passed.

No Hebert.

He would have to do it himself.

"There's your island. On the left." He cut the engine and gestured with one hand while the other reached surreptitiously into his knapsack for his gun. "It's not much of a place. The house is burnt to the ground, and look at that—"

He whirled with the gun in his hand and fired.

"What the—"

No one was there! Quinn's jacket and boots were on the bottom of the boat, but he was nowhere to be seen.

Then Dufour saw him, beneath the water on the left side of the boat, moving fast.

Shit. Lightning fast. Toward the boat, not away from it.

Dufour carefully aimed and fired.

———

Eve glanced at her watch. Jesus, it had been only fifteen minutes. It had seemed like an hour. She couldn't take this. What was she going to do? she thought bitterly. Go swimming after them through the swamp? She should never have let—

A shot.

Her heart leaped in panic. Joe didn't have a gun. It was here in her hand.

Another shot. Then another.

Oh, God.

"There's a very good chance he's dead, Eve."

She whirled to the right from where the voice had come, raising the pistol.

A bullet shattered the barrel of the gun, the force of the vibration whipping the weapon from her grip. She got a lightning glimpse of Hebert as she dropped to the ground. He was sitting in a canoe, pointing a rifle at her.

"So much violence. I would never have thought it of you." He cradled the rifle in his arm as he paddled closer to the pier. "And when I was trying to be merciful and give you a little more time. I could have killed you before you even knew I was here. You didn't hear me coming, did you?"

"No."

"That's because I don't believe in using motorboats when I'm in the swamp. A paddle can be whisper-silent if it's wielded by someone who knows what he's doing. Now, I'm going to get out of this boat. Don't move or I'll be forced to blow your head off." Hebert stood up and jumped onto the pier. "There. You can get up now."

Eve slowly got to her feet. "Where's Joe, Rick?"

"You recognize me? But then, my disguise wasn't that elaborate. I thought you'd been too ill that night to pay me much attention. Still, I did make Rick Vadim a likable fellow, didn't I?"

"Where's Joe?"

"The last time I caught sight of him, Dufour was going around a bend near the research island. I was going to take

Quinn out, but I couldn't get close enough to him without him seeing me."

"We thought you'd be waiting there on the island."

Hebert shook his head. "No cover. I had to get some distance away. But then I saw you weren't in the boat, and I knew he must have dropped you someplace. So I decided to let Dufour take his chances with Quinn and come back and find you."

"So you found me. Now what?"

"You heard the shots. We wait to see if Dufour comes back alone."

"Or if Joe comes back alone."

"There's always that possibility. I hear Quinn is very good."

"Better than you. Better than anyone." Eve's nails bit into her palms as her hands clenched into fists. "He's *not* dead."

"Then he'll come back for you. And I'll be here. You shouldn't have come here. It was useless. Do you think I wouldn't have come back and made sure there wasn't any evidence?"

"You're not infallible. You've made mistakes before. Evidently you made one here."

"I'm not the only one who makes mistakes. Quinn made a big one leaving you here."

"He thought I'd be safe. He wanted to protect me."

"And he's desperate to get back in your good graces. He wanted to fight the wicked monster and lay my carcass at your feet." Hebert smiled. "You know, I was sorry at the time that I had to pull you into the reconstruction by using your daughter, but it does keep paying dividends."

"Sorry?"

"I'm not made of stone."

"You're a murderer."

"So is a Medal of Honor winner who kills the enemy in battle. It's all a matter of means and ends."

"You're no hero."

"I never said I was. I just fight for what I believe in."

"And you believe it's right to kill me."

"I believe it's necessary. But I'm a little sad to do it. I admire your strength. I'll give you as long as I can before I put you down. I know how precious every moment can be." Hebert's gaze shifted to the bayou and he moved to the shadows at the side of the platform. "You just stand there where Quinn can see you when he comes around that curve in the bayou."

"And you'll pick him off."

"If Dufour hasn't done it for me. I paid him well enough to do the job, but I'm not sure he has the balls to tackle Quinn."

Eve drew a deep breath. "Joe doesn't have to die."

"Of course he does. You know better than that. He knows too much. It's my duty to keep the Cabal safe."

"The FBI already knows of its existence."

"Suspects." Hebert smiled faintly. "There's a difference. We have people in almost every FBI field office in the country. Evidence gets misplaced, information doesn't get to key personnel, agents who know too much have 'accidents.' "

"Like your brother. You killed him, didn't you?"

His smile disappeared. "He betrayed me; he betrayed the Cabal."

"How?"

"I made a mistake. Once I'd tracked them down, and found Bently and Simmons here doing research on fuel cells, I sent Etienne to work for Bently and Simmons to bring in supplies from the city. I thought it would be easier for him to destroy them and the prototypes from inside. They trusted him. Everyone trusted Etienne. He was everyone's friend."

"When he wasn't killing people?"

"He never killed anyone. I took him along because I hoped if the Cabal could see how loyal he was, they'd accept him. I taught him everything I could, but he had no heart for it. Still, I wanted him with me. I was lonely." He drew a deep breath. "I set the charge to blow up the facility, but Etienne was the one who went in to verify that they'd both been killed after the explosion. People were used to seeing Etienne go back and forth to the island, so it was less suspicious. He told me that he'd seen the bodies and buried them."

"He didn't?"

"He liked Bently and Simmons." Hebert's lips tightened. "He liked everybody. He was only a youngster, and it wouldn't have been hard for a smart man to manipulate him. I thought everything was fine. Until four months ago, when our sources in Detroit told the Cabal that there were new purchases being made similar to the ones that were bought by Bently two years ago. The order came from Louisiana."

"It could have been someone else experimenting."

"That wasn't quite all. During the last two months, three Cabal members from Louisiana have died under circumstances that were a little suspect. They could have been accidents, but all three were known to be against environmental restrictions. The Cabal doesn't like coincidences, and they don't like their members targeted."

"Revenge?"

"It was a possibility." Hebert smiled grimly. "Enough to scare Melton shitless. He was afraid he'd be next."

"But how would Bently or Simmons know who the Cabal members were?"

"Haven't you guessed? Bently belonged to the Cabal for over four years. He believed, as I do, that the power of the Cabal could work miracles. He was the one who brought Simmons's invention to our attention. He wanted our help. Then when it was decided that the fuel cell had to disappear, he dropped out of sight and took Simmons with him."

"They sent you after them."

"And I found them. I always find them."

"But this time you fouled up, didn't you? You failed your precious Cabal."

"I *didn't* fail them," he said, stung. "I made a mistake, that's all. A mistake I corrected. After we heard from Detroit, we had to make sure that both the research and the men who'd done it were destroyed. Melton asked me if I was positive Simmons and Bently were dead. Of course I was positive. Hadn't the person closest to me, the only man I trusted, told me that they were? But they asked me if I'd seen the bodies myself. What could I say? So they told me to go get the skeletons for DNA testing. I was in Barcelona at the time and I called Etienne and told him to re-trieve the skeletons and meet me at Sarah Bayou near Baton Rouge. Melton had already arranged for a forensic anthropolo-gist and DNA expert to meet us at the church, so that we could rush the tests." He was silent a moment. "When Etienne showed up with the coffin, I could tell something was wrong the minute I saw him."

"He didn't have the skeletons?"

"Neither one. Just that damn skull. At first, he told me that the skeletons had been stolen. Then when he could see I didn't believe him, he told me he'd destroyed both skeletons but had brought me Harold Bently's skull."

"Why?"

"He thought it would get me off the hook with the Cabal. He'd made sure the skull was almost impossible to identify, but he didn't want to get me in trouble. He was proud of himself for thinking of a way to save me and still keep the Cabal from getting what it wanted."

"But it didn't save Etienne, did it?"

"He didn't understand. I talked to him for hours trying to persuade him to tell me if we'd killed both men, and to whom the skull belonged. He wouldn't tell me anything. All he'd say was that what the Cabal was doing was wrong and we should do what was right. He wanted me to break with the Cabal." He shook his head. "He didn't understand. The world would be chaos without the Cabal to guarantee order. There have to be checks and balances. Someone has to guide our path."

My God, he actually believes what he's saying. "I'm with Etienne. I don't understand that concept, either. It's just propaganda. So you killed him?"

"You make it sound so easy," Hebert said bitterly. "You think I wanted to do it? I loved him. If there had been a way to save him, I would have done it."

"There's always a choice."

"I had to tell the Cabal what he'd done. It was my duty. He'd betrayed them."

"And they told you what to do."

"Yes, Melton said to find a way to lure him to the church and dispose of him there. It was isolated enough for our purpose, and for what I had to do." He paused. "I told Etienne that we'd find a way to fool the Cabal. I'd steal a skeleton from one of the old graveyards outside of town and put it in the coffin, so that we'd have something for the experts who were supposed to be waiting at the church to examine it." He swallowed. "It was easy. He thought it was a wonderful idea. He wanted to believe me. He always wanted to believe me."

"Until the minute he died?"

"Until the minute he died." Hebert's eyes glittered with tears. "It was a merciful death. He was happy until the end."

"No death is merciful."

"It could have been worse. Melton told me that I had to make him talk before he died. That's why he wanted me to take him to the church—so that I'd have all the privacy I needed. I'm very good at making people talk. I know every agonizing way. I couldn't do that to Etienne. He was very strong, very stubborn. It would have been a long, long time before he broke, and then he would have had to die anyway. So I disobeyed and killed him quickly." His lips twisted. "Melton wasn't pleased. I had to find a way to make amends for destroying any information Etienne might have given me."

"And you found me."

"I found you."

"But you couldn't know if Etienne had told you the truth about Bently's skull."

Hebert shook his head. "I thought I knew him well enough to know if he was lying about it—although he'd managed to fool me for two years. I could only hope." He paused. "But after you became ill, I knew that either Bently or Simmons must still be alive. One of them wanted you dead, so that no one would know that he was still alive and working on the fuel cells. I questioned Marie Letaux that night before she died, but she genuinely had no idea who had hired her. She got a phone call and then money in her mailbox, and the promise of a final payment when she'd done the job. She kept saying that it was only supposed to make you ill. That it wasn't her fault." He shrugged. "She was no help to me. I had to wait until you'd finished the reconstruction to find out which one had hired her."

"How did you find out the skull was Bently's?"

"A mole in Rusk's FBI office. Jennings told Rusk right before he died that your reconstruction was definitely Bently. All hell broke loose after Jennings was killed; it was easy enough to pick up the info."

"Then your mole must have found out what Jennings discovered about Boca Raton. What was it?"

Hebert smiled faintly as he shook his head. "So that you can ride to the rescue? You still think you're going to live through this, don't you? I've always found that no one really believes they're going to die until they do. I assure you, Eve, if I told you what was going to happen, you still wouldn't be able to save the old tiger. The plan's already in motion, and calculated down to the last gasp."

"Then you shouldn't mind telling me."

"But I do. Life still has to have some mysteries. You'd only fret, and your last moments should be worry-free."

"You're not worry-free. Even if you kill me, you're still going to have to contend with Simmons."

"I'll find him. I know who I'm looking for now. It's difficult for a man to hide in this world, particularly if the Cabal is looking for him." Hebert's glance shifted again to the bayou, and he moved to the edge of the platform. "Quinn's been a long time. I'm beginning to wonder if I should—"

He shrieked.

A machete blade had bitten through the bone and sinew of

the hand holding his gun. The weapon dropped from his almost-severed right hand, and Eve dove across the deck to get it.

"No!" Joe spat out the reed between his teeth. "Stay away from him." He lunged up from the mud beside the platform, grabbed Hebert's knees, and jerked him backward into the mud.

Hebert was struggling desperately. She suddenly saw a glint of metal in his left hand.

Oh, God, Hebert had a knife. And Joe had thrown his weapon at him.

Eve lifted the gun to aim at Hebert, but the two men were rolling, sinking, fighting in the watery mud. She might hit Joe.

She jumped off the deck into the mud and waded toward them.

"Joe, get away from him for a minute. I can't—"

Hebert's knife was gone, sent spinning into the mud by a blow from the edge of Joe's hand.

And then Joe was on top of Hebert. His hands closed in a stranglehold on Hebert's throat. He pushed his head under the mud and held him there. Hebert's arms and legs flailed helplessly as he struggled for breath. The mud was suffocating him.

"Joe," Eve whispered.

For an instant she wasn't sure he had heard her, and when he glanced sideways she flinched at the sheer blind ferocity she saw in his expression.

Joe drew a deep breath, and then his grasp strengthened and she heard a snap as he broke Hebert's neck.

He released Hebert, stood, and stepped back. "I expected a harder time with him."

"Why?" Eve drew a shaky breath. "You almost severed his hand when you threw that machete."

"He was pointing a gun at you."

She shivered as she stared down at Jules Hebert lying in the mud, his face submerged beneath the surface.

"Did he hurt you?"

Eve turned to look at Joe. Covered with mud, he was still almost as terrifying a figure as the creature that had lunged out of that muck and unleashed a spearhead of death, blood, and violence.

"Dammit, did he hurt you?" Joe repeated.

"He didn't touch me. How about you?"

"A few bruises. Not that you could tell under all this mud. You're almost as muddy as I am. Why the hell didn't you stay out of it?"

Because she couldn't stand by when she saw him in danger. "He had a knife."

"Did I look like I was helpless?"

No, he had looked absolutely terrifying. She tried to smile. "You reminded me of Swamp Thing."

"That's what I feel like." Joe grasped Eve's shoulders and glared down at her. "You listen to me. Never again. This is the last time I'll let you risk your neck. I can't take it. Screw women's lib." He turned, waded through the mud toward Hebert's canoe, and crawled into it. "I'll be right back. I'm going to take Hebert's canoe around the bend to where I left Dufour's motorboat. We'll go back to town and clean up."

"What happened to Dufour?"

"He won't bother us any more."

I was a killing machine. I could be again.

Eve shivered, and her glance shifted to Hebert. "And what will we do about him?"

"Let him rot." Joe grimaced. "Okay, I know. I'm an insensitive bastard about the dear departed. We'll tell the police in Houma where we left him."

"Not yet."

"No? That's a surprise."

"The Cabal doesn't know that he's dead and we're alive. It may buy us time before they send anyone else after us."

"Did he tell you anything about what was happening in Boca Raton?"

"Not much." Yet Hebert had said something . . . Surely there was some fragment of sense in his words that she could examine. "Maybe. He said something about a tiger and us not being able to stop it. That it had all been planned down to the last gasp." She rubbed her temple. "I don't know. I can't think."

Joe studied her. "I don't like the way you're shaking."

"I'm just cold."

"Chilled and shocked and wet to the bone. October is no time to take a mud bath."

"You did."

"Yeah, but I don't have a sensitive nerve in my body."

"That's bullshit."

"You really aren't feeling yourself if you're giving me credit for tender feelings. I've got to get you back to the hotel and a hot shower." Joe's paddle cut into the water. "Don't move a muscle."

Easy to say. It seemed that every muscle in Eve's body was trembling with cold and fatigue. She should try to think, but her mind was just as dulled as her body.

Fight it. There wasn't much time. Try to think what Hebert had said.

Tiger. Something about a tiger and his last gasp. That meant death, a killing. Why couldn't she remember?

She had to remember, or Hebert's death would mean nothing. He would still win and the killing would go on.

There wasn't much time.

————

Joe turned on the shower and pushed Eve naked under the warm spray. Another moment and he was in the shower with her, soaping her hair with shampoo.

"I can do it. Take care of yourself."

"Shut up." He soaped her body from shoulders to feet and then pushed her to the front of the shower to rinse off. "Just stand there and let the water warm you while I get some of the dirt off me."

"No time. Have to think. Someone's going to die, Joe."

"I know. You told me in the boat coming here. Several times."

"Did I? I hate death. I hate it."

"I know you do."

"I don't understand killers like Hebert. He didn't care about the death of anyone, except for his brother. It didn't matter to him about other people who have fathers or brothers or little girls . . ."

"Shh. Are you warmer now?"

"He was going to kill Jane and my mother. Two wonderful lives just snuffed—"

"Are you warmer?"

He had asked that before. She thought about it. The shaking was gone and so was that icy lethargy. "Yes."

"Good." He was out of the shower and reaching for a towel. "Then let's get you dry and into bed."

"I can—"

"Hush."

"You know, I didn't really believe in the Cabal before I heard Hebert talking about it. It wasn't real to me. I believe in it now. They're the ones who pointed Hebert at Jane and my mother and told him to kill them. Someone has to stop them. So much evil . . ."

"Yes."

"Jennings said it was right there before him, but he didn't see it. What didn't he see, Joe?"

"We'll figure it out later." He wrapped her in a dry towel and gently pushed her toward the bedroom. "Climb in bed while I dry off."

"If it was right there before him, then it was right there before us, too."

"The only thing right before you is that bed."

"I can't go to sleep. I have to put it together."

"You're not going to put anything together until you get some rest." He took her arm and drew her toward the bed. "Come on. I'll hold you and keep you warm, and you can think your little heart out." He slipped into bed, pulled her down beside him, and cuddled her close. "Better?"

Better? Warmth and safety against death's cold inevitability. "Don't let me go to sleep."

"No guarantees. You're on your own. The only promise you'll get from me is that I'll always be beside you to wake you in the morning."

Wonderful promise, beautiful promise . . .

Bittersweet promise.

"You're stiffening against me," he said. "Don't do it. Take this moment, Eve. I want to give it to you."

And she wanted to take it. She relaxed against him.

"That's it."

"This isn't a good idea."

"Shh." He stroked her hair. "Never argue with Swamp Thing."

God, she was actually smiling. Or was she crying? Maybe it was a little of both. "I wouldn't dream of it. If Swamp Thing will just shut up so I can try to think."

"That can be arranged." He kissed her temple. "Close your eyes; it will help you to concentrate."

He just wanted her to go to sleep.

She was very much afraid he was going to get his wish. Her lids were too heavy to stay open. . . .

No, fight it. Go over everything Nathan and Jennings had told them. Clear her mind and remember everything she'd learned from Hebert in those last moments before Joe had killed him.

And keep her damn eyes open.

———

HOUMA
3:35 A.M.
October 27

It was right there before me.
There's nothing you can do about the old tiger.
It's been timed down to the last gasp.
Royal weddings . . . The Olympics. . . .

"Oh, my God." Eve jerked upright in bed. "It's a funeral, Joe."

"What?" Joe rose up on one elbow. "What are you talking about?"

"It *is* a meeting of the Cabal at Boca Raton. But they had to have a reason. No Olympics, no wedding. It's a funeral. There's going to be a funeral so important in Boca Raton that it would validate the presence of dignitaries from all over the world."

Joe nodded slowly. "It's possible."

"Why else would the Cabal send their number-one assassin to Boca?" She felt sick. "Christ, I wonder how many important people have been killed to provide the Cabal a reason to meet."

"Wait a minute. We're not sure you're right."

"We're not sure I'm wrong." Eve swung her feet to the floor. "But Hebert talked as if his target wasn't dead yet. He said I couldn't stop it, but that means he's still alive. Maybe we can find a way to save him."

"Providing we can find out who he is."

"He's well known enough to attract worldwide notice." She was thinking quickly. "Probably not an entertainer or movie star. He lives in Boca Raton and has plans to be buried there. Otherwise the meeting would have been planned for somewhere else." She reached for her telephone. "What's Nathan's cell number?"

Joe reached in his pocket and brought out his phone book. "You're right, Nathan's a newspaperman. He should be able to track the target down."

"And he's in Boca right now." She was rapidly dialing Nathan's number. "Which is where we need to be. Will you call and get us reservations out of New Orleans while I talk to Nathan?"

Chapter Nineteen

CHRIST." NATHAN WAS SILENT FOR a moment after Eve had finished speaking. "It's got to be Franklin Copeland."

Shock rippled through Eve. "What?"

"I'm surprised you didn't guess. It's been all over the newspapers and television for the past couple days. The Old Tiger is a sick man."

"We haven't been paying any attention to the news."

"I can see how you've been a little busy."

"Old Tiger," she repeated. "That's what Hebert called him."

"That was Copeland's nickname when he was a colonel in Vietnam before he became president. War hero, ex-President of the United States, and for the last fifteen years, he's been known for his work with UNESCO. I'd say he'd warrant a pretty impressive guest list for his funeral."

"Is he supposed to be buried in Boca?"

"I don't know. I can find out." Silence. "Jesus, I met Copeland once when he was lecturing in New Orleans. I liked him. He's one hell of a guy."

Eve had never met him, but she'd liked what she'd known of him, too. He had seemed a warm, intelligent man with no delusions of grandeur.

"We're talking as if he's dead already," Nathan said. "What the hell can we do to save him?"

"What's he suffering from?" She inhaled sharply. "Anthrax?"

"No."

It had been her first thought, connecting Copeland's illness to the anthrax scare in Boca Raton a year or two ago.

"Then what is it?"

"Nothing suspicious. He has heart problems aggravated by severe asthma. The asthma seemed to be pretty well under control for the past couple years, but he's had several attacks in the past few weeks. He's been in and out of the hospital three times—the last bout of asthma triggered a heart attack."

"Asthma . . . What could trigger an attack? Some kind of poison?"

"Beats me. But the Secret Service should be able to find out, once they know what's happening. You're on your way down here?"

"As soon as we can get a plane. Find us a place to stay outside the city. We have to keep a low profile. We don't want anyone to know Hebert's dead."

"That's smart. Then you'll want me to go to Copeland's Secret Service team right away and tell them what we know."

"Right."

"I'm on it. Maybe they can save the old guy. Let me know what flight you're on and I'll meet you at the airport."

"God, I hope it's not too late." She hung up and turned to Joe. "Franklin Copeland."

He gave a low whistle. "It would fit. Not only famous, but loved by the masses."

"And they're killing him just for an excuse to have a god-damn meeting." She could feel the tears sting her eyes. "I wish they'd all burn in hell."

"It must be a pretty important meeting," he said thoughtfully. "Etienne told Nathan they never meet in person unless something critical is in the balance. I'd be interested in knowing what's on their agenda."

"So would I. We'll find out." She swallowed to ease the tightness of her throat. "But it's Copeland who's important right now. What time can we get out of New Orleans?"

"First flight is ten A.M. to Fort Lauderdale. It's about a forty-minute drive to Boca. There's nothing direct."

She started for the bathroom. "Then let's get out of here."

Nathan was waiting for them at the gate. She didn't have to hear his first sentence. It was all there in his face.

"Sorry. Copeland died two hours ago."

Disappointment flooded her. She had been hoping against hope that they could save him. She felt the tears sting her eyes. "I really hoped—"

"Let's get out of here." Joe took her arm and guided her

down the corridor. "What about the Secret Service? You got through to them?"

Nathan nodded. "For all the good it did me. It took me time I didn't have to convince them they had to take me seriously. They thought I was just some wild-ass reporter trying to drum up a story. Then they called Rusk at the FBI to verify there was an ongoing investigation about the Cabal."

"Did it help?"

He shook his head. "Rusk was killed in an automobile accident yesterday afternoon on his way home from the office."

She stiffened in shock. "What?"

"Hit-and-run as he was crossing the street to go to the supermarket."

Another death. No, another murder. Christ, would it never stop? "The Cabal."

"That's my guess. First Jennings, and then Rusk. They're plugging all the possible leaks."

"They didn't catch who did it?"

Nathan shook his head. "A witness said the car was an old beat-up Buick. The driver was possibly of Hispanic descent."

"But the Secret Service had to be suspicious that Rusk had been killed so conveniently."

"His death could have been unrelated. No one in Rusk's office knew anything about Copeland or anything that was going on down here."

Evidence gets misplaced . . . agents have "accidents."

Hebert's words came back to her with chilling impact.

"So they wouldn't listen to you," she said dully.

"I didn't say that. When they decided there was a small possibility the threat to Copeland could be genuine, they started to move. But it was too late. Copeland was already dead." He made a face. "I'm feeling guilty as hell I didn't get them to move faster."

"I don't know if we could have done any better," Eve said. "There's not even any proof Copeland was the target. Is there going to be an autopsy?"

Nathan nodded. "I hope so. I believe I convinced Copeland's Secret Service agent Wilson to do it. But any investigation will be done very discreetly. They don't want either his family or his high-powered friends to be on the attack if they find my story is bull-shit. They want Copeland's death to be as dignified as his life."

"So the funeral will go on."

Nathan nodded. "So it seems."

"And the Cabal has what it wants."

"At least the Secret Service knows that they may be meeting here." Nathan opened the passenger door of a gray Chevrolet rental car. "That could lead to something."

"Except they don't know who they're looking for." Eve got into the car. "And if they don't find any evidence Copeland was murdered, it may stop right there."

"But we know one member of the Cabal who will be here," Joe said. "Melton."

Eve shook her head. "If he even comes. Hebert said he was scared shitless that he'd be targeted by Thomas Simmons. Melton suspected that the deaths of three Cabal members from his state weren't the accidents they appeared. Melton thought he'd be next."

"A meeting of the Cabal probably doesn't happen that often, and it seems to be a pretty big deal," Joe said. "I imagine Melton would have to have cast-iron proof there was a threat to his life to be excused from coming."

"That's what I thought." Nathan backed out of the parking

space. "So we still have a ball game. We trail Melton until we find out where they're meeting, and then have the FBI close in."

Eve shook her head. "What good would that do? These are important people, leading citizens of their countries. How can we prove they're doing anything illegal? Do you think the FBI is going to take any action? It's our word against theirs."

Nathan's lips tightened. "I'm not going to let it go. I've been cooling my heels down here, searching for the Cabal, searching for Simmons, and now I have a lead. Okay, we may not be able to call in the big guns. But we can shine a bright light on their damn secret society. We can get names and faces."

"And maybe something more concrete," Joe said thoughtfully. "Long-range listening devices. Videos. Photographs."

"Their security has got to be fairly ironclad," Eve said. "It will be difficult to get that close."

"Their top man, Hebert, isn't on the scene. That may give us a little opening."

"I doubt it. They wouldn't rely exclusively on Hebert. And they're going to be suspicious when they can't contact him. It might make them be even more careful."

Nathan looked at Eve. "Are you saying you want to bow out?"

"No way. I'm just telling it the way I see it. We may not get everything we want, but I'll take whatever we can get."

Nathan smiled. "And, like Quinn said, it may be more than we think. I may get my Pulitzer after all."

The small, white beach house to which Nathan took them was a few miles outside the city. "This is the best I could do in the short time I had. I handled the rental over the phone with a broker."

"It will be fine." Eve got out of the car. "As long as it's private."

"I'll just take a look around the grounds. Be with you in a minute." Joe strode around the house and down to the shore.

"The key should be under the palm tree in a lockbox. . . ." Nathan found the box, pressed the combination, and unlocked the front door. "You go inside. I'll see if I can do anything to help Quinn check out the area."

"He doesn't need help."

"I'll do it anyway. I'm feeling responsible, since Galen isn't underfoot." He added fervently, "Thank God."

Eve wearily shook her head as she closed the door. All this concern for her safety, and yet no one had been able to keep that poor old man safe. Not even his Secret Service guards. How had Hebert managed to kill him?

She crossed the room and turned on the TV set to CNN.

Franklin Copeland's face appeared on the screen. They were running an obituary segment and she sank down on the couch to watch it. His wife, Lily, was still alive, and they showed her at the hospital when Copeland had suffered a heart attack a few weeks ago. She was a thin, elegant woman in her seventies; the bond between husband and wife was clear. Toward the end of the obituary they listed Copeland's many accomplishments and works for charity. It was an impressive list. She hadn't been aware that he was involved with Habitat for Humanity. She hadn't paid much attention to the details of the man's life.

But she'd damn well pay attention to his death.

Nathan and Joe came into the house a few minutes later. Joe dropped down on the couch beside Eve. "Anything?"

"The funeral is going to be at St. Catherine's Cathedral day after tomorrow."

"October twenty-ninth," Joe said.

"Right on schedule." She nodded at a TV shot of Kim Basinger getting on a plane in Los Angeles. "She traveled to Africa with Copeland for UNESCO. She's on her way to the funeral."

"I doubt if she's one of the Cabal," Nathan said dryly.

"Before her they showed James Tarrant, the British media mogul, hurrying from a meeting in London to the airport. He was quoted as saying the world had lost a great man, and he was going to pay homage."

"Touching," Joe said.

Nathan nodded. "It's going to be hard to separate the gold from the dross. But Melton may be the key." He turned to leave. "I'm going to the local newspaper office to see if I can find out when Melton is due to show up on the scene. I'll let you know as soon as I do."

"And we need some photos of Thomas Simmons. Can you get them for us?"

"Ah, the shadow man."

It was an apt description, Eve thought. Simmons had been lurking in the darkness all along, overshadowed by Hebert's looming menace. "That 'shadow man' tried to kill me, and evidently has killed at least three Cabal members. I want to be able to recognize him."

"I'm one step ahead of you. When I first came down here, I went on the Internet to the Cal Tech site and pulled off a staff picture and one from the college newspaper. I'll make a couple copies for you and Quinn."

"What was the name of Copeland's Secret Service agent you

talked to? Wilson?" Joe asked. "It's a little soon, but I'm going to see if they found out anything from the autopsy yet."

"Yeah, Pete Wilson." Nathan grimaced. "I hope you have better luck with him than I did." The door shut behind him.

Eve looked at Joe. "What next?"

"We need a car. We need surveillance equipment. We obviously need information. With any luck Nathan will supply the info. I'd better get busy on the rest."

"Wait." She hesitated. "Let's call Galen." She held up her hand as he opened his mouth to protest. "Among other things, Galen is a provider, and he does the job very well. He has contacts everywhere. I'll bet he could pick up a phone and get us anything from a space suit to an atomic bomb. We need him, Joe."

"We don't need him." He hesitated and then grimaced. "But we could use him."

Her eyes widened in surprise.

"I can work with him. He brought me into the picture in Baton Rouge because our personal differences didn't mean a damn to him if it meant keeping you safe. They can't matter to me, either. Do you want to call him, or should I?"

"I'll do it."

"Good." Joe headed for the kitchen. "I'll make coffee and then call Wilson and the precinct to find out if Carol's seen any forensic reports yet."

Eve nodded absently as she dialed Galen's number.

"Hebert's dead? Hallelujah," Galen said when she'd finished filling him in. "And what an interesting way for Quinn to kill him. I approve."

"I'm sure that will make him happy. Can you get us the items we need? It would be better if the Cabal doesn't know Joe and I are still alive."

"Piece of cake. Give me your address and phone number."

"I don't know what—" She saw the number on the phone and rattled it off, and then checked the address on the mailbox outside.

"Good." Galen said. "I'm moving. I think Jonas Faber is still in Orlando. He can help."

"Who's Jonas Faber?"

"Ask him no questions, he'll tell you no lies. Just accept that he can produce. And I'll work on finding out where the meeting will be."

"Nathan's already on Melton."

"Don't send a boy to do a man's job. I'll get on the tech stuff right away." He hung up.

"Well?" Joe stood in the kitchen doorway.

"He said he's moving. Did you find out anything from Wilson?"

Joe shook his head. "No autopsy."

"What?"

"The attending doctor said he knew exactly why Copeland died, and it was natural causes. He was allergic to mold, and lately the allergy had increased to a dangerous degree. He was tested a number of times in the hospital and it was always the same problem. They did everything to maintain sterile surroundings and keep mold away from him, but he refused to leave his home here in Florida or live in a bubble. Mold is everywhere down here."

"An autopsy might show something else."

He shook his head again. "He's not about to disturb the

family without concrete proof. The body could always be exhumed if the investigation proved he had been murdered."

———————

A black Chevrolet rental SUV was delivered to the door two hours later.

After dinner that night they received a phone call and then a visit from Jonas Faber. He was a small, cheerful little man who asked Joe very politely to accompany him to his van.

Joe came back twenty minutes later shaking his head.

"Something wrong?"

"Not if I want to open a spy shop or start trading in small arms. The FBI doesn't have as sophisticated surveillance equipment as Faber brought us. He parked a damn tech van in our backyard." He smiled. "Complete with tutorial. He's not going to let me go until he's sure I know how to operate every single camera and piece of equipment. He even wanted to show me how to use an AK-seven. I told him I wasn't exactly an amateur with firearms."

A tech van? She had only asked for surveillance equipment. "It seems when Galen said he was moving, he meant it."

———————

Nathan called an hour later. "Melton is in Boca. He arrived two hours ago, and went directly to Copeland's home to pay his respects to the widow. Bastard."

"You're following him?"

"Every step."

"Be careful."

"Hey, no problem. I value my neck."

"I have a favor to ask. I'm going to the funeral service day after tomorrow."

"Why?"

"I want to be there. I want to look at every person who goes into the church and be able to recognize them later. Will you find me a black hat with a dark veil?"

"You probably aren't going to accomplish anything by going."

She knew that. She also knew that she wanted to pay her last respects to Copeland in person. He had been a great man, and along with regret she felt a sense of . . . connection. "It can't hurt. I don't want to sit here and do nothing. Joe's going to be busy familiarizing himself with that surveillance equipment."

"You'll have to stay out with the crowd in the street. You have to be on the A-list to get inside."

"I'm going to be there."

"Okay. I'll drop your hat and Simmons's photos by the house after I'm sure Melton's tucked into his hotel for the night."

————

"Here's your black hat." Nathan handed her a plastic bag. "It wasn't easy. The regular stores were closed, so I went to an all-night drugstore and bought a black straw beach hat and a black sheer scarf. You'll have to rig a veil out of that."

"I'll manage. Thanks, Nathan."

"No problem." He reached in his pocket and pulled out an envelope. "Simmons."

She drew out the pictures. One was an informal photo taken in front of a building. The other was a close-up in the college newspaper at the time Simmons had been hired by Cal Tech. Professor Thomas Simmons was thirtyish, with regular features except for a slightly pouty lower lip. He was wearing horn-rimmed glasses and smiling confidently into the camera. "Nice-looking. It's hard to believe he's a murderer."

"Maybe he popped his cork when the Cabal tried to blow him up." Nathan looked around the room. "Where's Quinn?"

"Out back in the tech van." She made a face. "He's fascinated by all that equipment. He's decided to make me the audio tech."

"Pretty complex stuff."

"Not really. Faber made sure it was user-friendly."

"Well, then, I'd better get back to the hotel and keep an eye on Melton so that you'll have something to record." He turned to leave. "I'll keep in touch, but I'm going to stick close as glue to Melton now that he's on the scene. I'll meet you day after tomorrow in front of the church."

"Right." After the door closed behind Nathan, Eve took the hat and scarf out of the plastic bag. Both items were cheap and flimsy, but it didn't matter. They would keep her from being recognized and wouldn't appear out of place.

"Did Nathan bring the photo?"

She turned to see Joe standing in the kitchen doorway. "Two." She held out the envelope. "Finished for the night?"

He shook his head absently as he gazed at the photos.

"Clean-cut. I told Nathan that it was hard to believe he was a murderer."

"I'm not having any trouble. But I've seen more murderers than you have."

"Maybe I'm just confused by this whole scenario," Eve said wearily. "Thomas Simmons was probably a very good man with a wonderful future. Now his life's been twisted out of shape and he's become a killer. It's difficult to understand."

"Not to me. Killing is a choice. You make a decision and then you weigh the consequences. I'm a cop, but I have no problem scraping up the remains of some of the scum out there on the streets." He jammed the pictures in his pocket and turned away. "But he made the wrong choice when he tried to kill you."

———

BOCA RATON
October 29

The crowds were six deep on the roped-off streets outside St. Catherine's Cathedral. It took Eve a few minutes to locate Nathan standing near the back of the throng and then make her way toward him.

"Eve?" Nathan peered at her features through the dark veil.

She nodded. "Is Melton inside?"

"Thirty minutes ago. He probably wanted to get his share of the limelight before the President arrived."

"The President is here?"

"Arrived ten minutes ago." Nathan nodded at four dark-suited men in sunglasses, standing on the steps. "Secret Service."

"I hope they can protect the President. They didn't do a very good job with Copeland." She stared at the door of the church. "I'm glad President Andreas is here. Copeland deserves all the honors he can get."

"You're taking this very personally."

She shrugged. "I guess I'm feeling a little guilty. If I'd figured out the situation here sooner, maybe we could have saved Copeland."

"And maybe not. You didn't know that Hebert was targeting Copeland until it was almost certainly too late for him."

"Minutes can matter when a man is dying." She watched blindly as limousine after limousine pulled up before the church and deposited their passengers. "I don't know if— My God." She grabbed Nathan's arm. "Tell me I'm crazy. Is that Thomas Simmons?"

Nathan stiffened. "Where?"

"Across the street. Green polo shirt. Hell, he's not three yards from that Secret Service man." Her gaze clung to the man staring intently at the arriving guests. Same pouty lips, same horn-rimmed glasses . . . "It *is* him, Nathan."

"If not, it's his double." Nathan was edging toward the front of the crowd. "Let's see if we can get closer."

Eve pushed after Nathan through the crowd. Simmons. My God, Simmons . . .

Thomas Simmons suddenly lifted his head and looked directly at Nathan, who was only a few yards away now.

Nathan smiled. "Hi, could we have a few—"

Simmons turned and dove back into the crowd, pushing people out of his path. As the crowd thinned out down the street, he broke into a run.

"Shit." Nathan took off after him.

Eve tried to run, too, but she was slowed by the crowd until she reached the end of the block. Had they gone around the corner?

Yes, she could see Nathan. . . .

She broke into a sprint.

Almost a block away, Simmons was diving into a beige Toyota.

Nathan's pace increased. "Stop. You can't get away. Let me—"

The Toyota peeled away from the curb and down the street.

Nathan stopped and was cursing a blue streak as he watched the car vanish out of sight.

"It was him, right?" Eve was beside him now. "It was Simmons."

"I think so." Nathan reached in his pocket and took out a notebook. "And I hope to hell I remember that license number." He scrawled down a number on the pad. "Not that it will probably do us any good if it's a rental. Do you think Quinn can check it out?"

She nodded as she took the paper. "But what was he doing here?"

"Who knows? If he did kill those other Cabal members, then he could be picking out his next target. Or he could be following Melton, like I am. Or if he's a total wacko, it could be any reason." He leaned against the wall and tried to catch his breath. "Jesus, I've got to lose weight. That run almost killed me."

"At least we know he's here."

"Well, he's definitely not a shadow." He wrinkled his nose. "And he's in far better shape than I am." He straightened away from the wall. "Now I've got to get back and wait for Melton to dry his crocodile tears and come out of the church. Coming?"

She shook her head. "I'll phone this license number to Joe and go back to the house."

LAKE COTTAGE
ATLANTA, GEORGIA
3:05 P.M.
October 29

The funeral service had already started when Galen switched on the television set. Jonathan Andreas, the President, was standing at the podium giving the first eulogy.

Full house, Galen thought, as the camera panned the audience. There must be at least fifteen hundred people at the service. He recognized several dignitaries: Tony Blair, Norman Schwarzkopf, Colin Powell. With this kind of firepower, it would be perfectly reasonable to have—

"Could I see you for a minute, Galen?" David Hughes was standing at the doorway.

"A problem?"

"Maybe." He was frowning. "I just don't understand. It's not right. Come and take a look."

Chapter Twenty

IT'S NOT A LOCAL RENTAL CAR." Joe hung up the phone. "They're running a computer search now. It shouldn't be too long."

Eve frowned. "I hope not. The idea of Simmons hovering makes me very uneasy."

"If we can nail down where he is now, I guarantee he won't ever make you uneasy again."

She had a sudden chilling memory of Joe and Hebert struggling in the mud. "Why do you always think that you're the one who has to—"

Her cell phone rang.

"Saved by the bell," Joe murmured as she pressed the answer button.

"I've found it." Nathan's voice was shaking with excitement. "After the funeral, Melton met with a man outside his hotel. It was at the newsstand and it was only for a few minutes. I knew Melton was going to be surrounded by reporters, so I took a chance and followed the guy."

"Where?"

"Fort Lauderdale Airport."

"What?"

"Well, not actually the airport. There's a deserted naval air station down there. It's being fought over by the local historical society and the airport. It's the base from where those flyers took off in 1945 and were lost in the Bermuda Triangle. There's a big concrete building that is evidently going to be the meeting place. It's enclosed by a chain-link fence, completely private, and guarded by at least five men besides the guy who met with Melton."

"An airport," Eve murmured.

"It's perfect. The members leave Boca separately sometime after the funeral, presumably to fly out to their homes. They congregate at the naval base, have their meeting, and then go on to the airport at a staggered pace and board their flights. Very smart."

"But when?"

"Probably the middle of the night. They'd want the area absolutely deserted. I'll know when Melton moves, and I'll call you. Let me talk to Quinn."

Eve handed the phone to Joe.

He was on the phone for only a few minutes. "I'm on my way." He hung up the phone and turned to Eve. "He wants me to take the surveillance equipment to the naval base and set it up outside the fence. He said there's no way of getting near the building with all those guards, but there's cover close to a drainage ditch a little distance from the base. Shouldn't be a problem. The camera and audio equipment have a range of over a mile."

She nodded. "Let's go."

"Eve."

"Don't you say a word. Ever since I got here I've been twiddling my thumbs, watching all those hypocrites on television tell the world what a fine man just died."

"Some of them were sincere."

"But which ones? I need to find out." Eve headed for the door. "I need the whole damn world to find out." She glanced over her shoulder. "And there's not going to be any leaving me on the roadside or some deserted island. We're in this together. Do you understand?"

"Okay, but we have to—" He broke off as his phone rang. He punched the button. "Quinn." He listened for a moment. "What the hell?" He stiffened. "Plastic?"

———

FORT LAUDERDALE NAVAL AIR STATION
2:45 A.M.
October 30

The windows of the white concrete building were covered so that no light showed from the outside. Guards in dark clothing patrolled the area with Dobermans.

"Here comes the next one," Joe murmured as he focused the

video camera. He kept it trained on the dark sedan as the door opened and a man got out. "I recognize this one, too. Big time. Sheikh Hassan Ben Abar."

She nodded. "OPEC."

The last hour had been an incredible parade of well-known wheeler-dealers from every walk of life. Eve took the listening device from her ear. "I can't hear much right now. It's cutting out. Every time an airplane takes off I get static."

"Have you heard anything interesting?"

"Maybe. It's definitely not small talk, but I'm not a linguist. I need to zero in on a conversation between some of the English members." She adjusted the earpiece, turned one of the knobs on the panel in front on her. "That's better." She listened for a moment. "Something about a gorge. They need a clear majority because it's high risk. . . . What's high risk, dammit? Talk about it." She switched to another part of the building. "Tarrant, the British media tycoon. He's talking money and the ramifications for the World Bank. He's not sure how they're going to handle the repayments if the regime falls."

"What regime?"

"Shh." She held up her hand, listening. She suddenly stiffened. "Oh, my God."

"Eve?"

She shook her head. Dear God, she couldn't believe what she was hearing. Stop shaking. Do your job. Make sure it's being recorded. She glanced at the panel. Yes, it was okay.

Joe frowned. "You're white as a sheet. What the devil are—" He fell silent, watching her.

It was a full ten minutes before she took the earpiece out of her ear. "It's the Three Gorges Dam in China. Do you remember that PBS special we watched last year on the dam being built on the Yangtze River?"

"Yeah. The biggest project since the building of the Great Wall. It's supposed to generate eighteen thousand megawatts of electricity and control flooding."

She nodded. "Three hundred thousand people have died in the last century from the flooding of the Yangtze. It's a killer river." She drew a deep breath. "The dam is the target. They've decided they have to move fast before the first stage is finished. The construction is still in semichaos and will be easy to sabotage right now. But the Chinese government is pulling in the reins, and the security is going to be tightened."

"Sabotage?"

She nodded. "It has to be done before November third, when the increased security is going into effect. That's why they had to make sure to have the meeting no later than the twenty-ninth. As it is, they have only a few days to implement. If they don't get a majority and move fast, then they'll have to wait until the dam is completed and it will be much more difficult." She moistened her lips. "Can you imagine the devastation . . . ?"

"Too well. Why are they doing it?"

"The power generated by the dam will be a tremendous boost to the Chinese economy. The economy is moving too fast under the present regime, and the Cabal is having problems controlling it." Her lips twisted bitterly. "Control is clearly the name of the game with the Cabal."

"And, if the dam fails, the regime could fall with it."

"That's the plan. And the new regime would have a few high-placed Cabal members. Control."

"Nasty."

"Tragic." She closed her eyes. "God knows how many people will die as a result of the sabotage . . ." Her lids flew open; she straightened in the chair and put the piece back in her ear. "Let's see if they have any more dirty tricks in the works. We can't stop them if we don't know what—"

"Dirty tricks?" Nathan asked from behind them. He shut the door and came into the van. "What's happening?"

"Sabotage of the Three Gorges Dam in China," Joe said.

Nathan gave a low whistle. "So that's the agenda."

"That seems to be the subject of everyone's conversation." Eve turned another knob. "I'm trying to find out if there's anything else crucial going on."

"I'd bet it's gonna get more interesting," Nathan said. "Melton should be the next to get here. I followed him as far as the perimeter road and then cut around here. Did you get a count?"

"Fifty-two," Eve said. "And Joe got a shot of every one of them."

"Be sure you get Melton." Nathan lifted binoculars to his eyes. "Here he comes . . ."

"Bingo," Joe said as Melton disappeared into the building. "The good senator recorded for posterity."

"Your bright light is shining clear and true," Eve told Nathan.

"Truth is a beautiful word, isn't it?" Nathan's gaze fastened on the concrete building. "So clean and simple."

"Looks like that's it." Joe stood and headed for the door. "I'm going to scout around and make sure those guards are sticking inside the fence. We don't want to be surprised."

"Good idea." Eve adjusted another dial. "Because the meeting's come to order. Melton is giving a welcome address."

"They must all be here." Nathan moved toward the door.

"I'll go and give the FBI a call and then see if I can help Quinn."

"Wait, Nathan."

"We have to move fast now, or the whole show is—" He stopped as he saw the gun in her hand. "Eve? What the hell are you doing?"

"Franklin Copeland was a very good man. Didn't you feel even a twinge of conscience when he died?"

He gazed at her in bewilderment. "Why should I? I didn't kill him."

"You didn't kill him. You just let him die."

He went still. "I beg your pardon? I went to the Secret Service. They wouldn't listen to me."

"Joe called the Secret Service again this afternoon and did some more in-depth questioning. You went to them four hours after I called you. *Four* hours, Nathan."

"It took me a while to get in to see them. Red tape. It wouldn't have made a difference, anyway."

"It might have made a difference if you hadn't deliberately made the Secret Service agents think you were unbalanced. Agent Wilson said you were raving when you came to the house. No wonder they didn't believe you."

"I was frantic, dammit. I couldn't get them to listen. Not that they would have found anything suspicious, anyway. Hebert was too smart for us."

"Actually, they did find something—once Joe persuaded them to go to the house with him for a search earlier tonight. It was the filter on the vent in Copeland's bedroom. It was coated with a substance that reacted in his lungs like mold. Every breath Copeland took weakened his lungs and helped to bring on his asthma attacks."

"Diabolical."

"Hebert said it was planned down to the last gasp. I'm sure the doctors in the Cabal measured out the irritant to cause a final seizure no later than the twenty-seventh. That way the funeral could be scheduled for two days later, and it would be perfectly natural for all the members to be flying into the area before the twenty-ninth." She paused. "Copeland was a fine man. You shouldn't have let him die."

"I told you that—" His gaze narrowed on her face. "That's the second time you said that. Ridiculous. Why would I have let him die?"

"Because you didn't want the Cabal meeting to be canceled. You wanted them all here. You've been planning this from the moment Etienne told you that the Cabal was meeting in Boca Raton."

"But he didn't tell me."

"Yes, he did. Why wouldn't he tell you? He liked you and trusted you. You'd been working on him for two years to make sure he'd feel that way."

"Two years?"

"Since he came to work for you at the research center."

"What?"

"Oh, for God's sake, no more pretense. It's over. You're not Bill Nathan."

His brows lifted. "I'm not?" He tilted his head. "Then who am I? Now, let me see. A good reporter should be able to make a decent guess at where you're going with all this. You believe I'm Thomas Simmons?"

She shook her head. "Another red herring. How long did you think you could keep me from knowing that you were Harold Bently?"

A flicker of expression crossed his face. "What? Are you crazy?"

"Joe got a call from his precinct about the explosion that killed Jennings. The car wasn't rigged. The bomb was in the skull itself, and triggered by a remote device." She paused. "And the skull wasn't the one I worked on. It wasn't a human skull at all. It was a very good imitation, made of plastic and coated with clay. Now, it was obviously switched. I had to ask myself who had the opportunity to substitute the plastic skull for Victor, and why. Then Galen called us and told me Hughes had caught a glimpse of some kind of metal glinting beneath the porch at the lake cottage. He found a very small, very sophisticated long-range listening device. The rains had washed away the pile of leaves it was hidden under. Someone wanted to know exactly what was going on in our cottage, and there was no way Hebert could have gotten that close. But you were out there on the porch most of the evening, and you were on the steps when I came out of the cottage when Jennings's car blew up. You could have monitored Jennings's conversation with Rusk and then blown the car. It all began to come together. I asked Galen to find some pictures of Simmons and scan them into the computer. Lo and behold: Victor wasn't Harold Bently at all, but Thomas Simmons."

Bently was silent a moment. "Too bad. It seems the jig may be up."

"And you did some more swapping last night when you gave us the shots of the man you called Simmons. Computer substitution on those pictures from Cal Tech. It's easy these days, with a photo program. Who was the man at the church?"

"Just someone I picked up and hired on the local skid row. He cleaned up pretty well, didn't he?"

"Why did you go to so much trouble?"

"I thought you might become suspicious if I didn't give the 'shadow' substance."

"And when did you do the switch on the skulls?"

"When I packed up your equipment when we left Galen's house. That's why I had to go with you. I had to make sure you didn't take the reconstruction out of the case to do any more work on him."

"Because the plastic reconstruction was of you, and Victor was Simmons. You took a big chance."

"Not so big. You were so upset about the threat to your daughter that you weren't thinking of Victor. It helped that you always refuse to look at photos of your reconstructions. I knew you'd find out eventually, but I hoped it would be long enough."

"You mean you hoped Hebert would kill me before I did a photo comparison of the reconstruction."

"Hope didn't enter into it. It was just another tragic necessity in an already tragic situation." Bently grimaced. "I knew you'd have to die from the moment Hebert brought you into the picture. It's not something I wanted to happen. I respect and admire you."

"Is that why you bribed Marie to poison me?"

"I was playing for time. If you'd died, then they would have had to get another forensic sculptor. It would have delayed them. I needed that delay."

"But Hebert rushed in and killed Marie so that I wouldn't suspect I was targeted and be frightened enough to stop the work."

"Yes, damn his soul. You started the reconstruction, and I knew time was running out. If the Cabal found out I was alive, then they'd turn loose all their bloodhounds to find me. I know what kind of power they wield. It wouldn't have been a week before they tracked me down. I couldn't let that happen. All I needed was that two weeks and the Cabal would be here."

"And that's why you killed Jennings, too?"

"At first, I was only going to use him to throw the Cabal off my trail and onto Simmons. I was going to get him to ID the skull, and then blow it up and have Hebert blamed. But I could tell Jennings was getting too close to knowing about Hebert's plans for Boca Raton. I needed to stop him in his tracks."

"So many deaths." Eve shook her head. "Why the hell didn't you just take your fuel cell and leave the country? Work on it somewhere else?"

"Because I realized after the Cabal tried to kill me that they would never stop. That they'd find a way to bury me, the way they buried Simmons and his invention." His lips tightened. "Do you know what a miracle that fuel cell would have been? How many millions of people it would have helped? It would have cleaned up our planet. But the Cabal wouldn't let us do it. We were interfering in their profits, their control. They crushed us the way they crushed every other advancement that got in their way." Bently smiled bitterly. "Think about it. How many marvels of invention have you read about that just disappeared from view? Do you remember reading about the car down in Daytona with a super-efficient electric engine that met all the problems posed by the environmentalists? It was bought by Detroit and never heard about again. The inventors are always bought out, or scared out, or held up to ridicule by the media, consumer groups, or the government. They fade away as if they had never been. Well, Simmons and I weren't going to fade away. I had the funds and he had the fuel cell. We were going to make final refinements, and then I'd contact a few influential backers and we'd be on our way."

"Until Hebert set off that explosion."

He nodded. "Simmons was killed instantly. I was burned, but I crawled out into the mud and put out the flames. Etienne found me there."

"And helped you?"

"He took me to a shack in Houma and nursed me for months. I had plenty of money in a safe on the island, but he was afraid to call in a doctor. I almost died several times. When I was on the mend, I tried to think what was best to do. I wanted to try to continue Simmons's work, but it was too dangerous to confront the Cabal alone. Then the solution occurred to me: the media. What would a secret society fear most? The light of public attention glaring on them. I had Etienne phone Bill Nathan and ask him to meet me in secret, because I thought he'd be sympathetic to my cause."

"He wasn't?"

"Oh, he was sympathetic, as long as there was no risk involved. He was a miserable coward. I knew he'd probably go straight from me to Melton. I couldn't let him do that. Not after all I'd suffered."

"You killed him and took his identity."

"It wasn't too difficult. He was divorced and worked freelance, so he moved around the state a lot. I had a few facial burns and had to have plastic surgery anyway. I had Etienne buy a phony driver's license and passport for me, and I went to Antigua and had some work done. Nathan and I had similar features that only had to be made more similar."

"And you had the plastic skull made there?"

"No, that was later. After I failed to remove you from the picture, I realized it might be necessary."

"Might? I can't imagine you taking anything for granted. I'd bet you planned every detail."

"Well, I did know buying the fuel-cell components might attract attention. I knew enough about Simmons's invention to complete it, but I had to be prepared, in case the Cabal became dubious about my demise."

"Prepared to blow me up?"

"If the bomb wasn't used for you, I thought it might be a nice gift to give to the Cabal at their next meeting. But, as it happened, circumstances dictated that I use it in another way. Jennings. Kismet."

"Murder."

"Call it what you like. I was doing what I had to do to survive and bring something decent into the world." He shrugged. "The Cabal taught me that I couldn't be squeamish about the means of doing it."

"So you became like them."

"No!" Bently tried to temper the violence of his voice. "I gave up my wife and my children and a life I loved because I wanted to help the world become a better place. The Cabal tried to butcher me, and then made me hide like a wounded animal. I didn't even dare go home because I knew they'd target my family. Every act of violence I've committed is their fault."

Eve shook her head. "Murder is murder."

"It's easy for you to say. Sometimes sacrifices have to be made for the greater good."

"You sound like Hebert. In your way you're as twisted as he was. And you brainwashed Etienne until he was willing to do anything you told him to."

"Not anything. I couldn't persuade him not to take Simmons's skull to Jules. He was a simple soul; he wanted to please all of us."

"You knew Jules would kill him."

"If he hadn't, I would have had to do it myself. That's why I followed Etienne to Baton Rouge. I couldn't risk him talking."

She shook her head in amazement. "You're incredible. He saved your life. If you were there on the spot, you could have helped him."

His lips tightened. "But I needed the time. After Etienne told me what was going to happen here, I knew that opportunity was knocking. The only way to guarantee that the Cabal couldn't stop the research was to bring them down. And the only way to get them all was to make sure they gathered in one place like the vultures they are." His gaze went to the concrete building. "And now I have them all in there, roosting. Fifty-three of the most powerful and egocentric bastards on the face of the earth."

"They won't be there for long. Joe's calling the Secret Service man he talked to this afternoon. He asked Pete Wilson to be on the alert."

"I'm surprised he left you alone with me for the great confrontation."

"He didn't know about the confrontation. He thought I was just going to play along with you until the Secret Service came."

Bently smiled. "But you wanted some other recordings to give to the law, besides those of the Cabal. You've been getting our little conversation on tape, haven't you?"

"If you guessed, why did you talk to me?"

"Because I don't care. It's not going to matter. I have a boat waiting at a dock near here. I'll be on it and heading to a lab I have set up in the Caribbean. I watched Simmons every minute while he was creating the fuel cell. I can re-create his invention. Besides, you deserved to have some answers after all your hard work."

"Christ, I'm pointing this gun at you. It will matter. You'd have to be nuts not to—"

"Eve." The door had swung open and Joe stood in the doorway of the van. He resignedly shook his head as he stared at the gun in her hand. "I was a little worried about this happening."

"So you rushed back to safeguard the lady," Bently said. "And is the Secret Service on its way?"

Joe nodded. "Ten minutes, tops."

"Do you really think those Secret Service agents will do anything about the Cabal? No way. Hell, the Cabal will say they're having a private memorial for Copeland, and the authorities will question them very respectfully and then go away with apologies."

"But they'll know who was there. We'll have tapes and videos. They'll all be marked men. The Secret Society will no longer be secret. It's hard to organize the kind of power plays they've been doing when everybody suspects them. That bright light will push them out into the open."

"Spotlights don't last forever."

"Nothing lasts forever," Eve said.

"You're wrong. One thing is very permanent indeed." Bently looked back at the concrete building. "I became very skilled with explosives during my recuperation period. Etienne was an excellent teacher. He'd learned from a master. He knew how to rig bombs and place them where they'd go undetected. Do you know there are even ways to mask the scent from dogs? He was very proud of his knowledge."

Eve tensed as she realized he wasn't talking about the explosive in the skull. "You're bluffing. There was no way you could get near that building with all the guards."

"But the guards weren't here three weeks ago."

God, all the half-lies, half-truths. "Etienne told you exactly where the meeting was being held."

Bently nodded. "Did I forget to mention that? When you figured everything else out, I would have thought you'd guess."

She headed for the door. "For God's sake, you're going to—"

The tech van rocked as the night exploded.

The gun flew out of Eve's hand as she was hurled against the wall and the van lurched drunkenly. Joe was thrown backward from the door to the ground, stunning him.

Bently was already at the door as Eve straightened. He glanced back over his shoulder, his face alight with fierce satisfaction. "Death is forever, Eve. Nothing is more permanent. No more Cabal."

Then he was gone.

She grabbed up the gun, tore across the van and out the door.

"Stay here." Joe was shaking his head to clear it as he got to his feet. "I'll get him."

"Dear God." Eve stopped in shock as she saw the remains of the concrete building. What was left of the concrete was spread in huge chunks about the grounds; the remainder of the structure was enveloped in flames.

She tore her gaze away. Bently.

He was racing toward the drainage ditch. She started after him.

Joe was ahead of her, closing on Bently at a dead run.

Bently waded through the ditch. He was out and plunging into the brush.

Joe glanced over his shoulder at her. "Dammit, I told you to stay in the van. He could have set another—"

The earth heaved as another explosion rocked the concrete building. Concrete flew in all directions like deadly shrapnel.

"*Down*," Joe yelled.

Eve dropped to the ground as concrete missiles speared the air. Jesus, it was like being in the middle of an erupting volcano. She lifted her head, and her skin stung as a barrage of small rocks hit her face. "Joe, are you—

"*Joe!*"

Chapter Twenty-one

JOE WAS LYING CRUMPLED ON THE dirt. He wasn't moving.

She raced across the intervening ground and dropped to her knees beside him. "Joe."

Pale. Eyes closed. A cut bleeding at his temple. Was he breathing? He had to be breathing.

"Joe. You talk to me. Do you hear? You *talk* to me."

He didn't open his eyes.

Oh, God, don't let him die.

She reached into her pocket to get her cell phone. 911. Call 911.

Headlights.

A line of cars were pulling up in front of the burning naval air station. Secret Service.

Forget them.

Call 911 for Joe.

———————

Joe's eyes opened. "Hi. You . . . okay?"

Eve nodded. "And so are you. Concussion." She tried to smile. "You scared me. You wouldn't wake up. It's been two days."

He reached out and took her hand. "Sorry."

"You should be."

"Won't happen again." His eyes started to close. "Sleepy . . ."

"Then go to sleep."

"You going to stay here?"

"You bet."

"Bently?" His eyes were open again. "Did he get away?"

"He got to his boat and out on the ocean. After I told the Secret Service he planned to escape that way, they called in the Coast Guard. They intercepted him later that night."

Joe searched Eve's expression. "And?"

"The boat blew up before they could board it."

"Suicide?"

She nodded. "It's just as well the Secret Service didn't have to deal with him. They're having enough trouble trying to explain the deaths of all those power brokers."

"All dead?"

"They didn't have a chance. The authorities are even having trouble identifying most of them."

"Did it cause you any trouble?"

"Are you kidding? This thing is massive. Secret Service questioned me for a solid five hours. The FBI for another three.

You'll be on the carpet, too. Thank God, we had the surveillance tapes."

Joe yawned. "As soon as I wake up I'll talk to them, make sure they don't bother you any more."

"Joe, I'm handling it."

"A little help won't hurt . . ."

"Go back to sleep."

"Something's wrong." His gaze was searching her face. "You're not telling me everything."

"I told you everything that's been happening."

"No, I mean with you. You're worrying about something. What's bothering you?"

"I'm not worrying about—" Eve met his gaze. "It's what Bently said. He wondered why we hadn't figured out that he'd lie about Etienne not telling him the location of the meeting. I was wondering if somewhere in my subconscious I did figure it out, and just ignored it." She looked down at their joined hands. "The Cabal deserved to be destroyed, and we couldn't be sure that exposing them would be enough. Did I close my eyes and let Bently blow them up?"

"Bullshit."

"Did I, Joe?"

"No, you didn't." His answer was absolutely certain. "I know you. There were so many lies, red herrings, and half-truths floating around that this one got lost in the shuffle for you. As much as you might have wanted the Cabal to disappear, you couldn't do it. Death is the enemy for you. You fight it every single day." He lifted her hand and kissed the palm. "So forget it, okay?"

Eve moistened her lips. "Okay."

"Good." Joe's eyes closed. "Then let me go to sleep so I

can get enough strength to tackle those Secret Service assholes . . ."

"They're not assholes. They're just doing their—"

He was already asleep.

Eve sat there, holding his hand, staring at his face.

She was at peace again. Another gift from Joe.

But he had spoken only of her own lack of guilt, she realized suddenly. He didn't say that *he* hadn't figured out that Bently might have known enough to set a death trap. Joe was one of the smartest men she had ever known, and he had a memory like a steel trap. Had he known there was a possibility the Cabal would not survive the night?

Her hand tightened on Joe's.

It was a question she knew she'd never ask him.

———

"So Bently is dead," Galen repeated thoughtfully. " 'Down to the sea in ships . . .' "

"We'll be back at the cottage tomorrow," Eve said. "The questioning isn't over, but they're going to let us go home."

"Jane will be jumping up and down with joy. Is Quinn okay?"

"Headache. But that's to be expected."

"If I'd been there, it wouldn't have happened. You should take it as a lesson learned."

"I take it as another example of your inflated ego."

Galen chuckled. "Maybe. Are you going to call Jane, or shall I?"

"I will."

"Dammit, I wanted to do something to get into her good graces. She might be so happy she'd forget she considers me an ass."

Eve smiled. "Jane's always been a girl of impeccable judgment."

"Cruelty, thy name is Eve."

———————

"I have to go down to the precinct right away. They're feeling very cheated they don't know as much as the Feds." Joe put their bags inside the cottage. "Will you be okay?"

"Of course."

"Try to rest."

"I'm not the one who got knocked on the head." Her gaze wandered over the lake to the scorched trees where Jennings had died and then, compulsively, to Bonnie's hill.

"Shit." Joe's gaze had followed Eve's. "I know, dammit. No more threat, no more sword hanging over us, and everything is coming back to you. I knew it would happen. It's always going to be here."

"What do you want me to do? I can't forget it, Joe."

"I'm not an idiot. It's got to be faced. Just do me a favor," Joe said. "Don't think. Don't make any decisions. You're tired. Just try to live in the present until I get these next few days of red tape over with and we can talk."

She nodded. "I'll try."

He started down the steps. "And I'll pick up Jane, your Mom, and Toby on my way home tonight. They should keep you too busy to think of anything but them."

Eve took one last look at the hill as he drove off. She had

hoped the pain would go away, but it still lingered. Keep your promise, she told herself as she went inside. Don't think. Just live in the moment. It was the best advice she—

There was a note propped on the coffee table.

Eve,
I had a few things to tie up. I'll call you.
Tell Jane I didn't run away because she intimidated me.
She doesn't scare me . . . much.

Galen

She smiled as she put down the note. A few things to tie up? Now what the hell was that rascal up to. . . .

———————

It was two days later that Eve got the call from Galen.

"Where the hell are you?"

"I've been busy. I just thought I'd fill you in. I've called Hughes and told him he's to stay with you and maintain protective surveillance until the end of the week. That should keep some of the media away. Have you brought Jane back home?"

"Yes. I brought her and Mom back to the cottage." Eve's gaze shifted to Jane and Toby playing outside by the lake. "She couldn't be happier. Where are you, Galen?"

"Barbados. I felt the need for a vacation."

"Out of the blue?"

"My last job was very exhausting. You're not an easy woman to work with, Eve."

"Why are you in Barbados?"

"The sun. I got a little chill in my bones while I was at your lake."

"Galen."

He was silent a moment. "My suspicious nature. I don't think Bently was the type to commit suicide. And I found it very convenient that his death took place in the middle of the ocean, where his remains couldn't be retrieved."

"You believe he staged it."

"He's very, very smart. He would have to be, to fool me into thinking he was an ass."

"Your pride is hurt."

"Well, maybe. I'm just exploring possibilities. He got rid of the Cabal, his primary threat. He was obsessed with the idea of that fuel cell, and he told you he knew enough to put it together himself. Why not fake his own death to make sure he had the opportunity to work on it?"

"You believe Simmons's fuel cell may become a reality someday?"

"We'll have to see, won't we? At any rate, I don't think Bently's any threat to you. You're off his radar now. I'm just going to poke around and see what I can find out down here."

"And what if you find him?"

"I'll make a decision then. I don't believe in throwing the baby out with the bathwater."

"When will you be back?"

"Not for awhile. You're on your own. Well, not on your own. You'll always have Quinn. How's he doing?"

"Okay, I guess. I've scarcely seen him since we got back. He's been closeted with the Secret Service and the FBI from morning to night."

"Drudgery. I don't envy him. I like the easy life. If I don't find Bently, I may go on a real vacation. Then I'm going to get on with my life. I highly recommend it. Why don't you do the same?" He hung up.

Annoying bastard, Eve thought crossly as she pressed the disconnect. She had actually been stupid enough to worry about Galen for the past couple days. She should have known he'd pop up like some zany jack-in-the-box.

His lack of certainty about Bently's death was a little far out, but not totally crazy. Bently had actually told her about the boat and his preparations to get away.

So that she could tell the authorities and set his real plan in motion?

Let Galen worry about it. Eve and her family were safe, and she didn't want to think about Bently. She agreed with Galen that if Bently was alive, there was no reason for him to target her or Joe.

She moved onto the porch and stood looking out at the lake. The water looked beautiful and serene today. If she hadn't known Hughes and his men were moving discreetly around the property, it would have reminded her of the time before she had gotten that DNA report.

Her gaze lifted across the lake to the hill. Would she ever be able to look at that grave again without remembering Jules Hebert and his death in those swamps? Or that gravestone with her Bonnie's name crossed out and smeared with ugly red paint?

Get on with your life, Galen had said.

Sometimes things get in the way and you forget who you are and what you do.

Why did those words of Jane's suddenly pop into her head?

They had been spoken when Jane had been trying to convince her to go after Hebert, and had nothing to do with—

She stiffened in shock. "Dear God . . ."

She slowly moved down the porch steps.

———

Jane was sitting on the porch swing when Joe got home from the precinct. Toby was curled up at her feet.

"You must have worn him out." Joe bent down and petted him. The dog raised his head, lazily licking the back of Joe's hand. "I've never seen Toby this quiet."

"Yeah. He runs until he's ready to drop and then he collapses. Stop that, Toby. You're getting his hand all wet." She was frowning. "I've been waiting for you."

"Problems? Why didn't you call me?"

"Eve didn't want me to."

He stiffened. "Eve?" His gaze flew to the front door of the cottage. "What happened? Did she leave?"

Jane shook her head. "She just wanted me to give you a message. She wants you to go up to the grave."

"What?"

"That's what she said. She left the cottage over an hour ago. I asked her if she wanted me to go up there with her, and she said no."

"You're sure she went to the grave?" His gaze shifted to the hill. "Did she give any reason?"

Jane shook her head.

"How did she look?"

She shrugged. "Sometimes it's hard to tell what Eve's thinking. She didn't look mad, but she wasn't smiling. I don't know, Joe."

"Then I guess I'd better go see for myself." He turned and started down the steps.

Jane's voice followed him. "I hope everything's okay, Joe."

"Me, too." He started down the path around the lake. "Me, too . . ."

———————

Eve was standing beside the grave, staring down at the tombstone.

"Eve?"

She didn't look at him. "There are still the faintest traces of that red paint. I thought we'd gotten it all off."

"I'll do it tomorrow."

"No, it doesn't make any difference."

Silence.

"Why are you here, Eve?"

"I had to get my head straight. I thought I'd better do it here."

"It has to hurt to see that tombstone."

"Of course it does."

"And makes you even more bitter toward me."

"A little."

"Only a little?"

Eve's gaze lifted to meet his. "I'm trying to be honest with you. Galen called today. He's in Barbados."

"Doing what?"

"He thinks maybe Bently staged his own death. He's looking around." She studied Joe. "You're not surprised?"

"I considered the possibility, and was tempted to go down and scout around. I decided my priority was here."

"Galen says even if he's alive, he thinks we're off his radar." She paused. "And he recommended that I get on with my life."

"And what did you say?"

"I didn't get a chance to say anything." Eve looked back at the tombstone. "But it rang a bell. And then I remembered something Jane said when she was trying to talk me out of hiding. She said everything was getting in my way and making me forget who I really was and what I did. That struck a note, too. I've been running around, hurt and angry and so defensive I blocked out everything else."

"Who could blame you?"

"I blame me," she said fiercely. "I felt so much the victim that I forgot about who I really am and what I do." She gestured to the tombstone. "I only thought about Bonnie. I never thought about that little girl we buried in her place. She was one of the lost ones, and I didn't even think about her."

"You couldn't be expected to—"

"Bull. I made the choice years ago that if I couldn't help Bonnie, I could at least help the parents of other lost and murdered children. I've devoted years to doing that, and yet I allowed myself to be derailed because I felt so sorry for myself. The little girl in this grave was about the same age as Bonnie. She had everything to live for, and it was taken away from her." Her hands clenched into fists at her sides. "And I never thought about her. I had no right to be that selfish just because I was hurting."

"You weren't selfish. If you need to blame someone, blame me."

"I'm tired of blaming you."

Joe smiled. "Then I'm not about to urge you to do it. I know when I've gotten a break." His smile faded as his gaze went to the tombstone. "So why did you want me to come up here?"

"Because I wanted to know how I'd feel if I stood here with you."

He stiffened. "How do you feel?"

"Sad. Regretful. Scarred."

"And what does that mean?"

"It means you made a mistake and it hurt me terribly. It means I probably made a few mistakes myself. It means I have to heal and it will take some time." Eve met his gaze. "But I don't want to do it alone. I want you with me. Whether it hurts or not, I can't imagine life without you."

"Hallelujah," he whispered.

"I don't promise you everything will be the same. But then you said you weren't sure you wanted it that way."

"I would have taken it." Joe moved to stand beside her, but not touching her. "Tell me what you want from me."

"I want you to have this little girl disinterred. I'm going to do a reconstruction on her. Then I want you to help me find out who she is."

"Done."

"And I'm going to find my Bonnie. Will you help me?"

"For God's sake, of course I will." He paused. "I've never stopped looking. I've followed up on every report, every lead, even after I paid to have that DNA report sent to you."

She went still. "You didn't tell me that."

"I didn't think you were in the mood to believe me."

"Maybe I wasn't. Would you have told me if you'd found her?"

He smiled crookedly. "I asked myself that a thousand times. I think I would. I hope I would. I can't guarantee it."

"I hope you would, too. Because I want to trust you again, Joe."

"You already trust me. You just have to recognize that you do. Why else would you agree to start again?"

"Because I love you so much that life's not worth a damn without you," she said simply. "In spite of everything that's happened, that's the bottom line."

Joe drew a deep breath and held out his hand to her. "Yeah, that's the bottom line."

Eve hesitated, then slowly reached out and took his hand.

Strength. Comfort. Love. His touch was so familiar, and yet it had an element now that was tentative and entirely new.

Rebirth? Maybe.

Whatever it was, like Joe, she'd take it.

Her hand tightened around his as she turned away from the grave. "We'd better get back to Jane. I think she was worried."

"I know she was." Joe walked beside her toward the path. "She was afraid you were going to ditch me. She was probably concerned about who would get custody of Toby."

"Don't be silly. Jane would get custody even if she had to run away from home with that dog." She suddenly stopped to look back over her shoulder at the grave she had called Bonnie's all these months.

"Okay?" Joe asked gently.

She was beginning to think it would be okay. Hope was a wonderful thing, and they had that great bottom line. "Sure, I was just thinking about that little girl. I want to get to work on the reconstruction right away." She started down the path again. "I think I'll call her Sally. . . ."

Epilogue

I like the name Sally," Bonnie said. "One of my friends at school was Sally Meyers. Do you remember her, Mama?"

Eve looked over her shoulder to see Bonnie curled up on the window seat. "You had a lot of friends." She went back to measuring the child's skull for depth markers. "And if I'd remembered her, I certainly wouldn't have named this poor kid after her."

"Why not?" Bonnie giggled. "You're superstitious. You think it might be bad luck."

"I'm not superstitious."

"Yes, you are."

"I've just learned not to take chances, brat."

"Sally's fine. Her daddy gave her a car and she almost died in an auto accident last year. But she's getting well."

"I don't call that exactly fine."

"Well, she would have been happier on this side, but she's still fine."

"And I can't relate to your notion of a happy little afterlife, either."

"I know. It's out of your realm of experience. That's why you're so determined to find me."

"Don't be patronizing. I'm still your mother."

"Yes, you are." Bonnie smiled lovingly. "And I understand why you want to bring me home. It's just that I don't want you to hurt yourself doing it. You almost lost Joe this time."

"We're working it out."

"Yes." Bonnie leaned her head back against the window. "I can feel it in you."

"Feel what?"

"A sort of glow, a serenity . . ."

"Oh, give me a break."

"Have I embarrassed you? Serves you right for being such a cynic." Her glance shifted to Sally. "I hope you're able to bring her home. She's been lost a long time."

"How long?"

"Longer than me. Have you heard anything from Galen?"

"No, have you?"

"Do you mean, is he dead? I don't think so."

"I shouldn't have asked. I don't know why it even bothers me. He's a law unto himself. I refuse to worry about him."

Bonnie chuckled. "You'll worry." She was silent a moment. "I have to leave now. Jane and Toby will be coming up the porch *steps in a few minutes. She's going to show you a trick she taught him."*

"Is that supposed to prove you're clairvoyant? She teaches him a new trick every other day."

"Well, I thought I'd try. You're a tough sell. By the time they come in that door, you'll have persuaded yourself that you've just woken from a nap and started working on Sally again."

"Which is probably what happened." She could hear Toby scrambling up the porch steps and then shaking his coat. "He sounds like he's been in the water. We can't keep him dry. He refuses to stay out of the lake. The rascal's full of the devil."

"He's full of life. You could learn from him. Let life in, Mama."

The door was opening, and Eve knew if she glanced at the window seat Bonnie would no longer be there.

"Eve, you've got to see this!"

Bonnie was gone, but life was here, joyously bounding into the room with Jane and Toby.

"I can't wait." Eve wiped the clay from her hands and went forward to meet it.

IRIS JOHANSEN

Final Target

PAN BOOKS £5.99

A pacy thriller packed with international action, psychic intrigue and sexual tension.

Dr Jessica Riley nursed her sister back from a six-year withdrawal after the traumatic deaths of their parents, and Melissa has spent every day since living life to the full. But when Jessica takes on the treatment of Cassie, beloved daughter of US President Andreas, the lives of both sisters become more and more complicated. Cassie is suffering a nightmare-filled trauma after a foiled kidnap attempt. Her life was saved at the last minute, but the bloody affair has gone unpunished and her saviour, Michael Travis – the only man who holds any clues to the attackers' identities – has disappeared himself.

As the manhunt for enigmatic diamond smuggler Travis closes in, everyone is forced to bend the rules and trust those they would normally condemn.

This intense and lively thriller will keep you turning the pages to discover who is going to be the final target.

'Iris Johansen is incomparable'
Tami Hoag

IRIS JOHANSEN

No One To Trust

PAN BOOKS £5.99

In the heart of Colombia the US DEA and Colombian drug barons have for years been engaged in a war with no rules . . .

Rico Chavez is the most terrifying of killers: ruthless, cunning, charismatic. A man who always gets what he wants. And what he wants now is Elena Kyler. He wants her alive long enough to see him destroy every reason she has for living. He wants her to turn against everything and everyone she ever believed in. And then he wants her to commit the ultimate act of betrayal.

But Elena, herself, is an assassin trained by the military, and a loner. Now she finds herself on the run from one dangerous man and turning to another for help.

New York Times No. 1 bestselling author, Iris Johansen, raises the stakes and the heart rate in her new thriller that follows the harrowing trail of a ruthless killer – and the woman determined to hunt him down.

Iris Johansen's gripping new thriller
No One To Trust *will be available as a*
Pan paperback in December 2003.